True North

Bethany Brown
Ashlyn Kane

Dreamspinner Press

Published by
Dreamspinner Press
4760 Preston Road
Suite 244-149
Frisco, TX 75034
http://www.dreamspinnerpress.com/

True North

Cover Design by Mara McKennen

ISBN: 978-1-935192-42-8

Printed in the United States of America
First Edition
January, 2009

eBook edition available
eBook ISBN: 978-1-935192-43-5

For Alina, Melissa, and the rest of the girls' night crew; and for Brandon:

Without your relentless encouragement and support, this book could not have been written.

I love you all.

Chapter 1

"JACKSON STRANGE," the nurse read out, her eyes meeting his across the nearly empty waiting room. She checked something off on her clipboard. "The doctor will see you now."

Jackson stood, trying not to put too much weight on his left leg—and trying not to look like he was limping. Too late; Aunt Bella Bitoni was as perceptive as she was competent—and blunt.

"Stop right there, mister," the nurse told him. Her normally laughing black eyes were hard today, and focused completely on his leg. She pursed her lips and pushed a lock of silvering black hair out of her face. "Bobby, have you got the wheelchair in there?"

Aww, man. Jackson nearly groaned out loud. He hoped she wasn't going to write to his mother. "Bella, I'm fine—"

But Bobby, the teenaged evenings-and-weekends receptionist, was already wheeling the damn thing into the backs of his legs. They collapsed, fire shooting up from the left knee. "Dammit, Bella! Ow!"

"Thanks, Bobby," she said, ignoring him completely. The two other patients waiting snickered. "I've got it from here."

Jackson gave old man Bender from the grocery store an unpleasant glare as Bella wheeled him into an examination room. "Dr. Dan busy today?" he asked, mostly to keep her from lecturing him for walking on his injured leg.

"Dr. Dan's seeing about Star Hamilton's girl. She's due any day now." Bella didn't look up from filling in his chart. "We've got a new man in; he'll look after you." She put her pen down at last and scowled at him from behind her no-nonsense spectacles. "As for you, Jackson Strange, you should know better! No telling what damage you'll do to yourself next. And you'll break your mother's heart. Are you trying to get yourself killed?"

Damn it; why did she always have to play the mom card? "No, Aunt Bella," he mumbled. Did they teach guilt-tripping in nursing school nowadays or what?

Aunt Bella grabbed the chair at the computer desk across from him and peered around the monitor, spectacles obscuring her eyes. "What did you do to yourself this time?"

Jackson sighed. He would have to hope for doctor-patient confidentiality on this, or Bella'd be writing to Calgary in no time. "Some fool left his toolbox out. I tripped, cut my leg open on a raw girder."

Bella winced, but she was typing away. Probably checking whether his tetanus was up to date. "By the way you were limping you've either let it get infected or it's fresh and you're gonna need stitches."

"I'm not that stupid," he protested. He'd only let an injury get infected once; that had been more than enough, thanks.

"Hmph. Depends on who you ask." Bella finished her data entry and looked at him over the rim of her glasses. "You need a place to stay while you're recovering, you call your Uncle John or me, you hear? Don't let them send you back to work before you're ready."

He bit his tongue to refrain from pointing out that it was his own business—literally—to manage and he'd go back when he was damn well ready, which was usually right away. He didn't like leaving someone else in charge. "Yes, Aunt Bella."

Bella closed the door.

Jackson let out a breath he hadn't realized he'd been holding. It had been a strain, hiding the pain from his aunt. God, he hadn't needed to swear this badly since the Flames lost the Stanley Cup finals. He pressed his closed fist into his left thigh, grimacing and cursing under his breath.

The door opened, admitting a tall, slender man in a lab coat.

"Who the hell are you?" Jackson growled, not letting up the pressure. Detachedly, he noted a growing red stain above the knee of his jeans.

"I'm Dr. Piet," the man said, not too sharply considering Jackson's attitude. He consulted his chart. "You must be Jackson Strange."

"I go by Jack," he said through clenched teeth. "You'll forgive me for not standing up."

"Bella didn't give you anything for the pain?"

"She thinks I should suffer for being careless."

"Hmm. We'll have to agree to disagree." He went to a cupboard and sorted through the various medications. "How bad's the pain? On a scale of one to ten?"

Oh, thank God, Jack thought. *Morphine.* "I dunno. Seven? Worse than the dog bite to the calf, but not as bad as the time I accidentally set myself on fire in high school."

He could hear the sadistic amusement in the doctor's voice. "Are you accident prone?" Then, before he could even answer, the prick of a needle at the curve of his shoulder.

Almost immediately, he could feel the pain begin to dull. "Oh, Doc. I think I love you."

"I'll bet you say that to all the boys."

Morphine-sedated, it was hard to tell what he meant by that. The sudden respite from pain also gave Jack a chance to look up at his lord and savior.

Dr. Piet—Julian, according to the name on the lab coat—hardly looked old enough to have a medical degree. He had no facial hair to speak of, and his skin was smooth and fair over sharp cheekbones. He had dark hair—sort of long and unruly, for a doctor—and darker eyes, which were definitely at least a little bit amused. "Are you stoned enough for me to look at the injury yet?"

Jack stared at him for a minute. "You want me to take off my pants?" He didn't know if he could do it, even with the drugs to kill the pain.

"I could cut them off if you prefer, but it'd be easier if you stripped. More room to move around. And you won't have to walk out of here naked."

Jack blinked. "Am I harassing you, or the other way around?"

Dr. Piet gave a slight smile as he turned again. "How about I help you out and we call it even?"

The part of Jack's mind that would normally have sensed a bad idea and found an alternate path had been more or less rendered comatose by the drugs. It hurt to be helped to his feet—but that was apparently as far as the good doctor was willing to go. Too bad. Now that he was standing Jack could see that the man had a truly exceptional ass.

Dr. Piet led him to a handgrip screwed into the wall. "You can use this to keep your balance. I'll be back in a few minutes. I need to get a bigger needle."

Jack watched the door close behind him and wondered if that would have sounded as erotic if he were sober. Now, how to get his jeans off? Left leg first, maybe? He undid his belt and popped the buttons open, but there wasn't really anywhere for the denim to go; his jeans were glued to the bandage wrapped around his leg. He was just going to have to peel them off.

Wiggling the jeans down past his ass didn't present too many problems. Once he got them halfway down his thighs, however, there was a renewed surge of angry protest from his injured leg. Carefully, he sat again—on the examination table this time—and more or less kicked the jeans off his right leg. It made peeling them down the other much easier.

Just in time, too. Just as he'd balled up his jeans and tossed them in the corner, there was a knock at the door.

"I'm indecent."

Dr. Piet came in rolling his eyes, took one look at the makeshift bandage around Jack's leg, and made a face. "This was the best you could do?"

"It stopped the bleeding," Jack said defensively. "Well, for a while, anyway." He'd probably torn it open again walking in the waiting room.

The doctor pulled on a set of surgical gloves. "Let's have a look, then." He took a pair of plastic-wrapped surgical shears from a drawer and ripped the package open. The metal was cold against Jack's skin as he cut away the cloth and gently pulled it away from the injury. He held up the offending material. "What cowboy patched you up? Please tell me no one ever actually wore this."

"Johnson did it," Jack told him. "And what's wrong with my shirt?"

"Was it clean?" the doctor asked, going back for the bottle of alcohol. Damn, this was going to sting. "I mean, ever?"

"I'm an engineer! I do field testing!"

"So, what, hygienic considerations don't apply?" Dr. Piet grabbed a cotton swab and started sterilizing the wound.

Jackson was momentarily distracted from their banter by the fire in his leg. "Should that still hurt with the morphine?"

"Man of your size with the dose I gave you?" Dr. Piet looked him up and down speculatively, and Jackson did his level best to keep from reacting. "Yep."

"Just checking." Jack's stomach made an uncomfortably loud noise and he stopped watching the doctor's hands.

"You're going to need stitches," Dr. Piet announced, dropping the cotton swab in the hazmat trash can. "Surprise!" He held up two spools. "Would you like the pink thread, or the blue?"

"You're kidding, right?"

"Mostly; I don't think I have enough of the blue. How's the pain? Need another hit before I start sewing?"

Jack shook his head. "I've had stitches before. I'll be okay."

"That's what I love about cowboys. So macho." The doctor threaded the needle. "Out of curiosity, when was your last tetanus shot?"

Jackson watched the needle disappear into his flesh, then emerge on the other side. "Uh," his stomach twinged, and he turned away. "I'm not sure. A couple of years ago?"

"I'll check your records, but you'll probably need another, just to be safe. It was metal you cut yourself on, right?"

Jack nodded. "Gotta kick Harrison's ass for leaving his toolbox out like that."

"Or you could start watching where you're going," Dr. Piet quipped, slipping the needle through another few layers of skin.

Jack scowled. "They pay you to be funny?"

"It probably won't make the itemized list I send Blue Cross Alberta, no." He tied off a knot in the thread and surveyed the damage. "Mama would be so proud. It's hardly even going to scar."

Jackson had to admit, the pink stitches were not nearly as gruesome as the blue ones he'd had last time. "Thanks, Doc."

Dr. Piet was busy consulting his medical records. "That's my job." He pulled a small notepad out of his pocket. "I'm prescribing some antibiotics to prevent infection. Twice a day every day, with food, until they're gone. Any unusual side effects and you call me or Dr. Dan." He tore off the top sheet and handed it over. "I've got to grab the tetanus booster; they're in the supply room. Only had morphine in here out of sheer luck; last patient almost hacked his finger off chopping wood. It's supposed to be kept in back under lock and key. Damn fool should've gone straight to the ER in an ambulance, though. Be right back!"

Great, Jackson thought. *Injury, Aunt Bella, stitches, booster shot.* Good thing the doctor was hot or this'd be one hell of a day.

Easy, cowboy. This town was small enough already. No reason to risk shrinking it any smaller by giving the gossips something to talk about. Besides, the evidence that the good doctor might swing his way was circumstantial at best.

Anyway, his leg would put him out of commission for at least a few days.

Jackson heard the warning bells go off in his head, but he figured he could probably afford to ignore them—at least until he was no longer drugged to the eyeballs with opiates.

"Okay, where do you want it?"

Huh?

Jackson looked up to see that the doctor had returned—and was holding up a giant syringe. "What?"

"Left or right?" the doctor asked. Was Jack just imagining that teasing glint in those eyes? "Arm."

"Oh," Jackson said, hoping to God he wasn't blushing. On second thought, he probably didn't have enough extra blood to blush. *Please God, do not let me get an erection in the next ten minutes.* It was not a prayer he had ever thought he'd need in his entire life. Then again, he'd never been half-stoned and half-naked with a hot doctor he couldn't seem to stop picturing naked. "Left, I guess," he said, rolling up his sleeve.

"Just a little prick," Dr. Piet promised. Oh, he was so doing it on purpose, that little tease.

Jackson watched the needle pierce his skin distractedly. It was more of a pinch than anything else, really. Why were the edges of his vision going black? "Hardly felt a thing," he said woozily, having the sudden urge to just...close his eyes.

"You're not going to faint, are you?" the doctor asked.

Jackson's eyes rolled back. His head tipped forward. The last thing he knew as he passed out was Julian Piet's concerned touch, keeping him from sliding off the table.

Chapter 2

COWBOYS. It never failed. He couldn't even count the number of times some misguided macho man had ended up in his office unconscious. Julian caught his patient's head in one palm and his shoulder in the other and pushed him backward until he was lying flat on the table.

A quick check of his respiration and pulse told him the man was fine, probably just dehydrated. (And, a little voice in the back of his mind added, *way* beyond just plain "fine.") He pressed the button for the intercom, wondering why he hadn't used it earlier. It was so difficult to get used to a new set of exam rooms. The first day he'd hardly been able to find a damn tongue depressor. "Bella, I'm going to need an IV cart and a saline drip in two."

Poor Jackson; he was probably in for a lecture. Julian had only known the woman two days and he already knew not to cross her. Not that Julian was any more lenient with the people he loved injuring themselves. In fact, he was probably twice as bad as Bella, and he had a lot of experience with that. His college friends hadn't been the careful type.

As predicted, Bella arrived with the requested items in tow, pursed lips firmly in place. "I swear, that boy has a death wish."

"He's just dehydrated," Julian soothed, hanging the saline drip. He turned Jackson's right arm toward himself, noting without meaning to the obvious strength just beneath the surface, and slid the IV needle into the back of his hand. Easy. "He should be up at any minute. Make him sit there until the IV's done, and don't let him leave without seeing me. I have to put the fear of God in him."

Well, that was an exaggeration. It was more a fear of Not Being Able To Walk Without A Limp, but it was usually at least as effective.

Bella's only response was to harrumph in her crotchety old lady way as he let himself out.

"Hit me," he said to Barbara, the nurse manning what he always thought of as the dispatch station.

"Mrs. Jones is in one waiting for you; she's been having problems with her shoulder again."

"Right." Maybe he should have read all the active patient files before coming out here. There couldn't be that many. Taking the folder, he headed off into examination room one.

Mrs. Jones was a woman of forty-something years, immaculately groomed but with an air about her that said "mother of two." She looked up from *Canadian Home and Garden* as he walked in. "You're not Dr. Dan."

"So they keep telling me." He tucked the file under one arm and slid onto the little stool, facing her, holding out his free hand. "I'm Dr. Piet. Nice to meet you."

Mrs. Jones had a nice, firm grip, but he noted that she moved awkwardly when she reached forward to take his hand. "Same to you."

Julian held up her chart. "I see you've been having some trouble with your shoulder?" He'd hardly had time to go over her record in detail.

"I was in a car accident a couple of years ago and tore my rotator cuff."

He winced; shoulder injuries were not particularly forgiving in women of her age. "Since then?"

"I had chronic pain until I had it operated on about six months ago. The pain's not as bad as it was, but now it doesn't move too well. I thought I just needed to give it time, but now I'm worried I've waited too long."

Nodding, Julian flipped through the file for the X-rays. "Have you been seeing a physiotherapist at all?"

"The surgeon in Calgary told me I should get a referral, but I got busy. I just forgot."

Hmm. Julian bit his lower lip as he held the X-rays to the light. On the one hand, as a medical professional, it annoyed him that she'd ignored her doctor's advice. On the other hand, the surgeon should have done the referral his damn self. And after two years of undergrad, four of med school, and six of residency at a teaching hospital, he knew what it was like to be busy. "No need to panic just yet. Can you move your arm a bit for me, just to give me an idea of how much range of motion you have?"

He watched carefully as he directed her through a series of motions, gauging both her reach and her expression. Finally, he nodded again, double-checking her post-surgical X-ray. "That's fine, thank you." He squinted. "It looks from the X-rays like the bone damage has been contained, and you haven't got any major tendon or ligament damage."

Mrs. Jones looked like she didn't know whether to be relieved or worried. "What is it, then? Am I going to be stuck like this?"

He smiled. "Mrs. Jones, you've got what we call frozen shoulder. It happens often after shoulder operations, and like many other conditions, it can worsen with age. Luckily, it can also be improved with steroids and exercise."

He wheeled himself over to what he was beginning to think of as the Wall of Explanatory Pamphlets and selected, after several minutes of searching, one on the side effects and pros and cons of using corticosteroids to treat joint pain. "If you decide you want to go ahead with the steroid injections after reading this, just come see us during our usual business hours. We'll figure out the dosage from there." Julian dug a business card out of his pocket. "Meanwhile, you can start physio whenever you like. My sister Roz runs the local gym; she's got her PT. You won't need a referral. Just tell her Julian sent you."

She blinked. "That's it?"

He wondered if she thought he was dismissing her. "For now. I don't want you to make a decision on the steroids before you're properly informed. If you have any questions about the treatment once you've done your research, you can call me. But I think you should try the physio by itself for a while first, just to see. You might be surprised."

Mrs. Jones breathed a long sigh of relief. "Thank you, doctor."

Julian shook her hand again for good measure, and went to meet his last patient of the day.

Tom Bender was the slightly senile old man who ran the local grocery. He had rheumatoid arthritis in everything that could be remotely arthritic, coke-bottle glasses, a cane he probably didn't need, and a truly amazing sense of hearing for such an old man.

Dr. Matheson had told Julian he could expect him roughly once a week with some malady or another, ranging from an imagined nervous tick in his cheek to complaints of low energy to the insistence that he was suffering from any of a variety of brain cancers. Except for the arthritis, the man was literally a picture of health. Julian gave him some Tic Tacs in a prescription bottle and sent him on his way.

Bobby was forwarding the lines for the evening while Barbara disinfected the flat surfaces of the waiting room. Julian locked up the back, then popped back into examination room two to check on his patient. He opened the door just as Bella walked out, rolling her eyes, and poked his head around the frame before walking in completely. "Oh, good, you're awake."

Jackson blinked at the ceiling, squinted at the bright light and groaned. He didn't look so great, for a man who was ridiculously good-looking. "I fell asleep?" His voice was incredulous. Julian watched his movements carefully for any sign of further injury as he shuffled himself up onto his elbows.

"The medical term is *lost consciousness*." He said it with relish. Jack's reactions were too entertaining.

His patient stopped trying to right himself and stared at Julian. "I *fainted*?!"

"I take it this is a new experience for you." Yep, he was definitely enjoying this. It was totally innocent, he told himself. He was just amused by Jack's injured pride; that was all.

Jackson attempted a glower, then apparently thought better of it and laid his head back against the examination table.

Julian took pity on him and started to explain. It was, after all, he reminded himself firmly, his actual *job.* "It happens sometimes when people get dehydrated. For example, after a traumatic loss of blood. You're lucky you didn't damage your femoral artery." He padded over and carefully removed the IV. "Since you were unconscious, I took the liberty of re-hydrating you."

"Didn't know you cared."

"I'm that kind of guy."

Jack gave him a long, calculating look, and Julian tried not to chafe under it, instead holding out a hand to help him up. Jack hauled himself upright. "Is this the part where you tell me I should take it easy for a few days?"

Julian shrugged eloquently, dropping down onto his favorite of the clinic's rolly stool things. "Only if you like your leg." It was a flippant answer, but one that would doubtlessly get the point across. He pulled out his prescription pad again and wrote one for some slightly above-counter grade drugs. "Painkillers," he said, and handed it over. "I don't recommend taking them on an empty stomach."

Jack gave himself some time to adjust to the new blood flow before swinging his legs over the edge of the table—very, very carefully—Julian noted with approval. He probably didn't want to faint again, not that Julian thought he would.

"How did you get here, anyway?"

"Drove," Jack said shortly, like it was a dumb question.

Julian raised his eyebrows. *Dumb shit,* was his first thought. He could have passed out at the wheel and ended up in worse shape than he'd already been. Then again, people didn't generally do their best thinking while bleeding from a gaping flesh wound. "Just tell me it's not a manual."

Jack blinked, reaching for his jeans and managing to wiggle his left leg in without falling over. "I mean, Hamilton drove me. I think he wanted to have the rest of the day off to be with Mel. They just live around the corner."

Well, thank God he wasn't a total idiot. Julian let out the breath he'd been holding. As a doctor he would have had to advise strongly against anyone operating heavy machinery in Jack's condition. "Good. So, let's talk shop. I don't think you've got any irreversible damage, but you're going to be operating below capacity for a while. If you've got the time, I'd like to refer you to a physiotherapist. You wouldn't be going for a week or more. I just want to make sure the muscles heal properly. That all right by you?"

"There's one here in town?" He sounded surprised. Distractingly, it was just his ass hanging out of the bloodstained jeans now.

Julian guessed it wasn't all that unusual that not everyone knew Roz had completed her qualifications a few months ago, before she'd returned to take over the gym their parents had run for as long as he could remember when they retired to Florida. Truth be told, Jack probably didn't need the physio. He likely would have been just fine on his own. But his health insurance covered it, and anyway it was an easy way to keep an eye on the injury and forestall any future problems. "She's my sister," he explained. "And if you want a ride home from someone other than your Aunt Bella you'd better like her."

Jack huffed a laugh. "In that case, I think we'll get along fine."

"It's quitting time, so she should be here any minute." Julian flushed a little in spite of himself. Here he was at twenty-seven, getting picked up from work by his sister. "I had to sell my car when I finished my residency in Ontario. For one thing, it wouldn't have made the trip, and for another, it wouldn't have survived the winters anyway. The shit that passes for snow down there."

"Ha!" Sliding down from the table, Jack's tone was triumphant. "I studied engineering at U of T. You should have heard them whining every time there was the slightest flurry. You'd think they lived in Georgia or something."

For the first time, Julian caught the hint of an accent. "Not from around here, then?" Most of the local boys never got out of province for an education, but then again, most of them didn't need to.

Jack looked sheepish. "You couldn't guess, with a name like Jackson Strange?" The accent was suddenly a lot thicker. "Cape Breton, Nova Scotia. Worked my arse off to get in to U of T and out of the Maritimes; God knows the east coast's in poor enough shape."

Julian stared at him blankly for a moment before he came up with something to say. Jack's voice had an odd lilt to it now, a cadence that was somehow…he didn't know what to call it. It made him want to keep Jack talking. "You must really hate living in Alberta," he commented as they left the room, turning the lights out in the office as they went.

"Not as much as my mother," he said ruefully. The words came out sounding like *me mether*. "I think it breaks her heart a little every day she doesn't see the sea. But Cape Breton's tiny, and there were too many memories of my father, so she left, came out here to be close to me." He laughed self-deprecatingly. "Not that Calgary's that much closer, come to think on it."

"This place is rather isolated," Julian commented as he locked the door behind them. He shivered, shrugging into his coat. The long winter was already starting to make its presence known. Yuck. It was only September! He hoped Roz had the heater going. "It's not really close to anywhere. Where do you live, anyway?" Julian asked, fighting the urge to curl his hands up his coat sleeves like a little kid. He shifted from foot to foot, trying to keep warm.

Jack raised an eyebrow at him. He was probably wondering about the fidgeting, but didn't comment on it. "Few minutes out on Highway 77. Five kilometers, maybe."

"Don't much like the neighbors, eh?" Julian teased. Inwardly, he was a little worried, since the location was pretty remote, but if at his age Jack couldn't take care of himself there was certainly nothing Julian could do for him. Worrying obsessively didn't count, though it was a possibility.

"What neighbors?" the other man joked. "Everyone knows everyone in this town, anyway."

Julian was just about to disagree with him—he certainly didn't know everyone, not anymore and not *yet*—when he was saved by a dirty Silverado swinging around the corner. "That's our ride."

Roz pulled the Chevy up to the doors and put the thing in park…

which was when Julian remembered that the Silverado was a three-seater and not the extended-cab version they'd had when Mom and Dad were still in the country. *Balls.* It was about to get a little crowded. He opened the door.

"Hey, Beanstalk," Roz greeted cheerily. "Who's your friend? He looks familiar."

Julian sighed exaggeratedly and stepped aside. "Jackson Strange, meet my sister Roslin. I guarantee she's stranger than you."

The two shook hands, awkwardly through the height difference provided by the truck.

"Pleasure," Jackson said.

Roz eyed him up and down without any shame. "No kidding."

It was going to be a long ride home. "As cozy as this must be for you, Roz, we are freezing our balls off out here. Let us in, would you? I promised Jack a ride home."

"East or west?" Roz asked after they'd piled in.

Julian held his arms in close to his body, folding his hands awkwardly in his lap, but there was no way to keep his elbow from brushing Jack's. He chewed his bottom lip distractedly.

"West," Jack told her.

Roz threw the truck in reverse and backed up, making a left onto the main street. Julian considered telling her to stop at the pharmacy—Jackson was sure to be sore in a few hours, and Julian wanted to start him on antibiotics as soon as possible—but there would have been no point; the pharmacy closed at four-thirty on Fridays.

"You running a taxi service out of your office now, Jules?"

Julian scowled at her and considered using the excuse to shift closer to Jack but resisted, reluctantly. "Leg injury, lack of vehicle. What was I going to do, send him home with Mata Hari?"

Roz shot a look at Jack over Julian's head. "Bella's a friend of yours, then?"

"My father's sister," Jack said with a wry smile Julian could practically hear. "I take it you know her."

"By reputation mostly. My little brother's a dinner talker."

"Never would have guessed."

"I am sitting *right here*."

"Yeah. You're hard to miss, you take up so much room." Jack nudged him into Roz.

Flushing, Julian relaxed slightly, shoving back. The trick was in ignoring Roz's knowing look and the tingle in his shoulder at the same time. "How old are we?"

"Personal question," Jack barked teasingly.

"I'll show you mine if you show me yours."

"Would you two prefer to have this conversation somewhere private?" Roz broke in, pulling into a driveway. "This is it, right?"

Julian glanced out the window, mentally noting the location.

"This is me," Jack confirmed. "Thanks for the lift, Roz." A wink.

Julian rolled his eyes. "Take it easy, Jackson. I mean it."

"Yes, sir." He ripped off a mock salute.

"I like him," Roz commented after the door shut.

"You would," Julian muttered, moving over.

Dammit. The seat was still warm.

Chapter 3

THE alarm clock went off, and Julian rolled over with a sleepy smile, slapped the snooze button, and snuggled back into the pillows. Not being an intern was utterly fantastic. Normal office hours. Weekends off. *This* was why he'd spent half his life in school. To be able to, one Saturday morning, roll over and hit the snooze button and feel utterly guilt-free about it.

Ohhh, yeah.

Then the phone rang.

Groaning, Julian pulled the second pillow over his head. Maybe if he were lucky it'd stop before it annoyed him enough to pull him out of bed.

Apparently, today was not his lucky day. Julian wiped a hand across his eyes and reached for the cordless. "Hello."

"Doctor Piet, I presume."

"I go by Julian on weekends," he yawned, not recognizing the voice. He sat up a little, trying not to fall back to sleep.

"Julian."

Oh, well, that explained it. Julian didn't have that reaction to too many people just saying his name. "Jack. What can I do for you at this ungodly hour of the morning?" Under any other circumstances, he might've felt guilty about the snippy tone. But he was awake now, and he desperately wanted to be sleeping. "And how'd you get my number?"

"You live with your sister. You gave me her business card. Turns out it has a home number on it. Did I wake you? Sorry, Doc. I forget that not everyone's used to rig hours. Listen, I need a favor."

Julian stood and stretched, pointing his fingers toward the ceiling. "Do I need to be dressed?" he asked unthinkingly.

"For this one, yeah. I need someone to drive me to the pharmacy. My truck's still at work."

Balls. He'd forgotten about that. A morning without painkillers or antibiotics to keep Jack pain-free and healthy, and there was no way he could walk into town to get them. Not a good idea to let that state of affairs continue. Apparently doctors were never off-duty. Well, you lived and learned. "You don't sound so great this morning."

"I've had better nights' sleep, yeah," Jack admitted. "So...." He sounded embarrassed. "I'll be seeing you?"

"You can make me breakfast when we get back," Julian grumbled, grabbing a T-shirt from the floor and smelling it. It seemed reasonably clean. Now, sweatpants.... "I'll be there in ten minutes."

"Thanks, man. I owe you one."

Julian, still half-asleep, allowed himself to think of a couple of particularly naked ways he would like to collect on that favor, not that he ever would. "See you in ten."

Pants, pants.... There they were, half-hiding under his open suitcase. He should really get around to unpacking; he wasn't going anywhere now. Julian jumped into them, wiggling until he was comfortable, then thudded down the stairs to the kitchen. Keys.... Oh, thank God, Roz had left the keys to Dad's Sierra hanging from the rack by the front door. Good thing she'd thought to call and have the insurance reinstated; apparently she hadn't been planning on driving him around for long. Julian slipped on a pair of sneakers and half-stumbled, half-ran out the door to the truck.

Six seconds later he was running back in to brush his teeth, just in case.

Finally, hoping he remembered the way, Julian started the truck. It felt awkward in his hands at first—his little VW Jetta obviously handled differently—but it hadn't been *that* long. He took off in the general direction of Highway 77.

He pulled up in front of the white Cape Cod-style house eight and a half minutes later, not much more awake than he had been ten minutes ago. His stubble was starting to itch, and he wished he'd taken another few minutes to shave.

"Top of the mornin' to ya."

God, was his accent always this pronounced in the mornings? Julian spun around with a smile he couldn't help. "It certainly is the very beginning of what might be classed as morning hours, yeah."

"Lookin' good on it," Jack grinned widely. His morning hair was nearly as bad as Julian's own, but it was, in Julian's opinion, far sexier. Julian desperately wanted to touch it.

God, this was bad. Bad Julian! No crushing on the patients!

Aside from the hair, though, Julian had to admit that Jack looked pretty rough. There were dark circles under his eyes, and he was limping pretty obviously. Not that the leg-favoring was a bad thing; at least, not yet. The poor leg deserved a rest.

"You look like shit," he returned cheerfully, still more or less in doctor mode. It was always more difficult for him to be around new people without the official interface of his lab coat or scrubs. "That's karma for you. Got your prescriptions?"

Jack shot him the finger, then waved the papers in the air. "Got 'em. Ready when you are, Doc."

"Let's go then, I want my breakfast. I'm a bear before orange juice and food."

"The cuddly kind or the growly kind?"

Julian smirked as he hopped back in the cab, not letting the inward wince show on his face when Jack had obvious difficulties with the height. "The hungry kind," he answered. "It's not just all talk about breakfast, you know."

Jack was giving him a sly look, and Julian was pretty sure he could guess what for, so he broke eye contact and started the truck again. "So, where is it I'm taking you?"

"Truck first," Jack said. "Pharmacy's not open yet. Then breakfast. Pub's open for breakfast five-thirty to ten."

Julian shuddered at the ungodly hour, but that was life in northern Alberta for you. Damn early risers. "All right. Where'm I going?"

Jackson directed him back to town, and Julian followed the directions absently, feeling more than a little awkward. Roz had told him more than once that he was a completely different person in uniform, and he knew it was true. When he put on the coat, he was untouchable, and because of that he could do and say as he liked, joke around, make friends—because it was a built-in excuse to keep them at arm's length. Without it he was naked, vulnerable, and socially awkward.

"You can pull over here," Jack indicated, and Julian flicked the turn signal and pulled into the small lot dubiously.

"It doesn't look much like an oil rig."

Jack rolled his eyes at him. "This is just the engineering office. We're an R and D facility, really. New designs, new ways to get the oil out of the ground, environmental containment, that sort of thing. The test rig's a few clicks out yet. We carpool."

It was the most he'd said at one time since they'd met, and Julian had the sudden impression of how much the other man genuinely loved his job. He nodded as they both hopped down from the cab, Jack a little gingerly. The pub was only a few shop fronts away and he could already smell the bacon frying. Julian's stomach grumbled loudly.

"Christ, isn't your sister feeding you? I heard that all the way over here."

Julian laughed self-deprecatingly and waited at the sidewalk for him to catch up. "God, if Roz heard you saying that. Cooking isn't her strong suit, unless you want to live on baked goods."

"Mmm, cookies." They fell into step. "You been to Brenda's before?"

Julian had—but not for years. "When I was a teenager we used to go sometimes, try out our fake IDs. Too bad Gord knew all our parents. That was back when he tended the bar himself." He stopped, flushing, and remembered taking his very first boyfriend out to dinner here, Christmas the year he was eighteen. "And I just totally dated myself, didn't I?"

Jack chuckled. "Relax, kid. I'm older'n I look." He swung open the door and took a deep breath. "Only place around with decent coffee in the mornings." The tiny little town had yet to be invaded by Tim Horton's.

"It's the only place around *open* in the mornings," Julian pointed out. "In fact, it's the only place around, period. But at this point they could serve concrete with my orange juice and I'd be happy."

Jack rolled his eyes at his obvious preoccupation with food and waved at the proprietor, Brenda, as they made their way to a table.

Right away, a bottle-blonde teen with a bouncing ponytail popped over with some menus and a pot of coffee. "Get ya something else to drink?" she asked brightly, pen hovering at her notepad.

Julian ordered an orange juice, then amended it to two glasses as she filled Jack's coffee mug. He covered his own.

Silence overtook them for a moment as the girl bounced away, and Julian squirmed uncomfortably until he finally resigned himself and bit the bullet. "So," he said, injecting as much wry humor into his voice as possible, "you come here often?"

Jack snickered. "Like you said, nowhere else to go." He shrugged. "Besides, they've got pool, music, beer on tap…."

"He's a regular," Ponytail Girl—Bess, according to her name tag—confirmed as she set down two extra-large glasses of orange juice. "Usual for breakfast?" she asked Jack.

"Don't mess with perfection," Jack agreed.

"And you?"

Julian had been so busy trying not to be nervous he'd hardly glanced at the menu. "Um." Suddenly realizing he hadn't actually been to Brenda's since that Christmas, he scanned down the list quickly and decided on eggs, toast, bacon, and hash browns, then devoted all of his attention to the orange juice.

"No coffee?" Jack asked when he set down the glass.

Julian shook his head and licked a bit of pulp from his upper lip. "I always hated the stuff, but I needed it to get through medical school, and residents live and breathe that sewage. Detox was tough, but I swore off it once I pulled my last double shift. Got the shakes so bad my roommate wanted to take me to the ER."

Jackson looked a little horrified at that. "Thanks." He glanced down at his coffee and twitched, then laughed. "Moderation is the key."

"Never been any good at moderation," Julian admitted, nodding at his two glasses of orange juice, one already empty.

"I can see that."

Julian was just starting to feel awkward again when Brenda arrived at their table, topping off Jack's coffee. "Hi, guys," she said warmly, sliding into the booth next to Jack. "What brings you here before high noon?" she teased Julian with a grin.

Julian rubbed his eyes with one hand and pouted, pointing at Jack. He'd known Brenda since he was ten, and she'd always had a soft spot for kids, having none of her own.

"This mean old thing? Did he threaten you?"

"Oh, for God's sake." Jack nudged her in the shoulder. "I dragged him out of bed to get me to my truck, and the pharmacy. Ah…I might need tonight off work," he added sheepishly. "Sorry."

Work? Julian wondered, but opted not to ask.

"What did you do to yourself this time?" she asked him, her expression long-suffering.

"I, uh, I cut my leg open on a steel girder."

Brenda looked at Julian for clarification. Oh, thank God; the doctor side could take over for a while. He said, "He tripped. Fifteen stitches. Pink ones, actually."

Jack shot him a mutinous glare and aimed a kick at him under the table. "Thanks a lot, Doc."

"Jackson Strange, is that any way to treat someone who's doing you a favor?" Brenda tsked at him. "Honestly, Julian. It's good that you're getting to know him now. I swear he's in that clinic every other week with some injury or another. Usually only because we make him go."

Oh, boy. Julian wasn't sure if he was looking forward to seeing that much of the other man, or dreading it. Probably equal parts of each. "Guess I'd better order some more thread."

She chuckled. "That you should. Now, boys, I've got gossip to make. I'm sure you understand, and I think your breakfast is almost here, so I'll get out of your way. Jackson, you take as long as you need, you hear me? Let me know when you'll be back. We'll make a party of it."

Jack looked like he wanted to protest that he wouldn't be off *that* long, but Brenda never gave him the chance. She swanned off with the empty coffee pot in one hand, greeting the steady stream of customers trickling in the door for Saturday breakfast.

"Second job?" Julian finally had to ask, raising an eyebrow.

Jack squirmed a little at that. "I help out sometimes on Saturday nights. It's nothing major. I like it."

Whatever it was, it was pretty obvious he didn't want to talk about it with Julian right at that moment, so he let the subject drop. It was just as well, since their breakfasts had arrived, and Julian discovered exactly how hungry he really was, attacking his bacon-eggs-toast-hash browns with gusto.

When he looked up a half a minute later to grab the ketchup, it was to find Jack looking at him with an unidentifiable expression. "What?" Julian asked. "What? Have I got something on my face?"

Jack just shook his head and picked up his fork, digging into his own breakfast. There was some kind of biscuit, a stack of pancakes, and what seemed to be half a plate of breakfast sausage. "Nothing," he said innocently, his eyes betraying him.

"What?" Julian persisted, stabbing another forkful of hash browns covered in egg yolk and mushing them in the ketchup for good measure.

The part of him that was a doctor and sometimes had to remind people to count calories and think about what they ate switched right off.

"Just…" Jack waved his hand. "Where do you put it all, man? Are you always this… hungry?"

Julian nodded, swallowing. He didn't exactly look like a guy that could put away a plate of food in three minutes. "If I thought about how many calories I consume in a day, I'd have to put myself on a diet." He shrugged. "More fallout from med school. You learn quickly not to waste your time eating when you could be doing something useful, like studying or sleeping. It's not good for you to eat so fast, but old habits die hard."

"Some things need to be savored," Jack pointed out, spearing a piece of pancake. They did look delicious, and they came with whipped cream. Julian kept his mind firmly away from *that* dangerous path.

Well, he tried, anyway. He got points for that, right?

"I savor things," he defended himself. "Days off, for example. I will never again take them for granted."

"Remind me to call you early and wake you up on the weekends," Jack ribbed.

"You'd better not. I know where you live, and I could kill you and make it look like an accident." The threat was somewhat undermined by the fact that he said it between huge bites of egg-slathered toast. Just the orange juice left to go.

There was a lull in the conversation as they both finished up the last of their breakfasts. Then Jack asked, "So, your sister. What's the deal with that?"

Ah, crap. That figured. Julian had found someone he could hopefully safely crush on from afar and the guy was only interested in Roz. Typical. He shrugged, trying to mask his disappointment, annoyed with himself for being disappointed in the first place. "What do you want to know?"

"You look alike, and you act alike, and you even have similar jobs, but…" he trailed off. "Am I crazy? You can't possibly actually be her younger brother."

Julian sighed. Maybe he was just curious, just making conversation. It still wasn't something he particularly wanted to talk about, but he'd just find out from someone else in town anyway. "She's not really my sister," he explained. "We're cousins, but we were raised together. I'm actually a couple of years older, but her parents adopted me when I was eight and she was five. Since I'm newer to the family…."

"You got dubbed 'little brother,'" Jack finished. "Got it." He looked like he wanted to comment further, but for whatever reason he left it at that, and Julian was grateful.

"What about you? No brothers or sisters?"

"On Cape Breton, everyone's family," Jack said. "It's part of why I've always liked small communities, and why I like it here. But no, no siblings. My parents married late in life; maybe they didn't have time for two. I don't know."

Julian sipped his orange juice absently, having run out of things to say, and gazed out the window. The small town was starting to come to life, as much as it could on a Saturday morning. There were kids coming in from hockey practice and seniors playing bridge in the corner. He wondered if he'd ever get used to life in a small town again.

"You boys ready?" Bess was back at their table again, collecting their dishes. "Or are you stayin' for lunch?"

Jack shot her a smile that could have lit up the Arctic Circle in December. "I think we're done here." He looked over at Julian. "You're not going to eat another plateful, are you?"

"Not for at least an hour," he affirmed. Actually, he was feeling a little queasy. Maybe he should've taken time to breathe between bites.

Jack turned back to their waitress. "In that case, check, please!"

It was then that Julian started to panic. He flicked his gaze around the pub again, taking it in. The majority of the clientele appeared to consist of families—dads and daughters, mothers and sons. A few guys Julian thought he recognized as oil refinery workers or people he'd known in high school were sitting in the far corner, playing cards. There was the bridge club, and the Monforton brothers sitting up at the bar.

Okay. He could go out for breakfast with a man and nobody was going to call the feds to put him under what Roz eloquently referred to as homosuspicion.

It had been different in Toronto, of course. He had never felt the need to hide there. Most of his friends had either been gay, curious, or just plain easygoing. But this was Alberta, conservative to the core. It made him nervous.

Trying to squash the rising uneasiness he felt, Julian reached for his wallet—only to be stopped short by the warm hazel eyes across from him. Jack tipped his head. "I believe your terms were breakfast. This one's on me."

Oh, God. He didn't know how long his resolve would last if Jack kept giving him looks like that. His composure was already shot to hell. Now he was worrying if this was a date! Julian didn't know if he'd feel worse if it were or if it weren't.

Toronto had never been this complicated; but then again, he'd been far too busy when he'd lived there to date seriously, barring a very few notable, atypical exceptions. In point of fact, even the one or two short-lived flings he'd managed to fit in between classes, clinics, exams, and rotations had in no way prepared him for a situation like the one he was in now.

"Thanks," he managed.

Jack winked at him and grabbed the bill, taking it up to the register to pay, limping the whole way. Julian watched him without really meaning to, envying the easy manner with which he carried himself, the quiet confidence he had. Part of him knew how good it felt to be perfectly comfortable in his surroundings, firm in his belief in himself and his abilities; he'd been practicing medicine long enough. He just wished that same self-assurance would transfer over to his personal life.

"You all right, Doc?"

Julian started, blinking up and recognizing Jack standing over him at the little booth. "What? Oh, yeah." He shook himself, standing. "Sorry. I was somewhere else."

"I could tell." He held the door, eyes curious. "Anyplace interesting?"

Shuffling out onto the sidewalk, Julian shook his head, squinting in the morning sunlight. ""No place I've got any business being. Thanks for breakfast, again."

"Thanks for the lift, again," Jack returned. The inquisitive look had nothing if not intensified. "You wanna talk about it?" he hedged.

I'd like to drink it right out of my system. He didn't want to lie, but he wasn't just going to come right out and say it, either. "Nah, thanks. It's sort of personal." He laughed softly, though he was anything but amused. He was trying desperately not to think about how much Jack reminded him of someone he used to know. "Apparently I'm even a bear after orange juice."

"The grumpy kind or the cuddly kind?"

He glanced up to find Jack's eyes shining with some kind of warm amusement, and he shook his head again. "Depends on the company, I guess."

Wait—was that disappointment? Whatever the flash of emotion had been, it was gone almost as soon as it had appeared. But the tone was light. "Lucky me."

Julian opened his mouth to say something, anything; to apologize, or to clarify. But he couldn't come up with something that didn't sound wrong. "The broody kind, apparently," he sighed. "Look, I'm sorry I'm not great conversation this morning. You've got your truck. I'll catch up with you later, all right? You should come in for a check-up, maybe Tuesday, to see how you're healing up."

"Yeah." A muscle in Jack's jaw twitched, and the warmth seemed suddenly to be gone from his eyes. "I'll do that, Doc. Think I might just take the drugs and sleep away the weekend."

"It'll be good for you," Julian promised, and wished he meant something else. "See you Tuesday, then." Not wanting to be any ruder than he already had been, he extended his hand for the man to shake.

Jack eyed him for a second before grasping it, his grip dry and firm, but not crushing. "Later, Doc."

Julian waved as he turned, shoving his hands into the pockets of his sweatpants and wishing he'd worn a coat. Somehow, the day that had appeared so fair and warm from the truck this morning seemed cooler and darker now. Climbing into the truck took the rest of his energy, and he sat there for a minute wondering what to do before starting the engine. He headed home.

∿Chapter 4

JACKSON slammed the truck door shut and stomped inside, nursing a giant headache, a throbbing leg, and a really foul mood. His dog Robot met him at the door, her tail wagging unflaggingly, and he ruffled her ears absently before continuing to the kitchen.

Relax, he told himself. *Deep breaths. You're overreacting.*

When would he learn to leave well enough alone?

Pouring himself a glass of water, he glanced briefly at the directions on his prescriptions before shaking out the appropriate dose and knocking them back. Hopefully this was close enough to breakfast time to count as "take with food."

Utterly disgusted with himself, Jack almost threw the water pitcher back in the fridge before slinking into the living room and flopping down on the couch. Robot could obviously tell he was in no mood. Ordinarily by this time she'd have some toy or another in her mouth and be absolutely begging to play, but today she was standing almost indecisively in the doorway to the kitchen, her tail still going slowly.

He sighed. He was such a jerk. He was taking out his groundless frustrations on the only being in the universe that was consistently happy to see him. "Come here, girl," he said softly. She padded over and sat down, her head nudging his hand.

Jack rolled his head back against the pillow and stared at the ceiling, petting her absently. He'd been happy enough earlier this morning, considering the pain he'd had to grit his teeth through and the fact that he'd barely slept. Julian—Dr. Piet—had been interesting enough company to keep his mind off of it, most of the time. That was the problem, really. Jack didn't like to need people. He especially didn't like to need other men in this part of Alberta.

He *would* have liked to sit around the entire day half-stoned on pain medication and fantasizing about that ass, though.

Except that Jack was a realist, more or less. He could tell when something made someone uncomfortable, and while Julian hadn't struck him as particularly homophobic or even unreceptive—he couldn't have been, not with the constant innuendoes and sly smiles of the day before—he was certainly…awkward this morning. It made Jack wonder what on Earth he was running or hiding from all the way out here in the middle of nowhere.

That, Jack decided, was what Julian had done this morning. Run. He'd seen something that had scared him and made his excuses as quickly as he could. It was a far cry from the doctor he'd met yesterday, a man who gave as well as he got and then some, a tease and a flirt. The dichotomy sent up giant red warning flags in Jack's brain that said that even if there were some way of determining whether Julian might be interested in making a house call every now and again, it was probably a bad idea.

This sucked.

Any other time if something like this had bothered him he'd have just hit the gym to work it off, or gone for a jog with Robot, or found a reasonable substitute. None of those things was going to help him work it out this time, though. He was effectively under house arrest until further notice.

God, maybe there was some porn around here somewhere, he thought hopefully. At least then he wouldn't be bored.

Just five more minutes, he thought to himself. Five more minutes just laying here, petting his dog, and then he'd find *something* to do about getting his mind off of the pretty doctor.

Just…

five…

minutes…

Then the medication and lack of sleep the night before took their toll. Jack's eyes fell closed, his arm hanging limply off of the side of the couch, boots on. Robot curled up on the rug beside her master with her head on her paws and followed him into unconsciousness.

SOMEWHERE, a phone was ringing.

Jack grumbled, not wanting to get up, resolutely keeping his eyes shut against the noise. He shifted onto his side, rubbing his face into the pillow—

and sat up before he fell off the couch. Damn, that upholstery was rough on the skin. He made a mental note and sighed, glancing around for the phone.

Mental note: Do not call people early in the morning.

Jack stood stiffly, his left leg nearly buckling under him as he did so, and limped to the phone cradle. "Hello."

"Geez. Sorry, man. Who shit in your cereal?"

Jack grunted. "Hamilton. What the hell time is it?"

"Five-thirty. Did I wake you up?! I thought you got up before the sun!"

"I didn't actually go to bed last night, I don't think." He limped into the kitchen, rummaging in the fridge for something to drink. His mouth was drier than the Gobi desert. He grabbed something without looking and pulled it out, squinting. Orange juice. It'd do. He tried to put Julian out of his mind. "Five-thirty? Shit."

He'd slept for almost eight hours; no wonder he was hungry and lightheaded.

"Jack? You okay, buddy?"

"Fuck, I think I'm still stoned."

"Dr. Dan fix you up good?"

"He wasn't in," Jack said, sloshing orange juice over the counter.

Crap. "Got some new guy to kiss it better." Damn, he *must* still be feeling the effects if that was slipping out of his mouth. Maybe he should eat something.

"So, are you coming to work on Monday, or what?"

"Doc's got me under house arrest 'til Tuesday," he said, opening the fridge fully again to check for orphaned leftovers. Excellent: leftover pizza. He grabbed the container and debated over adding a beer to his growing pile of items for consumption before ultimately deciding against it. "Be too damn stoned to drive anyway."

"Aww. Life's really tough. Want me to send you home something to do?"

Oh, thank God. "Would you?" he said gratefully, mouth full of pizza. Hamilton wouldn't get it. He was a nine-to-fiver, and a family man, and if he'd had the bad luck to get stuck at home for a few days he'd have had his wife and four-year-old to drive him comfortably insane in no time. Jackson was facing a weekend of quiet boredom and sleeping off the drugs, and even if he did manage to rustle up some porn there was only so many times he could do *that* in a day.

"You're nuts," Hamilton told him flatly, "but I have to go in anyway; left Mellie's pregnancy book in the office. Which project do you want me to bring?"

Jack swallowed, chasing the cheese, mushroom, and sausage with a mouthful of orange juice. "Bring in that new one GeOil just sent in. I want to look at the specs before we get it hooked up. Last one damn near burst, it was put together so badly." He bit off another piece of pizza.

"The modifications turned out nice, though."

They had. The company had made a tidy sum on that little patent-pending number.

"Yeah."

"Listen, I need a favor."

Oh, boy, Jack thought. *Here it comes.* "Yeah?"

"Melanie's scheduled for a C-section on Thursday at two o'clock.

Can you pick Jason up from his swimming lessons and bring him by the hospital?"

Well, if that was all. He could pick up the kid, sure; he was going to be at the gym to pick up his neighbor's daughter anyway, just like he did every weekday at five-thirty. "I can do that. I'll have to drop off Hallie before we head out to the hospital, though." It was an hour's drive on the best of days, and with the way Jack's luck was going, he wasn't prepared to count on a best day.

"Thanks, man. I appreciate it. I'll call the gym tomorrow to let them know."

After a few more moments of Star Hamilton's token whining about his pregnant wife, and a pointed remark from Jack that the two were not, in fact, officially wed (about as close to scandal as it got up here in the northern prairie provinces), they hung up, and Jack went back to wolfing down the pizza.

Making his way to the kitchen table, he winced at the stiffness in his leg. Damn. Maybe he'd need that physiotherapy after all. Then again, maybe he'd just slept funny. It wasn't often that he passed out with his boots on.

Wolfing down the rest of his dinner, Jack popped his medication, then checked his watch. "Come on, Robot. What do you say?" Jack stretched, attempting to work the stiffness from his leg without pulling any stitches. "Want to try a walk?"

Robot wagged her tail, then chased it in a circle. He figured on that for a yes.

Jack pulled a pair of gloves and an adjustable leash from the front closet, snapped the clip on Robot's collar and headed out the front door at about half the pace he would have just a few days ago. It felt like premature aging, and poor Robot was probably wondering why they weren't huffing along at their usual speed, but fresh air was definitely preferable to being cooped up in the house for another minute.

As the medication gradually kicked in, the pain in his leg lessened into a sort of dull ache, and Jack finally relaxed enough to let his mind wander. In this part of the country, the leaves on the few deciduous trees had already turned and fallen, leaving the ground covered in a slightly damp-smelling red and orange carpet. The sun was setting earlier and earlier each day, and the mornings came coated with a thin blanket of frost that, as Jack neared his thirty-sixth birthday, was just starting to annoy his joints.

Passing his nearest neighbor, he tugged on the leash, reining Robot in. "Should we stop to say hello?" he asked her.

By the way her ears perked up, she thought it was a great idea. They headed up the driveway toward the house. "Anybody home?"

Hallie Klein, the eight-year-old he drove home from swimming lessons, dance, or gymnastics every weeknight, waved at him from her bicycle. "Hi, Mr. Jack!"

"Hello yourself, Miss Klein," he said seriously, trying not to laugh. She had managed to get her pigtails to stick out the top of her bike helmet, and resembled a stunted alien. "How's the world treating you?"

"You're funny," she said with a smile. "My bike's all fixed now, see?"

Jack saw. A rough tumble a few weeks earlier had left deep scratches on the girl's arms and legs and made a bit of a tangle of the chain and spokes, but Jack had managed to sort it out for her. He'd also picked up a pair of elbow pads the next time he'd been in Calgary. "I'm glad to hear that. Is your daddy around?"

"He's making spaghetti. It's my favorite." Hallie hopped off her bike and laid it in the grass. "We can go say hello! Have you had dinner, Mr. Jack?"

Jack tried not to laugh as he let her lead him up the path to the house. "Yes, I have. I had pizza."

"With green peppers?" she asked suspiciously, wrinkling her nose.

"No, no green peppers," he promised. "Hey, Roy? You around?"

"Well, well, well. If it isn't the walking scar tissue."

Had Hallie not been present, Jack would have been tempted to make a rude gesture. Apparently news of his little accident had gotten around. Great. "Hallie here tells me you're setting the kitchen on fire."

"No!" she protested, covering her mouth and giggling. "Daddy, that's not what I said."

"Hmph," Roy grumbled, pretending not to have heard. "That's gratitude for you. Kids these days. You make their favorite meal and they go around insulting your culinary prowess." He smiled. "You eat?"

"Yeah, I just came by to say hello," he said. Robot punctuated his remark by barking once, happily. "Needed some exercise. Don't worry, though. I'm good to pick up the rug rat on Monday." *I might even stick around to talk to her swimming instructor.* He'd need to ask her what she thought about his physio, anyway—and with any luck, convince Roz to let him start early. He was already going mad from inactivity.

"Daddy, what's a rug rat?"

Roy shot Jack a warning look. "A very sweet, smart, cuddly little girl."

Jack feigned innocence, but ruined it with a wink and a cheeky grin. "Anyway, I'll leave you to your dinner. See you Monday, rug rat." He ruffled her ponytail over her helmet.

"Bye, Mr. Jack!"

He waved back at them, then half-staggered, half-limped down the path back to the road. Good grief, those drugs were doing a number on him. Jack stumbled up his driveway, eyelids heavy, and let Robot in the house. Then he sat down heavily on his front porch and took a few deep breaths.

No wonder the pill bottle said *Do not operate heavy machinery.* In this state, he could probably total a golf cart cornering at two miles per hour.

He was just about to get up and head inside when he heard the car door slam.

"Jackson Strange!" said a familiar voice. "What are you doing outside with no coat on? Honestly, you'll catch your death."

Jack looked up, astounded, and squinted into her face. *"Mom?"*

HELPLESS to do anything but stand and follow her into the house, he did so, wanting to offer to take her duffel bag but sure the gesture wouldn't be appreciated. What in God's name was she doing here? She was always complaining about how much work there was to be done in Calgary. She hardly ever took time off. "Mom, you're not a hallucination, are you?"

"Oh, for crying out loud," she said. (Mom had only been saying this since she'd started living in Calgary.) "What kind of drugs has Matheson got you on, anyway?" She picked up his prescription from the kitchen table and sniffed, then set it down. Evidently, whatever it was, it met with parental approval.

"Not Matheson," he said, feeling out of place in his own house. "New kid on the block."

"He at least seems to know what he's doing, I'll give him that." It was a burden, having not one but two nurses in the family. "Well? Let's see it."

"Mom, I'm not going to drop trou in the kitchen. Besides, I had it looked at yesterday. It's fine."

Flo Strange crossed her arms, tapped her foot, and raised one eyebrow.

Jack reached for his belt buckle. *For crying out loud* seemed to about cover it. He let his jeans pool at his knees. "Are you happy now?"

His mother flicked the kitchen light on and grabbed the nearest chair so she could get right up close. "Well, you certainly did a number on it. At least your doctor can hold a needle." Seemingly satisfied, she stood, patted him on the rear, and meandered over to the fridge. "But what's with the pink?"

Jack sighed, hiking up his jeans again. "Apparently they were out of blue."

"It suits you," she teased, pouring him a glass of milk and pressing it into his hands. She stood on tiptoe to kiss him on the cheek, then ruffled his hair. "You should visit more often."

His stomach twisted a little. He knew he should, and it wasn't that he didn't like to visit. It just seemed that he could never find the time. "You're here," he pointed out. He sniffed the milk, hoping it hadn't gone bad. That was his mom for you; trying to keep him hydrated and strengthen his bones at the same time. Supermom. "They kick you out of the neonatal unit or what?"

"Can't a woman take time off to see her only boy?"

That innocent act wasn't gonna cut it—especially since the first thing she'd done when she'd arrived was to examine his battle wounds. "Aunt Bella called you, didn't she?"

"She is just worried about you," she said, shaking a finger. "Even if she does overreact sometimes. Don't you have any food?"

"I ate," he apologized. "Store's closed. We could go to the pub for dinner, if you like."

"Oh, Jack," she tsked. "When are you going to find someone to look after you? What were you going to do tomorrow?"

"Live off the land," he said dryly. "This isn't exactly the middle of nowhere. That's at least four miles away. I can hit up the store in the next town over, or pick up some hamburgers and buns at the corner store. If you're feeling really crazy we could bum a meal off of Roy and Hallie. I'm sure they wouldn't mind."

"Don't make fun of your mother. You must have pasta or something, right?"

He was about to tell her that Roy down the street was making spaghetti, but decided against it. "Bottom cupboard to the left of the fridge. I think there might be some ground beef in the freezer."

Flo rummaged around for a few moments and came up with a bag of penne, a can of pasta sauce, and a half-pound of frozen meat. "It'll do."

While his mom busied herself in his kitchen, Jack picked up her duffel bag and carried it into his guest bedroom, careful to keep it in his right hand to avoid brushing against the stitches. He looked blankly at the bed for a few moments, wondering if he should change the sheets, then decided that if he tried it, he'd just end up asleep in the pile of blankets.

Man. These drugs were starting to actually suck.

By the time he made his way back to the kitchen his mother had nearly finished with her dinner. "Are you sure you don't want any?" she asked. "You're looking a little pale."

Jack shook his head and collapsed into a chair. "It's just the medication. It makes me want to sleep all day. Actually, it made me *really* sleep all day. Now it's trying to get me to sleep all night, too."

"Poor lamb," Flo teased, ruffling his hair as he slouched his head down onto his arms. "It's a wonder you survive up here by yourself."

"Mmph," Jack grumbled. He enjoyed his freedom, and he was fairly certain his mother would never ask him to move, but there was no sense in tempting fate. "I'm tough," he said. "I told you. Live off the land. Commune with nature." He paused, feeling the need to add something. "Shit in the woods."

"Yeah, you're a bear, all right," she said, sitting across from him with a giant plateful of pasta. "Drink your milk; it's good for you."

Jack did. Nobody could boss him around like his mama. She was a formidable woman, tall and lean with a shock of bright red hair that she'd kept short since his father had died. He suspected that it was artificial color now, since she was well past seventy, but he wouldn't have asked her about it for anything. In his much younger years, many a girlfriend had expressed her terror after having met her. Flo Strange was just that good at reading people's actions and intentions in a handshake.

He'd never really got around to telling her he'd decided women weren't for him. Since there wasn't anyone special in his life anyway, and probably never would be—Jack was more than comfortable in the closet—he figured it wasn't much of an omission.

He was in serious danger of falling asleep in his empty glass when the doorbell rang. He shot up straight, pulled something in his neck, and cursed under his breath.

"Jackson Strange! I know I taught you better than that! Swearing in front of a lady."

Jack's mouth dropped open to apologize—he'd forgotten for a

moment that she was there—but then he noticed she was having a hard time keeping a straight face. "That hurt," he whined, massaging the muscle he'd pulled as he went to the door.

It was Hamilton and his kid, with a file folder full of schematics the company damn well should've e-mailed instead of sending in hard copy and a USB jump drive on a keychain. "Brought you a get-well present," he said, holding out the bundle.

Jack took it. Work. Now that would be useful, especially if he had to come up with an excuse to get his mother to leave him alone. "Thanks, Hamilton. And Hamilton, Junior. Excited about being a big brother?"

Jason's expression made his opinion on the matter perfectly clear. "Dad says I won't be allowed to play with the baby for a long time."

Kids. They were so cute when they belonged to someone else. "Don't worry. By the time the baby gets here, you won't want to have anything to do with her anyway."

Hamilton shot him a warning look, but Jack just grinned at him. "See you on Thursday, buddy. Maybe Wednesday for you, Dad, if you're lucky."

"Tell your mom I said hi," Hamilton smirked.

Jack waited until Jason wasn't looking and flipped him off, then closed the door behind them.

JACK was laying on his back in his second-storey bedroom, staring at the ceiling and picking out patterns in the ceiling tile. He couldn't remember how long he'd been awake; it could have been five seconds or five hours. He didn't know what time it was. It was dark and warm, and his leg itched, but he couldn't scratch it.

Damn. Maybe that seven-hour nap had screwed up his sleep schedule, after all.

He was just about to give up on the idea of sleeping and find something else to do when the door creaked open.

Jack squinted. No, it was closed again. But he could have sworn that, just for a second, there had been a figure outlined in the light from the stairway safety light, tall and lean with a mop of unruly dark hair—

He breathed in sharply when he felt someone slide into bed beside him.

"Shhh," Julian whispered, putting a finger over his lips. "Don't want to wake anyone up."

"What the fuck?" Jack hissed back, fighting the urge to lick it. "What are you doing here?"

"If you don't want me here, I can go," the other man crooned quietly. His whole body was pressed against Jack's now. His apparently naked body. His apparently naked, *definitely aroused* body.

Well. Jack wasn't exactly in a position to complain, since he was equally naked and soon to be equally hard. "You're not going anywhere," he murmured, catching Julian's hand in his. He tugged sharply, bringing the younger man's body flush with his own. His left leg didn't so much as twinge.

Julian wriggled. There was no other word for it. The movement brought their bare erections into direct contact, and Julian made an absolutely delicious noise in the back of his throat. "Not unless you're coming, too," he agreed wickedly, licking a line up Jack's neck to his mouth.

"You are a bad influence," Jack groaned into the sloppy kiss, reaching between them to lend a hand to Julian's efforts. "I was perfectly happy in the closet until you came along."

"I'll make it up to you," Julian promised, breaking away slightly. Jack could see his eyes slide half-shut in the darkness, felt him thrust a few times counterpoint to the rhythm of his hand holding their cocks. Julian half-rolled to one side, leaning on his hand as his wet mouth traced a long path down Jack's chest and stomach, left hand leading the way. For the barest of seconds Jack felt the ghost of warm breath, then a hint of moisture. Jack's whole body tensed and jerked.

"God, Julian—"

Jack sat straight up in bed, breathing heavily. There was light streaming through the bedroom window. The bedroom door was open wide, and the smell of bacon was wafting up the stairs.

Jesus H. Christ, what a dream. He groaned, covering his face with his hands. Why couldn't he have stayed sleeping for five more minutes?

At least he could chalk this one up to the drugs. Damn, he was going to have to wean himself off of the pain medication. He couldn't keep waking up like this; he'd go completely mad.

Taking a few deep breaths, he stood and headed toward the master bathroom. It was going to be a long week.

Chapter 5

THE first time Jackson Strange had walked into his examining room, Julian had managed to keep himself at a mental distance for a few reasons. For one, Jack had looked like crap. Sure, he was good-looking in general, but that day he'd been pasty-pale, looking like he'd fall over or throw up at any second. For another, he'd only known him as a patient—a patient with a large, nasty, bleeding hole in his leg that had needed to be sewn up.

So he'd flirted, sure, but that was just his own peculiar bedside manner, something inside him telling him how to put different patients at ease. In Jack's case flirtation had been called for, not to mention that Jack had started it. It wasn't until later, after he'd pulled out the IV, that he'd started to almost *mean* the things he said.

Now, several days later—after a bizarre and somewhat awkward breakfast-maybe-date—it was a lot more difficult to keep his thoughts totally professional.

Especially since Jack was more or less half-naked as soon as he walked in the door.

"You don't waste time," Julian quipped, willing himself not to react. It wasn't like he hadn't seen men in their boxer shorts before. In fact, he'd even seen *Jack* in his boxer shorts before. Jack had just been slightly more stoned at the time.

"You're a busy man," Jack returned. "So? Do I get a clean bill of health?"

Rolling his eyes, Julian set down the clipboard. "I haven't even looked at you yet."

Jack leaned back on his palms, his legs hanging down over the edge of the examination table. "Well, by all means, Doc," he drawled, "feast your eyes."

Julian was way ahead of him, though he was hoping he could maintain the guise of clinical detachment. "How's the pain?" he asked, examining the stitches. They could probably come out in a few more days, the way the wound was healing. "Any side effects from the drugs?"

"Picture of health," his patient promised.

Julian doubted health had ever looked quite this obscene, but opted to say nothing. He pressed the backs of his fingers to the wound, checking the temperature of the surrounding skin.

Jack jumped about fifty feet in the air.

Whoops, Julian thought. *Should've warned him.* "Sorry, did that hurt?" he asked. The area *was* warmer than normal, but that was to be expected since Jack's body was working overtime to repair itself. It wasn't anything to worry about, and it didn't look infected.

"No, just—" Interesting; Jack's face had an uncharacteristic flush; maybe he was feverish after all? "Your hands are cold."

Oh, Julian thought, nodding and accepting the excuse, until out of pure reflex his eyes drifted back down to the gash. *Oh.* Well. That was definitely interesting, all right. "Sorry," he said, averting his gaze in what he hoped was a totally inconspicuous manner but had a feeling was completely transparent. "Doctor thing. We bathe them in ice water before each appointment."

"You're forgiven," Jack told him, voice just a little smug.

Concentrating on not blushing beet red, Julian grabbed his clipboard and scribbled a few notes. *I will not stare at Jack's erection. I will not stare at Jack's erection.* "It looks like you're healing up just fine. Unless you come across any other complications, you can start the physio whenever you're ready, and you can start back at work tomorrow." He looked up to get in a little dig. "Just try not to trip over your own two feet, eh?"

Jack made a face.

Rolling his eyes, Julian put the clipboard down. His mental disciplinary tactic seemed to be working. "Come back in a few days and I'll take out the stitches."

"Promise you'll be gentle?" God, he was batting his *eyelashes*. Either he thought Julian was totally oblivious or he was making fun of him.

Or else he just liked to watch his reactions. Julian was equally guilty of that. He was shooting back a reply before he'd even had a chance to think about it. "Please, you probably like it rough."

That shut him up, and damn effectively, too. Julian smirked, gesturing to the door, trying not to show how shaken he was by the ease of their casual flirting. "You're all set, Mr. Strange. Don't forget to collect your health card from Barb at the front desk."

Don't let the door hit your ass on your way out.

Not that Julian was giving that ass any more attention than it deserved.

"Can I put my pants back on first?"

"If you think it's necessary." *Whoops. Forgot about that.* Julian smiled at him. "Wouldn't want to deprive anyone of the view."

"That would be a shame," Jack agreed. "Thanks, Doc. See you in a couple days."

Julian left him to it. Watching Jack get dressed was just as bad as watching him strip for his concentration, and he still had a few hours of his shift left to go.

He let himself out and wandered over to the reception desk, leaning across at Barb. "Another one down." He purposely didn't follow his own train of thought down the path it was taking. Down. Right. That about summed it up. "Who's next?"

She handed him a folder. "Room two."

He saluted her with it and meandered down the hallway. He opened the door one-handed because the folder was open in the other. "Hello, I'm Dr. Piet," he said, still engrossed in reading the history. He slid into the rolling chair without looking up. "You must be—"

"Flora," a dry voice answered.

Julian looked up, chagrined. "Sorry. Bad habit, I know." He reached over to shake her hand.

Flora was an older woman with green eyes and startlingly sharp cheekbones. It was obvious that she had been a beauty when she was younger, and if Julian had been attracted to women at all, he was sure she still would have been stunning. "It's nice to meet you, doctor."

"So, I take it you're not from around here," Julian said. "I'm not really sure what to tell you. Based on your medical history…." He frowned slightly, turning back to the first page. An ugly suspicion was forming in his brain.

A quick double check more or less confirmed it. He took a deep breath.

"There's no treatment, doctor. Not at this point. I'm a nurse. I know that."

"So you're not here for a second opinion. That's good. Oncology isn't my specialty." What else could he say? *Sorry you're dying of lung cancer; by any chance, are you Jackson Strange's mother?* The names were the same, but he couldn't just *ask*.

She held up her pill bottle—empty. "I dropped them down the drain this morning during a coughing fit. I just need a refill. I'd have gone to my regular doctor, but I'm afraid I'm a bit far from home." Now that he was thinking about it, he could definitely hear the accent. He thought he could even see a family resemblance, in the eyes and the cheekbones especially, if not in the hair color.

For lack of anything else to do, he reached for his prescription pad. "Well, I can get you a refill. That won't be a problem." He took the bottle and copied down the medication and dosage, trying to keep himself occupied.

Flora, evidently, had no problem just coming out and saying whatever it was that was on his mind. "So, is it you I have to thank for the stitches on my son's leg?"

Julian froze, put his pen down, and spun the stool around slowly. "In theory," he hedged, "if I were the doctor who had stitched him up, I wouldn't be able to tell you anything about it." Just like he wouldn't be able to tell Jack his mom had been by.

"I was counting on it," she said. "Thank you anyway, doctor."

He opened his mouth, not sure what he was going to say. The hair on his arms was starting to prickle; little things were falling into place. It just so happened to be Bella's day off. He knew that, because he'd checked to have Jack come in on that day specifically. He hadn't seen Jack and Flora together in the waiting room. In fact she seemed to have waited until Jack was otherwise occupied to come in at all. "It's just my job." He handed over the prescription.

"Believe me, I've met enough doctors to know a good one when I see one."

Awkwardly, he scratched at the back of his neck. He might as well ask, since it was sure to bother him either way. "Mrs. Strange…Jack doesn't know you're sick, does he?" And if Jack didn't know, she couldn't tell anyone else, either.

Flora Strange was shrewd enough not to be particularly surprised by the question. Her reply was even and measured, rather than defensive. "And why should I tell him that? He's a big boy, and he's got his own life now. He should live it."

That was not the answer Julian had been looking for. He bit his lip. It wasn't any of his business, outside of the strictly medical aspect, but…. He sighed. His own parents had died when he was just a kid. He would have given anything for just one more hour with them, even just a few minutes to say goodbye or tell them he loved them one more time, but he'd never get it.

Jack could have it, though. Julian was a doctor. When he saw the chance to spare someone unnecessary pain, he took it if he could, and he wasn't ready to give up on this yet. For a few precious minutes, he stopped being Dr. Piet and became the eight-year-old boy who had lost his parents. "Mrs. Strange, don't you think your son deserves to know the truth? Doesn't he deserve a chance to say goodbye?" *Don't you want a chance to say goodbye to him?*

He was way beyond the bounds of patient counseling now, especially since she wasn't officially his patient, but she didn't seem to be taking offense. In fact, she was smiling softly. "You don't know Jack. When he was a boy, he was so outgoing. Hockey, student council, fifteen girlfriends a year. He was quite the charmer. But after his daddy died, he just shut off." She shook her head, running a hand through her short red hair. "I don't blame him, you know. His daddy meant the world to him, even if they didn't always see eye to eye. But it wasn't easy to watch him grow from the outgoing boy I knew into a total stranger, obsessed with his grades and not much else." Her eyes seemed to linger on the name embroidered on his lab coat for a moment before meeting his gaze again. She shrugged, her expression apologetic, then gave a little wheezing laugh. "Of course, that's also when he discovered he was gay, so that could have had something to do with it."

Julian breathed in so sharply he choked and started coughing. He hadn't exactly been expecting to get confirmation of Jack's sexual orientation from his mother. "Sorry," he gasped out, still coughing, chest heaving. It took a lot of effort not to laugh hysterically. "I wasn't expecting that."

Flora gave him a wry look. "I'm sure you never had any inkling at all."

"Uhhh…" *Only if by "never had any inkling" you mean "wondered every time I was in the same room with him and quite a few times I wasn't."*

"He doesn't think anyone knows, of course. So secretive these days. That's what I'm trying to say. He's finally coming out of his shell again, building a life for himself. He's happy. It could be weeks or months or a year before I die. I won't ruin his life for him by putting him back in that place any sooner than I have to."

Julian fought the urge to let his mouth hang open. "I…oh." He spun the chair in a circle, needing a few seconds to process. It wasn't a choice he would have made, or one that he would want made for him. The fact was that it was going to be a tough haul for him to carry this knowledge without tipping off Jack or anyone else, especially in a town this small, and *especially* if he got to see as much of Jack as he'd like to. But he could live with it. It was her decision, and she was making it out of love.

It must be very lonely for her.

"I…respect that, I suppose."

"Thank you. Of course, I'd appreciate it if this didn't get around."

He snorted at the irony. Yeah, he knew what being in the closet was all about. Not to mention the fact that he couldn't have told anyone about Jack even if he wanted to. There was that doctor-patient confidentiality thing again. "You've got nothing to worry about on that account, believe me."

Flora shot him a knowing look, and Julian was suddenly a little worried that he'd said too much. "Well, thanks for your time, doctor. I'm sure I'll be seeing you again."

Uh-huh, Julian thought, watching as she left the little room. He had the unsettling impression that something important had just happened and he'd missed it completely.

"ALL right, Beanstalk, spill it."

Julian finished chewing the mouthful of mashed potatoes he'd dutifully shoveled into his mouth despite his lack of appetite and put down his fork. "Spill what?"

Roz folded her arms across her chest. "Come on, Julian, give me a break. I'm your sister. I notice when things are bothering you. You stop eating. Julian, you *never* stop eating unless there's something wrong. So, just tell me."

He sighed, pushing away his plate. There was no point in pretending he was interested in the dinner he'd fixed them. "It…was sort of a tough day at work today."

"Oh?" Roz speared a piece of red pepper from his salad on her fork. "Wanna talk about it?"

Shaking his head, Julian sighed. "That's the problem. I *can't* talk about it. Doctor-patient thing."

"No wonder it's got you tied in knots." Roz grabbed their plates and set them on the counter by the sink. "What do you say we just skip to dessert and you can tell me whatever it is you can tell me?"

She'd baked cookies earlier. Julian had been able to smell them when he'd come in the door, and the dishes were still in the sink. It *did* sound good. A little chocolate went a long way. He refilled their milk glasses. "Doesn't sound like a bad idea."

"That's because it isn't one." Roz plonked a plate of cookies on the table. Suddenly, Julian was ravenous. "So, what's going on?"

He grabbed a cookie and dunked it liberally in the milk before shoving half of it into his mouth, feeling suddenly stupid. "It's nothing, really." In fact, it didn't concern him directly at all, which made him question his reaction to it. Situations like this came up from time to time, and he usually handled them with a lot more grace. Maybe it was just being home in town, in the house he'd grown up in, that made it hit him that much harder. "I had a patient in today who's dying."

That didn't happen to GPs too often, especially in backwaters like this, and he could tell Roz knew it. "Oh, Jules. I'm sorry."

Julian shook his head, swallowing the last of the cookie and reaching for another. "That's not it. People die. When you're a doctor, you have to accept that. It's just, she hasn't told anyone. Not her friends, not her family. And she doesn't plan to. She doesn't want them to know."

He could see the realization dawning on her face. Roz's parents had adopted Julian when his own had died in a car accident. They had been on their way to the airport to celebrate their fifteenth wedding anniversary in Cancun when an oil truck had lost control in front of them. They had both died instantly. "Julian...."

Unexpected tears stung his eyes when she reached for his hand across the table. He let her. His parents' deaths had hit him hard as a kid, and though he'd worked his way slowly through the grief as a teen and later an adult, sometimes the loss and loneliness sneaked up on him. Especially when he saw other people who didn't know what they had to lose. "Sorry." He blinked, clearing his vision. "It just sucks."

"I know. I miss them, too." Roz had hardly been old enough to remember her aunt and uncle, but she had shared the bits and pieces she could remember from time to time, helping Julian to keep their memory alive. "All you can really do is be there for whoever it is when they need you."

Julian washed down his third cookie with the last swallow of milk. "Yeah. Thanks. I needed to get that off my chest."

"That's what big sisters are for." She took the dirty plate and ruffled his hair with her other hand. "So, want to hear about my day? I had seniors' aquafitness, three hours of physical therapy I'm not supposed to talk about, and a level-three swimming lesson."

"Oh, geez." No wonder she smelled like chlorine today. "Nobody peed in the pool?"

"Not even Mr. Bender." Roz shifted the dirty dishes around to make room for a sink full of hot, sudsy water.

Julian rolled up his sleeves to join her automatically, reaching for the dish rag. "Well, that's good news. What's level three?"

"Eight- to ten-year-olds, mostly. I figured out where I recognized your new friend from. He's there to pick up little Hallie almost every day."

Huh. Jackson Strange never ceased to surprise him. "Must be a friend of the family," he said. "He doesn't have kids of his own." *Because he likes men.* Julian tried to quell the rising tide of hope that welled inside of him.

It must not have entirely worked, because Roz was giving him a sideways look. "What?" he asked. His sister just raised her eyebrows. "What?!"

"You *want* him!" she accused gleefully.

Julian could do absolutely nothing to stop the violent blush spreading on his cheeks. He grabbed the next clean dish and dried it dutifully. "You know, if I'd thought coming out to you would result in that accusation *every time* I made a new friend, I probably wouldn't have told you." Plus, the time she'd sent him a dildo for his eighteenth birthday really wasn't as funny as everyone seemed to think it was.

"Pff," Roz shouldered him gently. "Whatever. You can't fool me, Julian. That man is so hot you could probably smelt iron on his abs. I haven't seen that moon-in-your-eyes face on you for ages. Not since your first year of residency."

Julian's stomach went hollow. Those had not, in retrospect, been his best days. "I don't want to talk about it, Roz." He put another dry dish on the counter and reached for the next.

Roz didn't say anything, just kept handing him clean, wet dishes.

First-year residency. Now *there* was something Julian was better off forgetting. Just thinking about it made his fists clench. That nightmarish year had been enough to make him seriously rethink his specialty. Still, Roz didn't deserve to be snapped at for it. "Sorry. I just can't…. It's better if I just try to forget it, okay?"

"It's been six years, Julian," she reminded him quietly. "If you haven't forgotten it yet, do you really think you're going to?"

He didn't. That was the problem. He put down the last dry dish and turned to his sister. "I don't know. I want to, God knows. It's not that easy to just…throw yourself back out there." He gave her a small smile. "Especially in this part of the country."

"You needed a break from big-city living, and you know it. Fresh air, wide open spaces…" Roz's gaze was wistful. "You were lost, these last few years. I thought you'd never come back home. Hell, there were times I thought *I'd* never come back home, either. It hurts to lose people…but you need to get out and meet new ones. It's the only way to go on living. You don't *have* to fall in love again. Wanting to jump Jack's bones is totally healthy."

Actually, he contemplated telling her, *it's the other way around, mostly.* God. It sucked to get lectured by a woman three years younger than you. Julian sighed, knowing that she was right but not quite ready to follow her advice just yet. There would be time enough for that soon. "When did you get to be so damn smart, anyway?"

"Preschool," she said sassily. Her expression, though, was unfathomable. "We'll have to get you in on Wednesday's hockey games; lots of guys your age, you'll skate circles around them. That'll do for a start. Now put those dishes away and I'll let you beat me at a game of Scrabble."

Chapter 6

JACK flexed his leg gingerly, testing his strength. It had been over a week since his little mishap, and a few days since he'd started seeing Roz for physio. If he had still been interested in women at all, he had to admit that Roslin Piet would have held a powerful attraction for him. She was smart, sharp-witted, and beautiful, and anyone could see that she put in a huge effort to make other people feel good. She'd had him do some flexibility and endurance tests, then more or less thrown him into the pool to make sure he wouldn't have any problems with resistance.

His leg seemed to be holding up pretty well. The stitches had originally been scheduled to come out the week before, but between Star and Mellie's baby arriving slightly earlier than planned and his mother's visit, he hadn't really had the time or ambition to go to the clinic. Not that he was avoiding the new doctor; oh no. For all he knew, Dr. Dan was back in on clinic duty, taking care of the regulars like he always had.

But, well…. Jack wasn't really sure what to do with his newfound attraction for the young doctor. Julian was so hot-and-cold that it was impossible to guess what he was thinking or feeling. He was almost sure now that the other man was gay, bi, or at least *curious*. Normally, he would have taken that information and run with it, had some fun and tried to work the lust out of his system. He had a feeling that that wasn't going to be happening this time. Jack wasn't looking for a relationship. He didn't do well with them; hadn't even tried a steady friends-with-benefits thing since his university years—but he was starting to think that one night with Julian wasn't going to be enough. The man was getting under his skin, and the worst part was that Jack wasn't even trying to stop it.

He sighed and finished lacing up his skates. He wasn't sure if he'd play the whole game tonight, but a week off from hockey had been enough. He had to do *something* to tire himself out enough to sleep tonight, preferably without dreaming. One more guest appearance by Julian Piet would probably be enough to drive him right over the brink of insanity.

Jack removed his skate guards and stood up on the rubber mats. Not bad. After a few laps around the ice, he might not even feel the ache.

"Good to have you back, man," Brad nodded from across the room. "Hamilton gonna show?"

"His wife just delivered baby number two a week ago," Jack pointed out, grabbing his stick. "He'll miss at least another week."

That'd give them odd numbers, but it didn't really matter. It was just a pick-up game. Roz had free skates scheduled every so often, but every Wednesday night at eight was reserved for pick-up hockey for gym members. There were twenty or so regulars, but they didn't all show up every week.

"Hey, whose turn was it to bring the beer?"

"Mine."

The hair on Jack's neck stood straight up and his fingers clenched around his hockey stick. He turned around to see Julian standing in the doorway of the change room, a case of beer under one arm and a hockey bag thrown over his shoulder. He was wearing beat-up sneakers, jeans with holes in the knees, and a long-sleeved tee that fit him just right. With Jack on his skates, the top of the doctor's head reached the middle of his chest.

Christ. "Hey, Doc," he said casually. "Didn't know you played."

"Roz said I needed to get out more. Started last week." He set the case down in the pile of Zamboni ice outside the change room, then hauled his bag in after him. "Did she clear you to play?"

"I didn't ask her permission," Jack said dryly. As a matter of fact, it had been Roz's suggestion that he return to his regularly scheduled physical activities, saying it was the best way for him to make sure everything was working the way it was supposed to. Now he was suspicious. "But given the way she's been working me in physio this week, I should be fine." He swallowed hard as Julian pulled his T-shirt up over his chest, looking away. "I'm going to try a few warm-up laps," he said to no one in particular. "See you on the ice."

Twenty minutes later, the first period was well under way. Jack's leg barely even twinged at him, and he was keeping up with the younger guys pretty well. He tended to play defense, which was good—less balls-out skating; he'd probably be thankful in the morning.

Julian had turned out to be one hell of a hockey player. The kid was fast, and his stick work had Jack coming up with some really horrible pick-up lines. Unfortunately, he was playing for the other team, so to speak. So far he had one goal and an assist to his credit, leaving Jack's team trailing by a point. At least the first goal had been scored before Jack had hit the ice, so he didn't have to feel stupid about the way Julian waltzed right through the defensive line and put one right in the goaltender's five-hole.

"Incoming," Brad warned, skating backward from the blue line. Jack followed suit, keeping his eye on the speeding blur of a red jersey. Julian broke toward him, two other red players following behind looking for the drop pass.

With luck, they'd never get it. Jack's teammates were hot on their heels.

Jack knew he could never hope to match Julian in terms of speed, not with his injury and Julian's greater momentum. Instead, he found himself watching his skates, trying to get a feel for where he would go. Jack had to hand it to him; the kid could move.

Finally, he thought he could see what Julian saw, where the hole was. He moved to close it just as Julian tried to shoot a pass laterally across the ice and intercepted it with his stick, shooting around the back of the net with the puck on the edge of his stick.

Putting on a burst of speed, Jack felt his left leg burn a little as he leaned into the corner, shifting the puck to keep it out of reach of his pursuers. He snapped off a quick pass to Brad…

and wheezed as his body was pushed against the boards, the air forced from his lungs. He went down hard, sprawling onto his back, his stick flying out of his grasp. *Damn. What the hell?* They didn't play with a ref; it was pretty much "anything goes" with penalties decided by mutual agreement, but the games were normally pretty tame unless there was a rivalry going. He hadn't actually been boarded—the push had been gentle and he'd been too close to the boards to do himself any actual injury—but he hadn't been expecting it, and surprise as much as anything had caused him to lose his footing. Jack blinked and looked up, suspicions strong.

Sure enough, Julian was standing over him, expression totally innocent. Jack didn't buy it for a second. "Need a hand?" he offered, reaching down.

What the hell? Julian didn't seem the type to start shit on the ice. He was a nice guy, and a doctor to boot. Then again, Jack had never figured him for an athlete before he'd seen him on skates. Besides, he was clearly caught up in the moment. Enjoyment of the game had spread an attractive flush over his features and put a sparkle in his eyes. Jack was glad he was covered in pads from head to toe, or he might have had another incident like the one at the clinic.

Eyes narrowing, Jack reached out and tugged on the outstretched hand, sending the other man sliding on the ice beside him. "Thanks," he smirked, climbing to his feet and retrieving his stick before Julian had finished laughing.

A cheer went up at the other end of the ice, and Jack smiled. His team had just tied the score.

The rest of the game went along in the same vein. Competition was fierce, the two sides almost evenly matched.

Confrontations between Jack and Julian popped up whenever they were both on the ice. Jack had decided he needed a breather shortly after dumping Julian on the ice and had sat out until the second period, when he retaliated for Julian's first boarding by hip-checking him almost viciously, sending him careening into a teammate. Jack's team hadn't managed to score on that possession, but Julian's hadn't either, so he figured they were doing okay. They both rotated off-ice for a few minutes after that. Then, at the beginning of the third period, Julian leaned in so close when Jack had the puck he was almost tempted to call for a holding penalty. Jack had been so distracted at the thought of their bodies pressed together that Julian had stolen the puck almost before he'd realized it.

Now, with less than a minute to go and the score tied at three all, both teams were skating balls to the wall. Julian had the puck at his own team's red line, and was passing it across to Tim Johnson.

Jack waited. He was exhausted and his leg hurt, but damn if he was going to sit out the last forty seconds of the game.

The red team raced down the ice.

With thirty-eight seconds to go, Julian crossed center ice, and Jack fell back close to the net, holding his breath. Jack's left winger slid in to block the passing lane, snatched the puck out from under Tim's nose as he went, and slingshotted around the net to break the opposite way up the ice.

To Jack's left the team members not on the ice were hooting and hollering, kicking the boards and cheering madly. Jack focused on Julian, quickly gaining on the left winger, and abandoned his usual safe zone as a stay-at-home defender. He tore down the ice, ignoring everything around him except for the players between him and the puck.

Left, right, center, across the ice. Eric passed back to Brad, who cleared it up to Jack again. Jack directed it to the right winger, deflecting a grab for the puck with his shoulder. The right winger took the shot with a second left to go. The puck hit the crossbar just as the buzzer sounded, signaling the end of the game.

Damn. That had been a close one.

"Ooof." Something bumped into Jack from behind when he wasn't paying attention, knocking him flat on the ice.

Then it fell on top of him.

There was a smattering of laughter from the guys heading off the ice. Jack stayed where he was. "Julian, I am going to kick your ass. I know you can stop. I've seen you do it."

"Ow," Julian whined. "I think your skate is already violating my ass."

"It doesn't sound too serious."

"Fuck you."

"You first." Jack huffed. "You going to get off me, or what? 'Cause I, for one, need a beer."

There was a grunt, and then the weight on his legs shifted. "Okay, okay. I'm up. Need a hand?"

"I got it," Jack grumbled, wincing as he stood. He was definitely going to be sore tomorrow. "What was that for, anyway?"

Julian tugged off his helmet, and Jack could see that his red cheeks weren't entirely due to exertion. "Uh…I wasn't watching where I was going, actually. Sorry."

"Man, and people call *me* accident prone." Jack half-limped off the ice, already stiffening up. In more ways than one, unfortunately. "Where'd you learn to play? No way are you new at this."

"Right here in this arena, actually. Roz's parents owned the complex before they retired to Florida. But I played through high school and two years of undergrad. Once I hit med school I sort of ran out of leisure time."

"Yeah. Doing my master's felt like that." Jack shucked his helmet onto the bench in the dressing room, running a hand through his sweaty hair. Yuck. It was definitely shower time. If only he could keep his mind—and gaze—off Julian's body for long enough to preserve what was left of his dignity. He peeled off his gloves and started unfastening the rest of his equipment.

Beside him, Julian was sitting to remove his skates. He'd already taken care of his arm and shoulder pads, leaving him naked from the waist down. Shit, he looked even better without a shirt on. So much for keeping himself distracted. "Pass me a beer?"

Someone had carted the sweating beer case into the change room and set it on the end of the bench. Julian reached in and grabbed the last two. Evidently they'd been flat on the ice for longer than he'd thought. "Cheers."

Jack clinked his bottle against Julian's automatically before sitting back to take a long swallow. He wasn't looking forward to taking the hockey pants off; he had a feeling there were going to be some complaints from his injured leg. Still, he couldn't wait much longer; the gym was only open until ten on weeknights.

"How's the leg?"

How does he do that? Jack could see, from the corner of his eye, that Julian had removed the rest of his hockey equipment. Needing an excuse not to look at him, he started unlacing his skates. "It's been better," he admitted. "Not too bad, though. I was expecting to play less and be in a lot more pain."

"You got lucky," Julian told him. There was a flap of something that sounded like a towel and Jack thought it might be safe to look up. Julian was wearing it like a skirt. *Pretty.* Then, "Good God, you weren't kidding when you said you were accident prone."

Jack could actually *feel* his gaze on him, raking from his back and shoulders down his chest, making goose bumps appear on his skin. It was true; he'd had his fair share of incidents resulting in scars on his body. There was the small burn scar on the back of his right shoulder, the faint white line on his left arm from when he'd broken it tobogganing as a kid, and the twin scars on the right side of his abdomen from having his appendix removed, then the infection drained, when he was twenty-three. He'd been in bed for a week and a half after that, and his roommate had had to take care of him. "That one's not my fault," he said, pointing. He wasn't self-conscious about them, but then, no one had ever looked at them quite the way Julian was doing now. If he kept that up, bets were off as to how long Jack could keep his hands to himself.

"Yeah, I could tell." Julian's gaze lingered darkly on the appendix scar for a moment, making the hair on the back of Jack's neck stand straight up. Then Julian flashed a smirk at him, grabbed a plastic bag filled with soap and shampoo, and headed toward the showers.

Ohhkay. Jack took another deep swallow of beer, then peeled off his hockey socks and started working on the pants.

"You okay?" Brad asked, "You look a little off."

Jack shot him half a smile. "Leg hurts like a sonofabitch." It wasn't a lie, but it was a convenient excuse. He squirmed the rest of the way out of his hockey pants and grabbed his kit. "I'm getting too old for this."

Brad just laughed at him. "Whatever, man. Just try not to kill the new kid before I have a chance to play on his team. That fucker is fast."

"Tell me about it." Jack grabbed his towel and stalked off toward the nearest shower stall.

Dressing room showers were not meant to preserve anyone's modesty, and these were no exception. There was a wall more or less blocking the showers from the changing area to keep equipment from getting wet unnecessarily, but the shower area was basically an open room with shower heads on all sides, individual showers only marked off by a waist-high tile wall that served more or less as a place to put the soap.

Jack turned on the spray and stepped under, closing his eyes. The water was only lukewarm, but it felt wonderful to have the sheen of sweat he'd worked up washed from his body. He reached for the shampoo and scrubbed at his hair, noting how long it was. It had gone far beyond starting to curl at the ends; now that it was wet, it hung nearly to his shoulders in the back. Making a mental note to call Katherine to set up an appointment, he ducked his head back under the spray. It gave him an excuse to keep his eyes shut tight. He knew if he saw Julian naked he'd never be able to stop at just *looking*.

Finally he had to open his eyes again, having forgotten where he'd put the soap, so he took a half-step back out of the spray and wiped a hand across his face.

Jack noticed right away that most of the showers had been turned off; he could tell by the sound. The second thing he noticed was the bar of soap, a few inches from his right hand.

The third thing he noticed—and the last thing, because how could he pay attention to his surroundings after *that*—was Julian standing in the shower almost directly across from him, back to the spray, dark hair plastered to his head. Water was rolling in beaded rivulets down his defined, slender body, much the way Jack's fingers were now itching to do. Jack took in the vision before him, from the wet hair and relaxed expression to the flat, dusky nipples to the trail of fine dark hair leading down from his navel. Jack swallowed hard, wondering if he was imagining that Julian was half-hard, eyes closed in apparent bliss, hands caressing his supple body.

Breathing in sharply and forcing himself to turn around, Jack reached for the soap with one hand and the cold water tap with the other. This was *not* the place to get into a naked wrestling match with his doctor. For one thing, there were too many potential witnesses. For another, the gym would be closing any minute now and when he finally got his hands on Julian, he wanted to be able to take his time. Jack finished his shower in record time and practically fled from the showers back into the dressing room.

It was empty, the case of beer sitting on the end of the bench, drained bottles in place but for the two he and Julian had been drinking. Jack took one look at his half-empty bottle and downed the rest of it, replacing it in the case, then grabbed his towel and dried off as quickly as he dared for the cold September night. His hair was still damp, but he wasn't going to worry about it right now.

Jack pulled his usual post-hockey clothes from his backpack (putting them in his hockey bag would have defeated the purpose of the shower entirely) and slung his equipment over his back just as he heard the water cut off in the shower.

The evening manager, Marianne, was already turning out the lights when he left the rink area. She gave him a friendly wave. "You the last one?"

Jack shook his head. "Dr. Piet's still in there. I think he might've drowned in the shower."

"I'll give him a few more minutes before I head in and revive him. Drive safely."

Chuckling, Jack waved. "Night, Marianne."

The parking lot was nearly empty, with just two pickups and Marianne's old beat-up SUV left. It was also dark. The recent switch to daylight savings time had meant that dark was coming sooner and sooner, and apparently someone had forgotten to reprogram the streetlights. The night was lit only by the spillover from the recreational complex and the sliver of moon peeking above the distant mountains. Jack tossed his gear in the bed of his truck, debating.

Hell, what harm could it do? He double checked his own truck was locked, then sauntered over to wait by the other, shoving his hands into his pockets to keep them warm.

He didn't have to wait long. It wasn't two minutes before the door to the complex opened again, and a lean figure was silhouetted in the doorway for a moment before the main lights went out. Jack held his breath, willing his heart not to race.

"So you're stalking me now?"

The voice was calm, cool, almost unaffected. Julian heaved his hockey bag over the side of the pickup and stood back, face barely visible now in the faint moonlight.

"The conventional approach wasn't working," Jack shrugged nonchalantly, not knowing if the other man could see him or not. He leaned one arm against the truck, half-trapping Julian against the door.

Julian didn't back down. "You never thought I might just not be interested?"

Jack tried to remind himself of all the reasons why pursuing this conversation was a bad idea. One: Julian was so hot-and-cold it could drive even the sanest of men crazy. Two: it violated their established doctor-patient relationship. Three: they were in a tiny, conservative backwater town in northern Alberta. Four: Sex in a parking lot was a bad idea under the best of circumstances. Unfortunately, all his libido was telling him was *he wants you now*, and since that was fairly obviously true, it wasn't easy to ignore.

"You're interested," he said confidently, maneuvering closer. He left his right arm down by his side, leaving open an avenue of escape—just in case.

Julian didn't budge, but his tone was flirtatious, not flat. "*If* I was interested, what would you do about it?"

Hmm. This seemed like a time for showing rather than telling. Not that Jack was exactly in control of his actions at this point. He let the lust take control and raised his right hand to Julian's face, brushing callused fingertips across his forehead and brow ridge and down his cheeks, feeling the rasp of five o'clock shadow almost too fine for the eye. As Jack's thumb trailed over Julian's lower lip, the other man's tongue flicked out to trace hotly across the pad of his thumb. Julian never even broke eye contact.

Fuck it. Jack dropped his arm to Julian's elbow and stepped into his body, pressing him lightly against the side of the truck, reveling in the way their bodies aligned. Taking a sharp breath, he gave in to the pull and leaned in close, slanting his mouth down over Julian's.

Julian's lips were moist, a bit chapped, and opened almost immediately under his assault, allowing Jack's tongue to slip inside and taste the inside of his mouth. Jack swallowed the other man's moan as Julian's right hand fisted in the front of his shirt. The response from their bodies was both immediate and obvious. Jack could feel Julian's erection pressing insistently against his thigh, and subconsciously rubbed his own into the other man's hip. *God,* it had been ages since anyone had touched him, he thought hazily as Julian dragged his tongue sparking across his upper lip. He slid his right hand up the other man's arm to his hair and dug his fingers into the damp curls, tugging gently.

The sound Julian made when he did that was something between a groan and a mewl, and it went straight to Jack's cock. He needed to hear that sound again—preferably louder. Working on the general assumption that if one was good, two was better, Jack took his other hand from the truck and wound it in Julian's hair as well, then ground their bodies together, breathing hard through his nose. Julian gasped his way out of the kiss, knees sagging noticeably as Jack moved his teeth over an earlobe. "How's this?" he growled quietly, nipping at his neck.

"Uhh," he felt Julian swallow against his lips, "I'd say this proves my interest pretty conclusively."

Damn. "I'll have to agree with you." Jack licked a line up Julian's neck to his chin and closed his mouth around it, feeling Julian's prick jump against his leg.

"Maybe we should—"

The sudden slam of the complex door startled them both into stillness, and Jack dropped his hands almost automatically from Julian's hair, stepping back and taking long, deep breaths to try to calm himself. *Forgot about Marianne.* Luckily, engaging the lock on the big steel door made a surprising amount of noise.

Julian blinked at him mutely for a moment, then turned slightly away.

Jack could've killed himself for acting like he'd been doing something wrong; Marianne probably would never have seen him anyway. Still, he had been comfortably in the closet for twenty years. He saw no reason to change that now. "Continue this later?" he suggested, watching Julian's body language closely.

Julian's shoulders hunched, like he was expecting a physical blow. "I'm not sure that's a good idea," he said.

"You were pretty sure a minute ago."

Julian leveled an unfathomable gaze at him, eyes narrowed, posture defensive. "I'm sure we've all done things we regret in the heat of the moment," he said flatly. "Goodnight, Jack. See you tomorrow about those stitches. I noticed they're getting a little raggedy."

God, when had he had a chance to notice that? Jack was sure that now wasn't the best time to wonder about it. He didn't even manage a reply before Julian was in the truck, driving away.

Chapter 7

JULIAN looked down at the folder in his hands and pinched the bridge of his nose. He had purposely planned to be out of the office when Jack came in today so that Dr. Matheson could take out his stitches instead. That had backfired, of course; Dr. Matheson's oldest girl had a swimming competition in a neighboring town, and he had swanned off an hour early, leaving Julian with the arguably unenviable task of removing the stitches from Jack's leg and checking that it had healed properly.

Fantastic. At least this was his last patient of the day.

Julian pushed open the door to exam room one, tossed the folder onto the counter, and threw himself onto the rolling stool. "Hi."

He bit his lip a little. He'd meant to be hostile, but the greeting had come out sheepish instead. Julian exhaled slowly, rubbing his nose again. "Sorry. It's been a long day." Mostly because he'd been dreading this visit since last night before bed.

Jack didn't seem to be much more at ease than he was. He was even still wearing his pants. "Long couple of days," he admitted. "Sorry, Doc. Apparently I'm as skittish as you are."

All the tension seemed to drain from Julian's body. He could hardly blame Jack for backing off, since he himself had been behaving particularly bipolar around him lately. He was trying desperately to take Roz's advice and have a little fun, relax and let himself work through a casual relationship or two. The thing was, he just wasn't wired that way. Whether it was because he'd been orphaned at a young age or just because he was naturally prone to getting attached, Julian had never been very good at casual relationships. Right from his very first relationship, he had craved commitment. He didn't always get what he wanted—actually, that first relationship was pretty much a case in point—but after that first year, he found that he just wasn't able to settle for less. He'd had a few one-night stands afterward, and even a casual fling or two, but they always seemed to leave him unsatisfied.

He knew damn well that Jackson Strange just didn't want the same things out of a relationship that he did. In fact, the word "relationship" might even have been a stretch. That didn't stop Julian from wanting it all the same.

"Don't worry about it," he sighed finally. "Well, come on. I'd better get those stitches out before they permanently become a part of you or start rotting. Then I'll have to cut you open to get them out, and that won't be any fun for either of us."

"Gee, Doc, you really know how to sweet-talk a guy." Jack stood and had removed his jeans before Julian had even had a chance to suggest that he leave the room.

"What can I say? It's a gift." Julian tried to ignore the display and snapped on a pair of gloves, rifling through a drawer for a sterile-wrapped pair of scissors and tweezers. "You've been keeping this mostly dry except for the shower yesterday, right?"

"It was tough to get the hockey pants on with the damn thing bandaged, yeah, so I guess I forgot." Jack didn't look too concerned about it, and Julian privately thought he'd probably had enough stitches in his lifetime to know what he was talking about.

Grasping the tiny knot with the tweezers, Julian reached in with the scissors and snipped the suture. Carefully, he pulled the thread through its tiny holes, then deposited the somewhat grungy-looking thread into the biohazard bin. "Gentle enough for you?" he asked mildly, reaching for an iodine swab.

"Your bedside manner is excellent," Jack said, straight-faced. "Oh, that's cold!"

Julian couldn't help the wicked grin that crept up on his face. "And we all know the reaction you have to cold." He didn't bother checking if Jack was indeed getting hard; he was pretty sure, but didn't want to be caught looking.

"I'll let you in on a secret." The other man leaned forward, his face inches from Julian's own. "It's got nothing to do with the cold."

Julian's lips twisted into a wry grin, but his stomach fluttered. "Not much of a secret," he said, not as steadily as he'd hoped. He finished swabbing the cut, then applied some generic Polysporin and a bandage. He managed to keep himself in check by reminding himself that Jack's mother was going to die and hadn't told him—and that the secret was legally his to keep. That would cool off just about anyone. "All better. Keep an eye on it to make sure it doesn't get infected, and let me know if you have any difficulty with movement, but it should be fine."

"It was a bit sore this morning," Jack admitted, "but then so was the rest of me. You don't pull your punches."

Flushing a little, Julian protested, "I never punched you." Still, he knew a lot of people found it odd that a doctor would be such a physical hockey player. "Sorry. I tend to get caught up in the moment when I'm on the ice."

Jack gave him a teasing smile and reached for his trousers. "It's all right. I think the accidental hit did the most damage. I hurt everywhere; not just my leg."

Julian found himself contemplating offering a massage, and then lapsed into imagining said massage in vivid detail, Jack's powerful back under his fingertips, the contented noises he'd make, the way he'd tense up when Julian brushed his hands too close to his ass. He snapped out of it, relieved he'd worn his lab coat today rather than scrubs. "Try the hot tub at the rec complex," he suggested. "They can work wonders."

Jack's hazel gaze met his own, heavy with suggestion, and Julian could have kicked himself for bringing up a second provocative image of his patient in less than twenty seconds. It had to be some kind of record. For a minute, he thought Jack was going to make another offhand comment, but miraculously, he didn't. "Look, Julian, there isn't really a great way to say this, so I'm just going to lay it all on the table. I'm attracted to you, and it's pretty obvious that you feel the same when you let yourself. This isn't really the greatest venue on Earth to explore that attraction, but that notwithstanding, I think we could be good together.

Let's just take it easy and see how it goes, yeah?"

Julian breathed in sharply at that, heart racing with hope and confusion. Jack was looking for a casual fling, he reminded himself—by his own admission. He released the breath slowly. "Yeah, all right," he conceded, hoping his face didn't look as warm and flushed as it felt. He tried valiantly to ignore the little voice inside him telling him what a terrible idea this was, that he would get hurt just like last time. It wouldn't be like last time, he hoped. He'd manage to go without the attachment that he'd always thought was so integral to a relationship. He could do it. Hell, he *needed* to, unless he wanted to die of sexual frustration very soon. "Anyway, it's time to close up for the day. I'll see you when I see you, okay?"

"Sure thing, Doc." Jack's expression was utterly unreadable, but he seemed…what? Disappointed? "I'll see you around."

Julian waited until he'd closed the door behind himself, then slumped against it, eyes closed. *Great,* he thought, fists clenching. *What now?*

"WEAR the black jeans!" Roz's voice echoed from her bedroom down the hall. "Don't even think about the ones with the holes in them, mister. And for God's sake put on some underwear."

Julian stared into his closet, utterly bemused. It never ceased to amaze him how Roz could read his mind, even after twenty years as her brother. He could swear she should have been a psychic. "We're just going to the pub," he pointed out with a grumble, following her advice anyway. If there was one thing he'd learned about Roz it was that she had impeccable taste. "Yes, mother," he yelled back, just to tease her, and wriggled into a pair of boxers.

The jeans were sitting on the end of his bed, having been washed but not yet put away.

"Watch your mouth!"

Grinning, Julian zipped the fly. *Hmm.* Was he losing weight? Probably the lack of shitty, greasy hospital cafeteria food. Maybe a belt would be a good idea. "Hey, Roz—"

"The white one," she said from the doorway. "Retro suits you. Black socks. No, not those ones, they have holes. Honestly, why didn't you just throw them out?"

Julian flopped backward on his bed and waved his bare toes at her. "Roz, we're just going to *Brenda's*. You know everyone there has seen me in scrubs with two days' worth of stubble, right?"

"Just humor me," she sighed back, tossing a pair of shirts at him from the closet. "There's live entertainment Saturday night and you haven't done anything on a Saturday night since you got here. That emergency house call to Mr. Bender last week does *not* count. Besides, you're gonna need the dressing practice if Jack ever actually takes you on a date."

A small smile fought its way onto his face in spite of his protests. He'd hated to prove Roz right, but there were some things he just couldn't quite keep entirely to himself. That day when he'd come home from the clinic, she'd pounced on him the moment he'd opened the door and had wrangled the whole story out of him in less than a minute. "I'm starting to regret spilling the beans, you know."

His black leather watch smacked him in the stomach and he sat up. "This, too," Roz decided, flinging a surfer-style beaded necklace in his direction. Julian caught it left-handed. Then she disappeared down the hallway, no doubt to put the finishing touches on her own pub wear. "And wear the black Chucks, Julian!"

Sitting up, Julian resigned himself and followed her instructions to the letter. The white cotton belt went first, then the white long-sleeved shirt, followed by his red Tragically Hip tee. Julian didn't understand the point of wearing a long-sleeved shirt under a short-sleeved one, other than that it would keep his arms warm, but then, Roz was the fashionista of the family. By the time he'd finished with his socks and shoes, Roz was standing in his doorway again in a soft sweater that he had to admit fit her perfectly and jeans that might as well have been painted on. "You hussy," he teased, standing. "Well, do I pass?"

Roz looked him up and down critically for a few seconds before taking a step forward and running her hands through his hair. Too late, he noticed they were slick with some kind of product. "Roz! I can do my own hair!"

"Prove it," she said dryly, ruining the effect by pinching his cheek. "Perfect. Let me wash my hands and we can go."

Rolling his eyes, Julian snatched his wallet off the bedside table and stuck it in his pocket, heading downstairs to find his jacket and keys.

Julian slid into the driver's seat and started the truck, flipping on the defogger and the heated seats. Damn, leather got cold early in this part of the country. He flexed his fingers, wondering if he should've brought his gloves, but by the time he thought of it, Roz had hopped into the passenger side and was already buckled in. "Let's go."

He wondered if Jack would be there. He had said that he helped out on Saturday nights, though Julian wasn't sure what with. Maybe he helped set up the sound equipment for whatever live band was playing tonight. He was an engineer after all; he was probably pretty savvy with the electronics. Julian figured he'd probably be busy all night, which was fine with him. He wasn't sure what he'd say at this point, anyway. *Yeah, I'm still attracted to you. So, how about the Flames?*

"Hello? Earth to Julian? We're here."

Blinking, Julian unbuckled his seat belt, wondering how on Earth he'd managed to get them to Brenda's without realizing it. Doing his best to ignore the butterflies in his stomach, he grabbed the keys and locked the truck. "Here goes nothing."

ROZ pushed open the door to *Brenda's*, and Julian was more than a little surprised to see how packed the place was. It was only a quarter past eight, but most of the tables were full, with just a few spots left at the bar. The makeshift stage had been set up in the back corner like he remembered from when he was a kid, with a tall barstool and a microphone; in the back there was an amp and a couple of guitars on stands. He didn't see Jack anywhere, but that wasn't completely unexpected.

Julian and Roz grabbed the two barstools closest to the stage. "What can I get you?" Brad asked, polishing a glass.

Julian ordered a Keith's—it seemed a little early for vodka seven—while Roz flirted a bit, finally deciding on a rum and coke, and turned around to watch the room. "Quite the turnout," he observed. "Who's playing?"

Roz turned an amused glance his way, sipping her drink delicately. "You mean you haven't guessed yet?"

Oh, you're kidding, Julian thought, managing not to groan out loud. He'd figured on Jack being busy enough that there would only really be time for a short conversation or two. What he hadn't planned on was having no reason *not* to stare at Jack all night. This could be bad news. "Roz, I'm going to kill you."

His sister gave him a sweet smile. "You wouldn't do that. You still need me to dress you."

"It's okay. I can go back to dressing like a depressed rodeo clown. I'll even give you a ten-second head start. Ready? Ten—"

"Depressed rodeo clown?"

Roz's smirk was infuriating. Julian felt the flush rise up across his cheeks and ears and sighed a little resignedly. "Jack. If you could just look away for a moment while I murder my sister, I'd be much obliged."

"Sorry, no can do. Murder's bad for business." Jack waved over at Brad, who brought him a couple of bottles of water, and Julian took the time to admire the man. He was wearing dark blue jeans that fit him just right and a yellow T-shirt that proclaimed he'd try anything twice. Five o'clock shadow covered his cheeks, emphasizing a bone structure any movie star would kill for. "Thanks."

Julian resigned himself to a night of being uncomfortable. "When you said you helped out Saturday nights, this isn't exactly what I had in mind."

"Well, I think we can agree it's not my fault you got the wrong impression." Jack winked at Roz, who just grinned and took a sip of her rum and coke.

"I have been so set up," Julian realized. He was about to say something very rude when he luckily glanced down for a moment and noticed the girl standing slightly behind Jack. "Hello. You're very young for eighteen."

The little girl laughed. "You're funny." She looked up at Roz. "Hello, Miss Piet!"

Roz waved hello, then fixed a gaze on Jack. "They just keep getting younger."

Julian put two and two together. "You must be Hallie. My name is Julian."

The little girl stuck out her hand to shake, face solemn. "Nice to meet you, Mr. Julian."

Julian managed to keep from laughing—barely—as she pumped his arm enthusiastically. "The pleasure is all mine."

"Actually, that's *Dr.* Julian, kiddo," Jack corrected, scooping the girl up. It was obvious that the two of them were very close. "Now, where's your dad? Is he about ready to start yet?"

"He had to take a leak," Hallie informed them.

Julian put a hand in front of his mouth to keep his smile from showing. Roz put down her drink quickly, like she was afraid she was going to squirt some out of her nose. At least that explained what the eight-year-old was doing in a bar.

"Your dad's going to kill me," Jack sighed. He set the girl down on the barstool beside Julian. "You stay here, and *don't* say that again when your daddy's around, or I'll be in trouble, okay?"

"Okay," she agreed gamely, sitting criss-cross on the stool. Jack spared Julian one last, smoldering glance before hopping up on the stage.

Roz elbowed Julian in the ribs. He pointedly ignored her, face still burning.

"Good evening, everyone," Jack said into the microphone. The crowd responded with cheers and whistles. "I'd like to get started in just a minute, but before I can do that, has anyone seen my fiddle player?"

There was a smattering of laughter, and a man about Jack's age appeared behind him on stage, looking sheepish. Julian assumed this to be the little girl's father. "Sorry, sorry. Line up in the bathroom."

Jack rolled his eyes theatrically and picked up the guitar on the left.

"A likely story." He slung the strap over his shoulder and sat on the stool, strumming the guitar gently with his head turned slightly to one side before plugging it in. "What d'you think, Roy? Start out with the classics?"

"Boy, you wouldn't know classic if it bit you in the—" At the last second, Roy seemed to remember his daughter was in the audience. "Leg." He picked up a fiddle from a case on the floor and set it to his shoulder. "After you."

Jack miraculously produced a pick from somewhere and Julian grinned as he recognized the opening chords of Gordon Lightfoot's "Alberta Bound." Jack had more than just a passable singing voice, and the fiddle was an excellent substitute for the song's twangy lead-guitar riffs. The audience had obviously heard this version a multitude of times before, and it was clearly a favorite, especially the part about Toronto. Julian smiled. Albertans and Torontonians would be at each other's throats until the end of time. No wonder the song was a hit.

By the end of the song, the excitement in the room was palpable. Jack continued to appease the older crowd by playing his "classics." Roy picked up a maraca and Seger's "Night Moves" followed, setting the hair on the back of Julian's neck standing straight up at the sudden rasp in Jack's voice. He glanced sideways at Roz, only to find her oh-so-innocently sipping at her drink. When she noticed him looking, she nudged him back toward the stage.

Jack's eyes met his own with a spark that ran straight through him, lighting nerve endings all the way down his spinal cord, and Julian had to take a long sip of his drink. He was really glad that he was sitting down. He thought he might've heard Roz snicker, but he wasn't sure.

Jack and Roy worked their way through the rest of a ten-song set during which Roy played everything from a harmonica to a tambourine. After finishing a particularly popular Billy Joel tune, Roy beckoned to his daughter from the stage, bending to whisper something in her ear. Hallie smiled at him and walked back to sit with Roz and Julian—or so he thought. As soon as Jack hit the opening chords of "Bad Moon Rising," she turned to Roz and said, very seriously, "May I have this dance?"

Laughing, Roz allowed herself to be pulled into the crowded space that served as a dance floor, twirling the little girl around enthusiastically. Julian wasn't really sure who was the better dancer. He was fairly certain Roz had said Hallie took lessons; Roz had had to hire an outside instructor for the rec complex because of her own two left feet.

"You all right for drinks, Julian?"

Julian glanced at the dregs of his beer, then assessed Roz's rum and coke. "We could do with another round. Oh, and can we get some of those sweet potato french fries? Those things are delicious."

"Sure thing," Brad grinned. "Cute couple, huh?"

Julian turned back to the dance floor. Roz and Hallie seemed to be enjoying themselves immensely. "I think the age gap might be a problem."

"Good point."

Brad replaced Julian's beer with another, and he watched the girls dance for a few more seconds before becoming firmly distracted by the guitar player. Damn, the man had nice hands. How had he never noticed that before? They were almost surgeon's hands, with long, nimble fingers. The dirt Julian could see under his nails undermined the artistry he could see in the fingers, and he had to remind himself that Jack spent his time divided between working up computer models and taking apart and rebuilding heavy machinery in the field.

After the second song, Roz and Hallie headed back to the bench, Roz sweating slightly and grinning. "Ooh, you got me a refill. Thanks."

Julian opened his mouth to say *you're welcome,* but didn't get that far. Hallie Klein was tugging on his hands. "Dr. Julian," she said, "dance with me!"

Julian caught Jack's eye across the dance floor and gave him a dirty look. Jack just fiddled with the tuning of his guitar and grinned. Julian had the feeling that this kid was going to be trouble when she grew up. "All right, all right. Just a second." He took another swig of his beer, then reached down to hold her hand.

He was entirely too conscious of Jack's eyes on him as he started in on something Julian recognized only vaguely as a song from the '60s or '70s. For her part, Hallie seemed to be rather attached to him. She didn't let him sit down for the rest of the set. When Jack and Roy finally stopped to take a break, Julian glanced around the room. The older crowd seemed to be leaving, though they'd clearly enjoyed themselves. Julian had even seen old Mr. Bender sitting in the corner, tapping his foot out of time to "The Wreck of the Edmund Fitzgerald."

Despite the exodus of people, the pub wasn't getting any less crowded. The crowd itself just seemed to be getting younger, the older patrons being replaced by the next generation. They were like ships passing in the night, the forty-plus crowd going out, and the twenty- and thirty-somethings coming in, exchanging greetings as they went. Julian shook his head. How they all seemed to know one another just boggled his mind, even after almost twenty years of calling this his home town. He slumped onto the barstool, stealing the basket of sweet potato fries from Roz's dangerous clutches. "Mine."

"Grabby," Roz chided, popping another of the delectable snacks into her mouth. "God, these are fantastic. Think they'll give you the recipe?"

"Even if they did, they'd never be as good if I made them at home."

"True."

Julian was about to scowl at her for agreeing with his dismissal of his culinary skills when the hair on the back of his neck stood up again. He turned all the way around in his chair, just relaxed enough to let his legs fall open slightly. "Jack," he said with a sly grin, "I didn't know you played. You're pretty good with your hands."

Roz, who'd been taking a sip of her rum and coke, snorted into the drink and excused herself to go to the ladies' room.

She might as well have been invisible for all the attention Jack paid her. "I've had a lot of practice."

Julian snickered, noting with a slight rush of excitement that Jack was practically trying to eat him with his eyes. He'd have to let Roz dress him more often. "I bet," he said innocently, raising his beer to his lips. "Maybe I could sit in sometime."

The feather-light touch of Jack's knee against the inside of Julian's own had his blood rushing southward. That was a brave move for someone as obviously closeted as Jack. Then again, in this crowd, there was hardly room for anyone to notice. "I could even teach you a thing or two."

"I'm a fast learner," Julian told him in confidence, then sat back to take a sip, licking the beer from his upper lip slowly.

Jack laughed at that, relaxing a little, and settled onto the barstool beside him, downing his bottle of water. Watching the muscles in his throat move as he swallowed, Julian fidgeted in his seat. His whole body was starting to tingle. "I believe it," Jack said when he'd emptied the bottle and set it on the counter for Brad to collect. "How long'd it take you to get through med school, anyway? You don't even look old enough to be a doctor."

Julian shook his head, thinking back. "Two years of undergrad, four years medical school, six of residency. I'm twenty-seven." The two years of undergrad had been the craziest, between overloading his course load every semester and playing on the university hockey team.

From the look on Jack's face, the math wasn't adding up. "You're shitting me."

"Nope. I skipped second grade, then fast-tracked through high school and university." The open look of admiration on Jack's face was sweet. Julian managed to restrain himself from kissing it off. "I had a lot of ambition when I was younger." And not a lot of social skills, he added mentally. Those had started to come later, but it was still a struggle.

"Obviously." Jack's gaze appraised him frankly. "Why was your residency so long? I thought you only had to do a couple of years to be a GP."

Julian's heart skipped a beat. *It's okay,* he told himself. *You can work around this.* "Ah, well, see, I didn't do my residency as a GP."

"You didn't? That's what you are now, though, right? What did you do your residency for?"

"Ah, um." *Oh, fuck it.* "I'm a surgeon."

Jack blinked. "Well. I guess that explains the really neat stitches."

He cracked open the second bottle of water without looking at it. "And why, exactly, are you not…working as a surgeon?"

Julian fiddled with the fry basket, then pushed it away. It was empty, anyway. "I got lonely, I think. This is where my family is—well, where Roz is anyway; our parents are living it up in Florida. And the office didn't need a surgeon; it needed a GP. And I needed to come home for a bit. I'm more than qualified, so…." Jack didn't need to hear the rest of the story. Not yet, anyway. Nothing cooled a burgeoning romance—if that's what this was—faster than a story about how an ex-lover ruined your life.

Not to mention, it made him sound kind of pathetic.

"Hmm." The absentminded noise could have meant Jack wasn't really paying attention, or that he didn't quite believe the story Julian was telling. What difference it would make to him, Julian didn't know and couldn't guess. "They visit often?"

"Sorry? Oh, my parents." He'd stopped feeling guilty for calling them Mom and Dad years ago. "They were here for Thanksgiving, before I started work. It's a toss-up right now if Christmas will be here or in Florida. Dad's arthritis gets worse in the cold, but Mom likes to have a white Christmas." Wondering if he was tempting fate by even broaching the subject of Jack's parents, he said, "What about you?"

"Dad's been gone almost twenty years," Jack told him. Almost the same as Julian's own, then. "My mom was here last week to baby me. She's a nurse. I think Bella probably told her I was in a coma or something."

Ah, hell. Might as well go for broke. "Do you see her often?"

"Not as much as I should." Jack looked a little regretful, but didn't seem inclined to continue the conversation in that vein, so Julian let the subject drop. "Well, looks like everyone's ready. Better start before they get going without me."

Julian frowned around the room. "Where's Roy?"

"It's a one-man act from here on out," Jack winked at him. "Roy plays the first set with me, but he doesn't like having his daughter in the bar when these rowdies come in. It's past her bedtime, anyway, but he hates getting a sitter. He thinks he's not there for her enough as it is."

The way he said that made Julian sure there was more to the story than Jack was letting on, but the other man was already weaving his way back to the stage. "How's everybody doing tonight?"

A few smattered cheers and catcalls rang out into the crowd.

"Ah, maybe you didn't hear me. I said, how's everybody doing tonight?"

This time, Julian nearly covered his ears at the volume. Jack sure knew how to work a crowd. That probably wasn't the only thing he could work, either. Julian was distracted by the long, sure fingers on the fret board of the guitar again. Damn. He could almost feel those fingers like he had the other night, on the inside of his elbow, in his hair, on either side of his face. He could think of a lot of other places he'd like to feel them, too, but that would have to wait for later.

Jack started the second set off with a rousing and entertaining rendition of a pop song that had originally been recorded by a female artist most accurately described as a bimbo. With his energetic guitar and occasional falsetto, not to mention the fact that he wasn't taking himself too seriously, Jack lent the song new life, and had nearly everyone in the crowd singing along just for fun. Julian even turned around to order another beer and found Roz, who'd hated the original, lip-synching into an invisible microphone.

He wondered how long she'd been sitting there again. He didn't remember noticing her come back from the bathroom. Then again, he'd been pretty distracted. Jack toned it down a bit for the next two songs, ones that Julian didn't recognize but several other members of the audience seemed to. He supposed they were originals, and had that thought confirmed by Jack a few minutes later. "Like the last two, this one's an original number that I wrote about a friend of mine back in Cape Breton who fell completely in love with the bitchiest woman I've ever had the misfortune of meeting. No offense, ladies." He strummed a chord or two to cheers throughout the room. "This one's called 'A Really Stupid Kind of Love.'"

Julian listened rapt along with everyone else as Jack sung the tale of the wooing of a girl named Janice O'Toole. Roz was laughing so hard there were tears streaming down her cheeks. The applause was louder than for any previous number.

The set went along smoothly after that, and before Julian knew it the night was ticking away into morning. When Jack bent to put away his guitar, Roz nudged Julian in the shoulder, yawning. "So." She raised her eyebrows, expression betraying nothing but curiosity. "You coming home tonight?"

That was the million-dollar question, wasn't it? "We just met," Julian protested feebly, cursing himself for letting his hand shake a little as he deposited his empty beer bottle on the bar.

"Oh, spare me. It wouldn't be anything you haven't done before."

"It's not like that," Julian protested before he could stop himself. He raised his hand to his mouth to stop the words coming out, but it was too late. The damage was already done. The last time he'd jumped into bed with someone this soon, they'd ended up in a relationship for almost a year. Julian wasn't sure if he could handle something that serious right now. He wanted it; he just didn't know if it was a good idea. "I mean, it *can't* be like that. This isn't Toronto. People talk."

"People talk in Toronto, too, but that's because they want to hear all the juicy details." Roz sighed, patting his knee. "Okay, I'll let it slide this once, on one condition."

Sighing in relief, Julian was agreeing before he knew her terms. "Name it."

The sudden gleam in her eyes let him know he should've thought twice. "Invite him to lunch tomorrow while I'm at the gym and you have the house to yourself."

"I—"

"Do it, Julian." She looked over his shoulder, probably to get a bead on the herd of guys he'd known in high school that had been checking her out all night. "Here he comes. I'll just be conveniently elsewhere. Bye!"

"Is it just me," said Jack, coming up beside him with a guitar case in one hand and the portable amp in the other, "or is she a little on the flighty side?"

Julian smiled, offering wordlessly to take something, but Jack shook his head. "If by flighty you mean manipulative." The smile morphed into a grin. "Who says *flighty* anymore, anyway?"

Jack nudged him with the guitar case. "Watch it. I might be older than you, but I'm also bigger."

Raising his eyebrows, Julian declined to comment. "What're you gonna do, spank me?"

Woah, easy. Jack's eyes were caught somewhere between calculating and aroused. "One step at a time."

"That's what I wanted to talk to you about, actually." Julian grabbed the door for him and followed him out onto the street, wishing he'd brought his coat. He'd left it in the bar, draped over the back of his stool. "Um…."

Jack wasn't going to make it easy for him, he realized suddenly. "Yes?"

Hell with it. "Have lunch with me tomorrow. At my house."

Turning, the other man fixed him with a smirk. "Took you long enough to spit that out." He hefted the guitar and unlocked the back of the pickup, sliding it inside. The amp followed, settling on the floor on the passenger side. He must have seen the apprehension on Julian's face, or the way his hands were shaking, because he finally softened. "Relax, Jitterbug. I already told you, I'm interested. What time do you want me to come over?"

"About one-thirty sound good?" Julian hedged. Then: "Jitterbug?"

"That's what you were dancing with Hallie, isn't it?"

Julian decided to let it slide. "I was trying, anyway. I'm not used to having such a short partner." He ruffled a hand through his hair, not knowing what to do now that the hard part was over. Sure, he knew what he'd *like* to do—preferably without an actual audience, and he didn't think they were going to be that lucky. Now that the entertainment was over, people were starting to trickle out of the pub. "Do you know how to get to my place?"

"Big old farm house out on the tenth, two stories, lots of big trees, detached garage, balcony in the back?"

Surprised, Julian blinked. "Are you sure you're not stalking me?"

Jack grinned. "Nah. I was out there a couple of years ago helping your dad fix one of the exercise machines. Circuits got fried or something."

For some reason, it was odd to think that Jack had known his father longer than him. Putting it out of his mind, Julian shook his head. "Well, it's had a couple of coats of paint and a new roof since then, I think, but it looks more or less the same." He scuffed his Converse on the asphalt, stuck.

"I'll find it," Jack promised, looking both ways furtively before reaching out and grabbing Julian's wrist.

He let out a small *oomph* as their chests collided and all the breath was forced from his lungs, but he hardly noticed. For a few brief, blissful seconds there was nothing but Jack as his stubble-roughened mouth covered Julian's, burning his lips.

Jack pulled away far too soon, glancing in the direction of Brenda's. Someone was headed this way. "We have got to stop meeting like this in parking lots."

Tell me about it, Julian thought, adjusting himself as discreetly as possible. "I concur." He watched the approaching figure long enough to be sure it was his sister, then smiled. "That's my ride. See you tomorrow."

Chapter 8

JULIAN was in bed, having a really excellent dream involving a few stolen kisses, some groping, a serenade, and the promise of a lunch date, when Roz popped her head in the door and said, "Rise and shine, Beanstalk. Big day today; you don't want to be late."

His eyes snapped open as he realized that it was not, in fact, a dream at all (except for some of the creative embellishments about the groping). He had asked Jack over for lunch, and Jack had accepted, and Roz was leaving for work, which meant they'd have the house to themselves.

Paralyzed, Julian's mind could only hover between excited and downright terrified.

As if she was reading his mind, Roz came in and flopped beside him on the bed. "Relax. He wants you, you want him…. God knows you'd be easier to live with if you got laid sometime this decade…."

"You're mean," Julian mumbled into his pillow. "Where's the sister who's nice to me?"

"You upgraded to a sister who'll get you laid." Kissing his cheek, she stood again. "I went shopping, stocked the fridge. I won't be home until five, so the house is yours. You do plan on taking advantage of that, right?"

If she could see the tips of his ears, she'd have all the answer she needed. Not that she'd really need an answer, after what she'd probably seen and overheard last night. "If I get lucky, I'll give you the details later."

"Atta boy." Roz ruffled his hair one last time, and he heard her footsteps retreating down the stairs.

Breathing deeply, Julian sat up, swung his legs over the side of the bed, and pushed himself to his feet. He could do this. "Hey, Roz—"

"Your clothes are in the bathroom!" she yelled from the kitchen.

"I love you!"

"Safe sex!" Roz shouted.

Julian rolled his eyes. Knowing Roz, she'd sneaked in while he was sleeping and stocked his night table with condoms and flavored lubricant. "Bye!"

Grabbing a towel from the hall closet, he padded barefoot into the bathroom. Sure enough, Roz had left a pair of jeans out for him—the very jeans she'd forbidden him from wearing yesterday, in fact—as well as a blue striped button-down with a note pinned to it. *Untucked, sleeves rolled up,* it said. *Leave the top two buttons undone.*

She hadn't left him any socks, he noticed. Or underwear.

Shrugging, Julian stripped out of his boxers and started the shower running. He figured he had an hour and a half before Jack arrived, so he wasn't in any hurry. He stepped under the spray with a sigh, running through recipes in his head. He didn't want to do anything too fancy; it would seem like he was trying too hard. Pasta, maybe? No, that was too casual. He could dress it up with some kind of bread and salad, but that was too much, wasn't it?

Maybe a nice stew, he mused, reaching for the shampoo. Judging by the frost on the bathroom window, it was pretty cold out there. He'd been meaning to try out a new goulash recipe, and he was pretty sure he had all the ingredients, even if Roz hadn't stocked up.

Rinsing his hair, Julian had just decided that maybe it was about time for a haircut when a door slammed downstairs. Roz had probably forgotten her lunch again. That would make the second time this week.

Thinking nothing of it, he reached for the soap with one hand, adjusting the water temperature with the other. Roz always claimed that hot showers dried out her skin and made her feel drowsy, but she was a bit of a freak, so he didn't entirely discount the possibility that she actually just *liked* lukewarm showers. Julian, on the other hand, appreciated the luxury after way too many hospital showers.

He was just contemplating stepping out to grab himself a clean washcloth when he heard the bathroom door open.

"Hey, Roz, could you pass me the—"

The shower curtain opened. It was not, in fact, Roz in his bathroom.

"You're early," he said dumbly, flushing to his navel.

Jack's gaze was frankly appraising, running from head to toe and lingering appreciatively in the middle. "Actually, it looks like I'm right on time." Julian could have drowned in the look he was getting. Especially since he was pretty sure his mouth was gaping open and the shower was still running. "Your sister left a note on the kitchen table."

Julian swallowed hard, hyperaware of the way he was being appraised. His cock stood up and took notice. His brain was a little behind the game at this time. "What?"

Jack held up a piece of paper so he could see.

Beanstalk:

I thought you might need a little nudge, so I changed the clocks an hour and a half and waited around for Jack to show up. Surprise!

Love, Roz

Oh. Julian finished reading the note and swallowed again. Jack tossed it aside and reached for the hem of his shirt.

Fuck that. He'd got this far on Roz's meddling; he could do the rest himself. Julian reached out and grabbed Jack's wrist and yanked him under the hot spray.

Jack clearly hadn't shaved since Julian had seen him at the pub, and what he figured had to be three days' worth of beard growth on his face rasped against Julian's neck as he struggled with the now-wet denim of Jack's jeans. "Hello," Jack said, biting down on Julian's collarbone and sliding one hand up and down the plane of his stomach. "I think we skipped that part."

What? Julian thought blindly as Jack scored a thumbnail over one of his nipples. Oh, right, the greeting part. "I don't know about you, but *parts* of me remembered." He managed to wriggle his hands down the back of Jack's jeans and contented himself with getting a good grope in.

Jack's hands fisted in his hair for a moment, and the larger man backed him up against the shower wall. The contrast between the cool tile and Jack's hot body pressed against him short-circuited something in his brain, and that was before Jack crushed his mouth down over his, licking and biting at his lips and tongue, tugging at his hair and rubbing their groins together.

It was all a bit much for Julian, especially when Jack's jeans reached critical saturation and started sliding down his hips of their own accord. Julian felt it the second Jack's thick cock slipped free of its confines to press against his stomach and the sensation went right to his dick. He could think of nothing he wanted more at that moment than to take Jack into his mouth and make him make the kind of noises that had haunted Julian's sleep for two weeks.

It was a forward move for him, but then again, Jack was the one who'd purposely walked in on him in the shower. What the hell? His knees were already giving out, anyway. Julian slid down the tile wall, trailing his fingers over Jack's nicely defined stomach as he went, fingers skittering a bit when he reached the scar on the right-hand side of Jack's abdomen. When he was eye-level with Jack's crotch—give or take a few inches—Julian dug his hands into the wet denim and pulled the jeans the rest of the way down, sharply. Leaving Jack partially immobilized by the fabric around his ankles, Julian leaned forward, grasped Jack's hips in both hands, and guided his cock to his lips.

Jack's hands twisted in his hair almost immediately, and the nearly inhuman sound Julian had been hearing in his imagination for two weeks filled his ears as he ran his tongue around the head of Jack's cock. Just tasting the smooth, hot skin like that wasn't nearly enough. Holding Jack's hips steady with both hands, Julian surged forward, letting the thick member slide into his throat.

"Jesus Christ."

Julian chanced a look up and found Jack's gaze fixed on him, smoldering. His mouth was open, his dark hair plastered to his head by the steady stream of hot water still spraying from the shower head as he slowly thrust in and out. Julian breathed hard around his mouthful when Jack's fingers disentangled from his hair to trace down his cheeks and outline his lips.

Long before Julian was ready, Jack pulled away sharply, reached down and pulled him to his feet. He pressed Julian up against the tile wall again, reached between them and grabbed both of their cocks in one oversized hand.

Julian's eyes rolled back and his knees nearly buckled. Jack managed to keep him vertical by virtue of the fact that there wasn't actually any room for Julian to go anywhere. "I wanna taste your mouth when you come," Jack said, tugging his earlobe into his mouth. "That all right with you?"

He'd have answered verbally, if that were physically possible, but he couldn't seem to make his mouth do anything except latch onto Jack's with all due enthusiasm, digging his fingers into Jack's bicep. "Uhhh…." His feet slipped a bit on the tile floor, and he shot his left hand out to steady himself on the ledge.

Something clattered to the ground, and Julian jerked in Jack's grip. His fist closed reflexively. What on Earth…?

Jack licked into his mouth, then pulled away briefly, blinking. "We need—"

Julian regarded the bottle he'd accidentally grasped with a blank expression. Lube. Roz had put *lube* in his shower. "This do?"

"Been planning this?" Jack panted, eyes glazed.

"Someone has." Julian flicked the cap open and turned the bottle over, drizzling the cool liquid over their erections.

Jack slid his hand up and down their shafts, holding Julian's gaze evenly. Panting, Julian slouched backward, leaning his head against the wall. He ran his eyes down Jack's body, taking in the well-defined chest and abdomen, down to the lazy grip Jack had on their cocks and moaned. "That kiss you wanted," he said. "Is now a good time for you?"

Jack's face darkened with lust. He leaned his left hand up against the shower tile and scraped his stubbled jaw across Julian's cheek, spreading fire down his spine. A wet tongue snaked out and traced a path from the pulse point in his neck up to the shell of his ear. "There's no hurry," he said languidly, breath rasping across Julian's skin.

"Are you kidding?" Julian groaned, unable to resist the urge to thrust up into Jack's fist any longer. "I've had a hard-on for you for two weeks." He reached down and added his hand to Jack's, noting how small it appeared in comparison.

"Shit." Jack's eyes flicked down to their joined hands, then back up to Julian's face. Breath hitching, he pressed his forehead against Julian's, then sealed their mouths together hotly.

Julian kissed him furiously, not bothering to hold back the whimpers that were fighting to come out. "Jack—"

"Do it," Jack bit out, closing his teeth around Julian's lower lip.

"Fuck, yes," he breathed. The muscles in his body tightened, his skin suddenly too small. "Jack—"

The world narrowed to the two of them, the pounding water and the soft sounds of flesh on flesh. Julian arched his back, dug the fingers of his left hand into Jack's bicep and came, vision blackening at the edges. Half a second later he felt Jack's hot semen spurt against his stomach.

Slumping backward, Julian noticed for the first time that the water was getting cold. He reached forward and turned the spray on them briefly, cleaning their stomachs and legs before shutting off the water.

"Well. That was unexpected."

Jack looked down at his sopping wet jeans, then back up again, a wry smile on his face. "You're telling me." He stepped the rest of the way out of them awkwardly. "I don't suppose I could borrow a towel?"

Mouth quirking up in a half-smile, Julian pulled back the shower curtain. "I don't know. I kind of like you wet and naked."

Jack bent to pick up his jeans. Not-so-covertly, Julian checked out his ass. Nice. "Considering there's no chance any of your clothes will fit me, I don't think you need to worry about the naked part for a while. A gracious host would do the noble thing and stay naked with me."

Gee, what a hardship that would be. "As long as I don't have to cook any food unprotected, that should be fine."

As if on cue, Jack's stomach rumbled. "This theoretical food you speak of…"

Laughing, Julian grabbed his towel. "Roz went shopping. God only knows how that turned out, but we should have *something* to eat, at least." He eyed Jack head to toe again, feeling lighter than he had in ages. "You'd better stay there until I grab you a towel, or Roz'll kill me."

"I'm not going anywhere," Jack promised idly.

Not if Julian had anything to say about it. He dried himself quickly, trying not to blush as he felt Jack's gaze linger appreciatively on his ass.

Ten minutes later (after having conscientiously closed the blinds on the first floor, just in case, and tossing Jack's jeans in the dryer), the two of them wandered into the kitchen. "How did Roz get you to sleep in until one, anyway? Even if you did think it was eleven-thirty…"

Julian shrugged, making his way over to the fridge. The towel he'd slung around his waist for the sake of decency flapped around his legs. "I don't suppose you like—"

He stopped, staring at the fridge's interior.

"What?" Jack prodded.

Lost for words, Julian opened the fridge the rest of the way and stepped out of Jack's line of vision, showing off the contents. "This is what happens when my sister goes grocery shopping."

The fridge was stocked, all right. With fresh strawberries, raspberries, sliced pineapples, whipped cream and chocolate sauce. There was a bottle of sparkling wine on the rack. A glance at the counter revealed a jar of honey and two spoons and a note that said, *Check the freezer.*

Julian did, revealing ice cream and three different flavors of popsicles.

"Damn," Jack said, impressed. "She thought of everything."

Shaking his head, Julian closed the freezer. As he did so, his eye caught on the box slightly behind the honey. He took a closer look. Wet naps, condoms, and those individual packets of lubricant that were hell on the environment. *Thank you, Roz.* "I think she expects us to have sex in every room of the house."

"That's not so bad," Jack said. "What's for eating?"

Julian looked at him sitting there, knees spread, naked but for the towel, and had a few really excellent ideas. "I'm sure we'll come up with something."

Jack flashed him a grin, eyebrows raising. "Looks like," he said.

Flushing, Julian glanced down. His towel wasn't going to hold up much longer at this rate, that was for sure. God, it had been a long time since anyone had looked at him like that. He could definitely get used to it. "Strawberries and cream?" he suggested.

Half a second later he was pulled sharply downward until he was seated, haphazardly, in Jack's lap. The towel gave up all attempts to cling to his hips and puddled on the floor.

"Might I suggest we take this somewhere a little more comfortable?"

Julian threaded his fingers in Jack's damp curls. "Bedroom's upstairs," he said a little shyly. It felt frankly ridiculous, considering what they'd just been up to in the bathroom…and were apparently about to continue.

Jack stood and set him on his feet, his gaze drifting down Julian's body. Then he stalked off toward the stairs, towel slipping dangerously low on his body. When he'd reached the stairwell, he turned back. "Bring the strawberries."

"DON'T move them," Jack instructed, and Julian's arms shivered at the command. He curled his hands around the bedposts loosely, closing his eyes halfway, looking down the plane of his body at Jack at his knees.

It was a sight to behold. Jack had strawberry smeared across his mouth and chest, matching in hue to the red blotches that covered Julian from his lightly defined pectorals to the insides of his splayed thighs.

Julian had to bite his lip hard to keep from squirming as Jack dribbled one last, thin trail of warm honey across one nipple and down his sternum to his navel, and even then he could feel his muscles twitching involuntarily. Jack drew one finger through the sticky substance, never taking his gaze from Julian's, and licked it off slowly. The scents of sex and honey filled the air, and Jack's hands returned to play in the thick syrup.

"God," Julian groaned, straining into the touch. He couldn't remember the last time anyone had touched him like that, looked at him like that. "Jack, please—"

Ignoring him, Jack dipped his head and followed the trail from Julian's nipple down his chest and across his hip, nipping lightly at the curve of it, cleaning every drop of honey from his skin. Julian wanted to wiggle away and arch into it at the same time. His breath came in shallow pants. "Yes?" Jack asked, running his hand up the inside of Julian's thigh.

God, what a tease. The problem was, Julian liked it. A lot. Jack's carefree nature was nothing if not addictive, and it didn't hurt that he knew his way around the bedroom. Julian got the idea that Jack was a bit of a philanderer, but at that particular moment he couldn't quite bring himself to care. Under Jack's heated touch he was starting to forget why he'd been single so long in the first place.

The fingers of Jack's left hand trailed down Julian's thigh and back and up, sliding into the crease of Julian's ass. Jack lightly bit the flesh of his thigh.

Julian's whole body arced as if he'd been electrocuted. "Fuck, what are you waiting for? An engraved invitation?"

Jack rewarded him for his cheek by sliding his index finger closer to Julian's hole. Julian's cock jerked, begging to be touched as much as the rest of him, and he moaned, his thighs falling farther open.

Jack breathed in sharply. "Lube," he demanded.

Julian let go of the headboard and turned the top half of his body, hands shaking as he rummaged in his bedside table for the necessary supplies. He passed them to Jack quickly, noting that Jack's hands were shaking every bit as noticeably as his own.

It seemed that it took Jack ages to open the cap and coat his fingers, but it couldn't have been longer than a few seconds. He pushed himself up onto his knees, spreading Julian's thighs further. "Quit squirming," he admonished.

Completely incapable of doing any such thing under the intense scrutiny Jack was giving him, Julian continued to writhe, needing to put his body in as much contact with Jack's as humanly possible. "I *can't*," Julian almost whispered, jumping at the first touch of a slick finger against his entrance. The muscle loosened immediately, and Julian's breath hitched. "Oh, God."

Jack slid his left hand up Julian's thigh to hold him steady and circled his hole again, firmer this time. Julian had to grasp the headboard again with both hands to ground himself, his whole body quivering in anticipation.

Finally, Jack pressed a finger inside of him, pushing deep on the first stroke, and Julian groaned, lifting his legs to give Jack more room. Then Jack put the tip of his cock in his mouth and found Julian's sweet spot with his finger, and a hoarse shout escaped him. With a Herculean effort, he managed not to thrust down Jack's throat—but only because he was paralyzed by the desire to push back against his fingers. "More."

Jack didn't need to be asked twice. He quickly coated another finger in the lubricant and pressed back inside, stroking Julian's prostate again.

"Like that. *Fuck!* Uhhn." Having Jack inside him felt so good. Julian bit his lip, valiantly trying to keep his eyes open. "God, Jack, you have to fuck me now."

Jack's movements paused, and Julian had a bad moment where he thought the other man would make him wait even longer. It seemed like he'd been hard for hours; it might well have been.

Julian heard the rip of the little foil packet being opened and half-sat to watch Jack roll the condom on one-handed, reaching for the lube again with his left. He licked his lips as Jack hurriedly slicked himself. Taking his cock in one hand and holding Julian's hip with the other, Jack pushed forward slowly.

Throwing his head back, Julian hissed as the head of Jack's cock breached his hole. It stung—Jack was fucking *huge*—but it was a good pain, and he enjoyed the burn.

"Fuck, you're tight." Above him, Jack had stilled, eyes closed.

Julian could not wait a second longer to have Jack's prick seated inside him, all the way. He planted his heels on the bed and angled his pelvis upward, bearing down until Jack's balls rested against the curve of his ass. An inhuman sound escaped his lips and Jack curled his fingers into Julian's hips, swearing under his breath.

Half-mad with need, it was all Julian could do to keep breathing. "God, Jack, *move*." God knew Julian couldn't—not much, anyway. He didn't have much leverage with his feet just barely touching the mattress.

Jack's eyes snapped open again, a hint of amusement seeping through the lust that was so blatantly written there. He reached upward and grabbed one of Julian's hands, pressing the palm flat on the bed, and leaned over, trapping Julian's cock between them. A frisson of energy shot through Julian as the movement caused Jack's dick to brush across his prostate. "You are so bossy," Jack said, sliding his cock slowly back out and snapping his hips forward again.

Biting back a groan of pleasure, Julian did his best to follow the movement, but he was effectively trapped by Jack's greater mass.

"More, Jack. Move, Jack. Fuck me harder, Jack," Jack mocked, keeping up the steady and slow pace as Julian thrashed and arched below him, trying anything to get him to speed up. God, even his *voice* was hot—especially when he was right up close like that. "Quit your whining," he commanded, licking a wet path up Julian's neck to his ear that went straight to his groin, "and take it like a man." Jack angled his thrust upward, striking Julian's prostate and sparking a long moan.

"Make me," he gasped, using whatever leverage he could to match Jack's every movement.

That was all it took to break Jack's tenuous control. Eyes like storm clouds, Jack let loose, pounding Julian's ass furiously. Julian's breath came shallowly as every thrust seemed to strike his prostate just right, sending bolts of electricity over his spine. Noises of encouragement spilled from his lips without his permission, along with words that would have made him blush in any other circumstance. His head fell back against the pillow, and his cock leaked steadily against his stomach.

Jack continued slamming into him, punctuating each advance with a small groan. He nipped sharply at Julian's lips and he reached a hand between them, grasping his erection in still-slick fingers, and Julian cried out at the contact. His hips seemed to move of their own accord, rising up to meet Jack's own, driving him closer and closer to orgasm.

Leaning down, Jack covered his mouth in a sloppy kiss, then flicked his thumb across the head of Julian's cock and latched his mouth to his neck. "Come on, Doc. Come for me."

It was all too much. Julian's whole body tensed, curving right off of the bed, mouth open, eyes closed, toes curling. His whole body shook as he came and hot, sticky semen shot all over their chests and stomachs. Distantly, he heard Jack cry out, felt his cock pulsing in his ass as he followed Julian into oblivion.

Breathing erratically, Jack managed to pull himself together enough to withdraw from Julian's body and tie off the condom. Then he nudged Julian to the side and practically collapsed next to him, saying nothing.

God. Julian didn't blame him. It had been a long time since he had had sex like *that,* and he didn't think he had ever been quite so lost to sensation. It was terrifying and exhilarating all at once.

Beside him, Jack seemed equally at a loss, or else he just didn't know what to say. What was there to be said, anyway?

"Holy shit," Julian finally admitted. Jack snickered. After a few long seconds Julian made a whiny sound and reached for the box of Kleenex next to the bed, then wiped up the seed he'd managed to splash liberally over both of them.

The two of them lay there a long time without moving. A muscle cramp tried to start in Julian's thigh, but he wasn't having any of it, and wiggled it until it went away. He was going to be sore tomorrow, that was for sure. And it would be worth every pulled muscle and suspicious bruise.

There was a noise like a giant diesel engine firing and he forced himself to open his eyes and look down at himself in disbelief. God, he hadn't realized how much of an appetite he'd worked up. They never did really have lunch.

"Jesus Christ," Jack said, obviously impressed. "Was that your stomach?"

Julian's stomach repeated itself. "I think that was a yes," he said, flopping back down. His voice sounded like he'd been screaming for a solid hour, which was close enough to the mark. He swallowed a few times, trying to get rid of the raspy feeling. "God, I'm starving, but I do not ever want to move."

Jack snickered again. He didn't seem like he was in a rush to go anyplace himself, which was a bit of a relief, though Julian was unsure how long it'd last. He was willing to bet Jack, too, had worked up quite an appetite, and not just for food. "Think my jeans are dry yet?"

Julian turned to face him, smiling distantly. "If they aren't yet, they may never be again. It's been almost three hours."

"I would say that the time for lunch has passed." Jack's stomach put in its own assessment, agreeing with Julian's. "You don't happen to have any real food squirreled away?"

Sitting, Julian shook his head. "Nope. Roz wasn't supposed to let me sleep so late. I mean, she wasn't supposed to let me sleep until eleven-thirty, never mind one. I wanted to go to the grocery store, see if there was anything good." He glanced around the room, flushing. She'd done well, though. Strawberries, chocolate, sparkling wine.... "Not that Roz didn't do a fantastic job or anything."

"Can't fault her taste," Jack agreed. "Is she always this manipulative?"

"Only when it's in your best interest," Julian said honestly. He was going to have to make her an extra special dinner, or something. He noticed Jack watching him appreciatively as he stood, stretching. Yeah, he was going to be sore tomorrow, all right. That was fine by him. Unfortunately, there was still dinner to think of, and since Roz hadn't bought any actual *food*.... "I don't suppose I can take you out for dinner instead? I feel bad for not feeding you."

"Oh, believe me, I was plenty satisfied anyway." Jack stood up, knees cracking a bit, and stretched out. Julian's mouth watered a little. "Dinner out it is," Jack agreed, running a critical eye over himself in the mirror on the inside of the closet door. "Do you mind if I borrow your shower for a minute first?"

JULIAN didn't move when he heard the door slam, announcing Roz's arrival back at home. He stayed right where he was, nice and comfortable and warm, and pulled his knees in a little closer. All right, maybe he wasn't exactly *comfortable;* he had a couple of pretty good muscle aches going, especially his abs. He just wasn't ready to move yet. Moving seemed to be the only thing he'd done all day.

Dinner with Jack had gone reasonably well. Brenda's hadn't been very busy, four-thirty being a bit early for the dinner crowd. They'd sat in the booth by the window, which made Jack squirm a bit. He was pretty obviously not ready to be outed, which didn't bother Julian too much since the only people in the entire town who knew without a doubt that he was gay were Roz, Dan and the pub owner herself. Aside from the squirming, though, they'd had a good time. Julian had no real reason to be running through today's events over and over in his mind, no justification for the slightly sick feeling in his stomach.

Or at least he hadn't, until Jack had dropped him back off at home again, and the same awkward tension that had been running between them for two weeks returned with a vengeance. Jack had pulled up at the back door, flashed Julian a wicked smile, and thanked him for *lunch.* Julian had laughed it off at the time—he hadn't had much choice, really—but the fact that Jack hadn't kissed him goodbye seemed fairly indicative of what he could expect in terms of future encounters.

He shouldn't have been surprised. Hell, he shouldn't have been *bothered*; he'd certainly suspected Jack to be the love 'em and leave 'em type. He didn't have to like being right.

"Julian?" Roz called from the kitchen. There was a muffled *thump* as she set something down on the kitchen table. "You home, little brother?"

He debated whether to say anything. If he did, he'd have the benefit of her advice and perspective, which usually made him feel better; on the other hand, he'd probably have to fend off some personal questions in order to get there. If he didn't, there was no telling how long he'd be sitting there in the dark before his mood improved—if it ever did.

He was saved from having to make the decision when Roz appeared in the living room, purse clutched in one hand. She dropped it when she saw him. "Julian?" She took another step toward him. "Should I bother asking why you're sitting here in the dark?"

She didn't seem to expect an answer, because she didn't wait for one. Instead, she crossed over to the gas fireplace and flicked it on, then toed off her shoes and left them in the middle of the room before squishing down beside him. "It's cold in here," she commented, making a show of shivering before wrapping both arms around him and leaning her head on top of his. "Tell me what happened."

Relaxing against her, Julian felt some of the tension ease away. "What do you think happened?" he said dryly. "What are you now, my pimp?"

"I'm sorry, Julian. I shouldn't have pushed so hard."

Julian shook his head slowly. "No, you were right. I needed you to, and I'm glad you did. God knows I can't spend the rest of my life like I have the past year. I won't make it to thirty if I do." There were a fair number of friends scattered across various provinces who would attest to that.

Roz's arms tightened around him. "Don't say that."

"It's true, though. You saw what a mess I was last December. I couldn't even get off my couch or choose something to watch on TV by myself. All I could think about was how Derek had cheated on me, how Richard had used me. Roz, if you hadn't driven up to see me, I don't want to think about what I might have done."

"Julian," she said, more urgently this time. "What *happened?*"

Sighing, he rolled his head so that he was facing the ceiling, leaning on her shoulder. "I'm not sure. We were having a good time until four o'clock or so—" Roz made a vaguely impressed noise—"but then we got hungry. By the way, next time you go grocery shopping, could you pick up some actual food? Not that I don't love strawberries and chocolate, but after a while I start to crave something a little more filling."

"Yeah, yeah, duly noted. You were saying?"

Julian picked at the hole in his jeans. "We went out for dinner, for one thing. Roz, the man is so far in the closet I don't know if he'll ever come out. He hardly even looked at me. And the way Brenda was watching us, I'm sure she knew."

"Brenda's always known about you, though, hasn't she?"

"Yes," Julian agreed, "but I haven't taken anyone there in years, you know? I could sort of tell that she wanted to say something to Jack. And I think maybe he noticed, too."

Roz seemed to weigh this for a moment. "Brenda's not one to spread gossip. She only listens to it."

"I don't think that's the point. Not for him. I just…."

Pulling back slightly, Roz wiggled until she could look into his eyes. "That's not it. It's something else that's bothering you. Something that happened before, or after? Do I have to beat him up?"

Sometimes it was nice, having a sister who could read your mind. Always, it was unnerving. In this case, it was also a little uncomfortable. "When he dropped me off again, it was just that. He went home to take care of his dog. No *I'll call you,* no *See you Wednesday.* No goodbye kiss." He stopped, unsure of how that sounded aloud. "God, I think I just spontaneously grew a uterus."

His sister nudged him with her elbow. "Julian. This is obviously a big deal for you. It's okay to be upset."

"It's just, I knew he wasn't interested in anything permanent." The explanation made more sense when he heard it spoken. "So I'm kicking myself for being disappointed." He should have learned his lesson the first time.

Roz wrapped her arms around him again comfortingly. "Believe me when I tell you that if he never asks you on a date, or walks you to the door, or kisses you goodbye, or falls hopelessly in love with you, it is *his loss* and you're better off without him. But I'll be really surprised if he doesn't come around. Whatever else you want to say about him, Jack's not stupid. Stubborn, maybe, but not stupid. He knows a good thing when he sees one."

"Thanks." Julian didn't exactly feel *better,* but he didn't feel *worse,* either, and now that he'd voiced his thoughts he was no longer going around in circles trying to figure out where he'd gone wrong. "How come you're home so late, anyway?"

"Oh, *now* he wants to know about my day." She smiled. "I popped out of work for an hour or two to get some actual groceries, so I had extra paperwork to catch up on. And I had to drop off my overdue library books. That satisfy your curiosity, *Dad?*"

Julian raised his hands palms-out. "Hey, I'm just looking out for you."

"My hero."

"And don't you forget it." They sat together in the flickering firelight for a few moments more. "Thanks, Roz."

She squeezed his hand. "You're welcome."

Chapter 9

JACK strolled into the recreation complex for his final physiotherapy appointment with a spring in his step despite the achy muscle in his left thigh. He thought he might have overextended himself a bit the night before, but he was happy enough with the results that he didn't much care.

He did feel bad about the way he'd treated Julian afterward, though. He'd been rude and insensitive, and he was starting to realize, with a healthy mixture of fear, apprehension, dread, and reluctant excitement that he wished he'd asked for a second date, walked him to the door, kissed him goodbye or just taken the doctor home with him.

Waving at the daytime receptionist, who raised both eyebrows at him inquisitively, Jack made his way past the double doors and opted to take the stairs up to the second level, wanting to stretch out the kinks in his leg before starting physio.

It was about three o'clock in the afternoon, and he was a few minutes early for his appointment with Roz. Still, the airy room that served as a waiting room for physiotherapy patients was empty, not to mention equipped with an especially fancy coffeemaker. Jack walked in and poured himself a cup, inhaling the delicious scent.

He never even heard the door open behind him.

"You've got a lot of fucking nerve."

Jack whirled around so fast the hot coffee sloshed over the edge of the cup, burning his fingers. He dropped the cup, sticking his fingers in his mouth. "Fuck! Roz, what the hell? You just about gave me a heart attack!"

"I'll try harder next time!" she snarled, stalking into the room. The door slammed shut behind her. Shit, she was definitely hacked off. Her green eyes flashed, and he was suddenly aware that this was no small woman—at 5' 10", Roz was just an inch shy of Julian's height—and that it was her job to be in excellent shape. Not to mention, she knew about his recent injury. If she really wanted to kick his ass, he doubted he'd be able to stop her without causing them both serious bodily harm. The bottom dropped out of Jack's stomach. He knew just what he was in trouble for. "Who the hell do you think you are?" Her eyes lit on the bouquet he'd set on the waiting room table and her voice went dangerously quiet. "Are those for me?"

Jack doubted there was anything he could say that wouldn't get him into deeper trouble. "I brought them to thank you for yesterday," he said, holding his ground through sheer force of will. "It was really sweet of you to go to all that trouble—"

Before he could go further, Roz picked up the bouquet and whipped her arm sideways, sending up a spray of leaves and petals around Jack's head. She repeated the motion again, and he put his arms up to fend off the blow. The whipping of the bouquet across his blistered hand stung badly enough to bring tears to his eyes. "I am not a fucking *pimp*, Jackson Strange. Do I make myself absolutely clear?"

Aw, shit. Jack froze, apparently stunning Roz enough to make her realize the absurdity of her actions. Of course. She was angry with him for the way he'd treated her brother. Well, she'd have to get in line. Jack had hardly slept last night, his conscience had been bothering him so badly. He didn't know what his problem was. After all, he was sure Julian had known the score beforehand. He could have walked away from Jack at any time, but he hadn't.

Roz must've sensed the change in his demeanor, because she took one look at the remnants of the bouquet and snorted, tossing it in the garbage bin. "Let me see your hand."

Reluctantly, Jack held it out. She took a cursory look. "I'll get the cortisone. Don't move."

Jack contemplated making a break for the door when her back was turned, but decided against it. She'd probably torch his house. The worst part was, he almost felt like he deserved it. "Listen, I was sort of hoping you could give me some advice."

"I'm not your goddamn therapist." A drawer slammed in her office, and Roz came stalking back out again, brandishing a tube of cream. She threw it at his head; Jack only just managed to catch it with his unburned hand. "You want advice, write to Dear Abby."

"Dear Abby's not Julian's sister," he said, working off the cap with some difficulty and applying the cream. He started to feel better—physically, anyway—right away. "And before you hit me again, I'm not just looking for a way into his pants, okay? Though I'm not going to rule it out."

Roz flopped down onto her leather sofa and looked up at him. Jack felt like he was some kind of specimen under a microscope. "I wish I could tell you he never wanted to see you again."

Hope—and guilt—sparked inside him. "I deserve that," he admitted. He hadn't been one hundred percent honest with Julian—or himself—about what he wanted, which was a first for him. "Look, I know I'm not good at," he gestured helplessly, "talking about relationships. Or having them. Or thinking about them. Or wanting them. I don't know the first thing about them. Hell, I hardly know anything about Julian!" *Except that he has a really hot birthmark on his stomach and he* really *likes strawberries.* Jack managed to tear his mind away from that dangerous path. "All I know is, I made a mistake, and I'd like the chance to correct it if I can."

Roz eyed him with obvious mistrust, then got up and went to the wall, closing the blinds to the hallway. "Take off your pants."

Jack dropped the little tube of cortisone. "What?!"

"Take off your pants," Roz repeated slowly, as if to a little child. "I need to make sure your leg's not infected after all you probably got up to yesterday. Then we can get on with your appointment and maybe, if you're very lucky, I'll mention to Julian you'd like to grovel for his forgiveness and answer the phone when you call later tonight. Around seven-thirty. After he's had a chance to decide whether he wants to talk to you or not."

Oh. Right. He supposed that was really the best he could ask for. "Thanks." He undid his belt and hopped up onto the table Roz sometimes used for therapeutic massages, though never on him. He wasn't actually sure she did those herself. "I think it should be okay."

"Yeah, it looks fine," Roz agreed after a cursory inspection. She stood back, as if looking at something else. "Oh, for Christ's sake."

Jack followed her eyes. There was a purple bruise on his right leg, just below his boxers. He blushed a little. "Ummm...."

"Never mind; I'm not going to ask. I have the feeling that that one wasn't an accident."

"He did seem to have his heart set on getting *all* of the chocolate off. And I just didn't have it in me to tell him no."

Roz rolled her eyes, then reached for the clipboard she kept with all of his various strength and flexibility exercises on it. "Why do I get the feeling I'm going to need to invest in a good set of earplugs?" she teased. "Come on; get your workout clothes on. I'm going to work you hard today to make sure you can take it. Probably not as hard as you worked Julian yesterday, but it won't be as much fun."

Oh, boy. Why did he have the feeling Roz was going to razz him as badly as she'd ever gone after her brother? "Before you do, I just wanted to mention...."

"That your little affair with Julian doesn't mean you're coming out of the closet anytime soon?" she finished for him.

What is this woman, psychic?

"Don't worry. I won't be outing you. In case you hadn't noticed, Julian's not exactly forthcoming about his sexuality, either. Except in select circumstances. Now move it! I've got another appointment at four and I want to see you *sweat*."

JACK swooped down and caught the running girl in both arms, swinging her up onto his hip. "How's my girl?" he asked, wincing a bit. He thought he might have overextended himself this weekend—not that he was regretting it in any way, shape, or form—and Roz's intense physio session wasn't helping matters. He knew he needed to keep pushing himself, and with any luck, next time it'd be with Julian, instead of his sister.

"Miss Jacqueline is going to teach us ballet!" Hallie said excitedly, throwing her arms around his neck. "And we're going to have a recital and I get to wear pink shoes!"

"Pink shoes, huh?" he said fondly. "Sounds stylish. Got all your stuff?"

Hallie nodded, and he set her down gratefully.

"Okay, let's go. Say goodbye to Miss Piet, Hallie."

Roz waved over at them from the front desk, then stood. "Oh, I almost forgot." She pulled an envelope from the stack in the message tray and handed it to Hallie. "That's for your daddy. Okay, sweetheart?"

"Okay," the little girl said cheerfully. "Bye, Miss Piet! See you tomorrow!"

"Talk to you tonight?" Jack asked, voice serious. Oh yeah. He was totally fucked. He was already way too nervous about how wrong this could potentially go, and he was doing it anyway. *Shit.*

Roz nodded at him. "Seven-thirty. Don't forget."

Grasping Hallie's hand in his own, Jack nodded to her and headed for the doors.

Ten minutes later, they pulled into Hallie's driveway. Jack helped her down from the truck and grabbed her dancing bag from the back. "What do you think, half-pint? Has your dad got supper ready yet?"

"We're having shepherd's pie," Hallie told him, taking his hand again like it was second nature. "It's my favorite."

"I thought spaghetti was your favorite?"

"Uncle Jack, I have *two* favorites."

Grinning to himself, Jack pushed open the door to the kitchen. "Is that so?"

"Yes! Shepherd's pie is my *other* favorite." Spotting her father taking dinner out of the oven, Hallie ran over, flinging her arms around his legs. "Hi, Daddy!"

"Hi there, half-pint. What's that in your hand?"

Hallie handed him the envelope proudly. "It's a letter from Miss Piet. She knows Uncle Jack, Daddy!"

Uh-oh, Jack thought, panicking a little.

Roy met his eyes across the room. There was something a little odd about his expression. "Oh she does, does she?"

"Uncle Jack," the little girl said, crossing the room to stand by him again, "are you and Miss Piet friends?"

Great. Jack should definitely have thought twice before buying her those flowers. Now people were going to get the wrong idea entirely, and he wasn't sure Julian would like it. Hell, he wasn't sure Roz would like it, although she would probably just find it all very amusing. That was the sort of person she was. "Yes, we are," he hedged, looking to Roy for help.

None came. Roy looked like he was trying not to laugh.

"Are you going to get married, Uncle Jack? Can I be in the wedding?"

What the hell? "No, Hallie, Roz and I are not getting married. We're just friends. Sometimes," he said, glancing up to glare at Roy for laughing through this impromptu twenty-questions session, "sometimes, a man and a woman can just be friends. They don't have to get married just because they're friends." *Especially if one of them is gay.*

Hallie deflated a little, then brightened. "But if you ever do get married, I can be in the wedding, right? My friend Jessica is going to be a flower girl in her sister's wedding. She gets to wear a pink dress!"

"Well, if I ever need a flower girl, you'll be the first one I'll call," he said, managing to keep a straight face (ha!) somehow. Yeah, right. Even if he wanted to get married, he doubted many people would want to attend. "How about that?"

"Okay," Hallie agreed begrudgingly. "But don't wait *too* long, Uncle Jack. In two more years I will be too old to be a flower girl!"

He grinned sheepishly, having no idea where the girl got these notions, but gladder than he usually was that he could just escape the questions by running home with his metaphorical tail between his legs. "I'll try to hurry and find the right one. Deal?"

"Deal." They shook on it.

Roy was still snickering behind his hand. Jack leveled a look at him that said, quite clearly, *you're next*. He stopped laughing. "Jack, we've got plenty of food. You're welcome to stay for dinner."

Jack thought of Robot waiting at home to be let out, and the groveling he was going to have to do later, and decided against it. "Thanks, man, but I've got to run home and let Robot out, and I've got a ton of stuff to get done tonight. Rain check?"

"Sure," Roy said easily, waving jauntily. Jack was already making his retreat. "See you tomorrow, Jack."

"Bye, Uncle Jack!"

Jack returned the wave, absently closed the door behind him, and walked back to his truck. He had some serious thinking to do, and only a few hours to do it in. Steeling himself, he started the engine and headed for home.

"MR. STRANGE, I presume?"

Jack's stomach coiled into a tense little ball. "Hi, Roz." If she was answering, did that mean Julian didn't want to talk to him? Had he fucked up already? "How'm I doing so far?"

"You usually only get points for remembering your date's name, not his sister's," she pointed out. He could almost picture her lounging carelessly on the sofa downstairs, reveling in making him sweat like she did in physio.

"I mean, do I get a chance to apologize?"

Jack really did feel like an ass. He'd screwed up a really good friendship with sex in college when his roommate had started developing feelings for him. Jack hadn't known how to deal with that then, and he still wasn't sure. The thing was, he kind of wanted to learn, and that was terrifying.

Especially since he might not get the chance.

"Hold on." There was a rustling sound, like something covering the receiver, and a few moments of silence.

Jack held his breath.

Finally: "Hello?"

Sagging in relief, Jack sank into a chair at his kitchen table. "Julian, it's Jack. Listen, I wanted to apologize for yesterday. I'm not very good at, uh...."

"Manners?" Julian suggested a little coldly. Still, at least he was talking.

I deserved that. "Yeah, I'm a little out of practice. Or I never had any to begin with."

There was a long sigh on the other end. "It's all right. I'm not exactly the picture-perfect gay man myself, seeing as you are now the fourth person in town to know I'm gay."

It looked like he might be forgiven, after all. "Really? I know Roz knows, but who are the other two?"

"I told Dan before I took the job at the clinic. And Brenda walked in on my boyfriend and me making out in the bathrooms when I was eighteen."

Jack had to laugh at that. Oh, to be young again. "Classy. Very discreet."

"I was young and in love," Julian defended, a little wistfully if Jack was not mistaken, "and horny all the time. What can you do?"

"Make out in public restrooms?" Jack suggested. He was thinking of the hockey game, when he'd nearly jumped Julian in the shower. It was a dangerous train of thought if he actually meant to have a conversation.

"Exactly."

There was an awkward pause as Jack tried to work out what he wanted to say next. He was sure he hadn't quite resolved everything just yet. "Can I…." *Call you sometime?* No, that was wrong; he was calling him *now*. *Take you out* implied, well, *out* and he knew he wasn't ready for that. Fuck it; this was why he wasn't an English major. "Can I see you again?"

That seemed to be the right one. He thought Julian might even be smiling. "I, um, yes."

Cute. Jack smiled, relaxing into the conversation. Maybe this could work out, after all.

"WHERE the hell did you two come from?" Brad panted, drinking his beer like it was going out of style.

It was Wednesday, and Jack and Julian had played on the same hockey team this week. Apparently they worked together well outside of the bedroom as well as in it, because they had completely dominated the match, even though they'd staged a few checks just for the sheer fun of it. Jack had gotten in a particularly good one when Julian was looking the other way, resulting in the other man falling flat on his behind.

Jack caught Julian's eye and winked, reaching for his own beer. "I've been giving him pointers," Jack grinned.

Julian rewarded him with a roll of those chocolate-brown eyes. "I taught him how to skate on the weekend. Just another in my big bag of tricks."

Choking on his beer, Jack spluttered, nose burning as the liquid tried to exit through his nostrils. Brad and the other guys were laughing, but Julian was smirking. It was sexy as hell, especially since Jack knew just what he meant. Jack adjusted his towel surreptitiously, glowering at Julian a little.

"You're funny, Doc. Tell me, who's going to stitch you up after I get you back next week?"

"Brad'll do it," Julian said automatically, fluttering his eyelashes. "Won't you, Brad?"

Brad put on a highly affected seductive expression. "Sure, baby. I'll kiss it better."

Jack snorted. Bartenders. They just loved being in the middle of things. In Brad's case, hopefully not literally. Jack was not prepared to share Julian with anyone—even if it would be kind of hot.

Glancing at his watch, Jack realized how late it was getting. Poor Marianne would be wanting to close up soon. "Guess we'd better get our butts in gear. Don't want Julian's sister to beat us up for keeping Marianne out all night."

That drew a couple of raised eyebrows, and Jack winced inwardly, making a mental note to never again mention Roz when he didn't need to. These guys were like vultures, waiting for him to mess up and betray the slightest detail. More than likely they were also a little jealous.

"She could probably take you," Brad said with a grin.

Jack flipped him off and dropped his towel to dress. The other guys filed out, one by one, until it was just him and Julian left in the changing room.

It could have been awkward, but it wasn't. After an embarrassingly honest apology on Jack's part that had revealed a lot more about himself than he'd honestly wanted it to, Julian had agreed that they should give a relationship of sorts a chance. Jack had the feeling that there was still a lot they weren't telling each other—he knew for a fact he was holding rather a lot back—but that was okay. He wasn't exactly looking for a lifelong commitment.

They hadn't seen or spoken to each other since Sunday evening, except for their too-brief telephone call. Roy had dropped Hallie off in the middle of the conversation so that he could run some errand or other, and they'd talked on the phone for a moment or two before it simply became too awkward. The important things had all come out, and now that the tension between them seemed to have disappeared for good, Jack couldn't have been happier about it. It was nice, not having to hide from everyone.

"What're you thinking?" Julian asked him as they slung their hockey bags over their shoulders and made for the doors.

Jack gave him a sideways look. "I'm thinking maybe you'd like to come home with me," he said slyly. "Got something I want you to take a look at. Do you make house calls?"

Snorting, Julian held open the outside door, then followed him out into the night. "Oh, like I haven't heard that one before."

Jack pouted. "I thought it was good."

"Cliché," Julian corrected. He took his bag off of his shoulder and put it in the bed of the truck. Looking around the parking lot, he must have noticed how far away Jack had parked, because he raised his eyebrows. "Felt like a hike?"

Hardly. Jack had had one thing in mind when he'd parked so far away, and one thing only. He held his tongue, waiting for Marianne to close and lock the doors to the complex. She waved as she got in her car and drove away into the night. Then he started leading the way back to his pickup. "Not really. Hey, Doc, do you think it's cold enough to get frostbite?"

It wasn't, and both of them knew it. The past few days had been unseasonably warm, a kind of almost-Indian-summer that Jack knew, from years of experience of living in Alberta, meant that the first snowfall could only be a week or so away. The cold would snap back any day, and with a vengeance. But for now….

Jack tossed his hockey bag into the bed of his pickup, then turned around and grabbed both of Julian's hands, pulling him tight against his body. "Damn. I don't know how I thought I could ignore this. Or why I was convinced I wanted to."

"Not the swiftest fish in the barrel," Julian teased, mixing his metaphors beautifully. Jack growled at him and bit his lips, then soothed the imaginary hurts with his tongue. Julian's mouth opened right up, welcoming the invasion of his tongue and greeting it with his own.

"I'll show you swift," Jack mumbled through a mouthful of Julian, turning quickly and pressing Julian up against the truck almost as if in homage to their first physical encounter. "How's that?"

Julian hummed happily into his mouth, his hands creeping up the back of Jack's shirt under his jacket, raising goose bumps along the skin there. Jack returned the favor by loosening his grip on Julian's shirt, instead spanning his hands across Julian's chest until he found the two almost-flat nipples and tweaked them, eliciting a moan.

"Very swift," Julian admitted, back arching at the contact, exposing his long throat. Jack licked it. "But not as swift as this."

Julian hooked his thumbs into Jack's belt loops and pulled, sending Jack crashing into him, crushing their bodies together against the truck. Jack could feel Julian's erection through the material of the loose sweatpants he was wearing, and having surreptitiously watched him dress, he knew damn well Julian wasn't wearing anything under them. The thought affected him more than he'd expected and he moaned, his own hard prick jerking against Julian's belly.

"Jesus," he said appreciatively, running one shaky hand up Julian's neck and face to nest in those soft, dark curls again. God, he loved Julian's hair. He wasn't sure what it reminded him of, but it was fucking hot.

"I wasn't finished," Julian complained, eyes flashing suddenly. Before Jack knew it, he'd reversed their positions so that Jack was leaning heavily against the side of the pickup, and Julian was pressed flush against him.

Not that Jack was complaining. Far from it. The uncharacteristic display was a definite turn-on. "How about now?" Jack growled, yanking him closer by the hair and pulling his lips into a bruising kiss.

Julian moaned into his mouth, rubbing his erection into Jack's thigh. Christ, this kid was going to be the death of him. Julian's hands skimmed down Jack's chest and stomach, fingers probing the waist of his jeans. "Nope."

Fuck. Jack groaned appreciatively as Julian popped the button on his jeans open one-handed, peeled back the denim and slid his hand inside, grasping his erection loosely. Jack managed to grab a generous double-handful of Julian's ass as the younger man stroked him firmly, mouths still locked in a searing kiss.

After another few seconds, Julian shoved him roughly away, slithering down Jack's body until he was kneeling on the pavement. He reached up and hooked his fingers into the waist of Jack's jeans and tugged them down, taking his boxers with them.

Jack's cock jutted proudly into the cool night air, a drop of pre-come oozing from the tip. Julian wasted no time before leaning forward and taking Jack deep into his mouth.

Cursing, Jack leaned back against the truck, his hands fisting in Julian's hair again, guiding that hot, perfect mouth down over his throbbing shaft again and again. Julian made a contented noise that reverberated all the way up Jack's cock and sat tight in his testicles. "Fuck, that feels fantastic."

Julian reached a hand around to cup Jack's balls, rolling them gently in his palm as he suckled the head of Jack's dick. His tongue felt amazing, licking little circles around the slit, then tracing back down to outline the pulsing vein on the underside. Julian's right hand curled around the base of Jack's erection, holding him steady when all Jack really wanted to do was let go and thrust down that luscious throat.

Someone had fixed the streetlights, and Jack could look down and see everything clearly, from the dark gaze in Julian's eyes to the slender fingers curled around his prick. Jack took deep, gulping breaths of the rain-fresh night as Julian sucked him, feeling the slight scrape of teeth against his glans. The dark was filled with the soft noises of sex, shallow breathing, muffled groans, and wet suction.

Jack watched, fixated, and Julian watched *him*—dark gaze unwavering, rhythm never faltering. When he moved his hand away from Jack's shaft, Jack hissed in protest—until Julian opened his throat and took him all the way down, swallowing the head of his cock and moaning. Jack was almost too caught up in the sensation of wet heat enveloping his dick to notice Julian reaching down to pull his own erection out of his sweatpants.

It was a ridiculously erotic sight, and it made Jack twist Julian's curls between his fingers even harder. "Damn," he groaned, unable and unwilling to keep himself from pumping his cock in and out of those full lips. "I had no idea you were such a cockslut."

The answering moan left little doubt as to exactly how much Julian was enjoying what he was doing. Mouth open, Jack stared down at Julian, stomach tightening as Julian simultaneously sucked him off and jerked his own dick. He would have sworn he could smell the pre-come leaking from the tip of the younger man's swollen member.

In a haze of lust, Jack bit his lip hard, fucking Julian's mouth.

"Fuck, baby, you're so good," he crooned, feeling his balls draw close to his body. His toes curled up tight in his running shoes. "God, I'm so close, gonna come. Wanna come in that sweet mouth of yours."

Julian jerked against him, and Jack's breath left him in a rush as he realized Julian had just shot his load all over the pavement. His knees nearly gave out as he thrust one more time into the wet cavern before his balls emptied into Julian's throat.

Jack leaned against the truck, insensate, trying to catch his breath, for God knew how long. After an indeterminate time period Julian rose and joined him, leaning his head on his shoulder, pulling Jack's jeans up as he went, but not bothering to fasten them.

"Should you be doing that?"

Julian gave him a sheepish look. "As a doctor, I should know better, yeah."

Somehow Jack knew that wasn't the end of it. "But....?" he prompted.

"As your doctor, I've seen your test results, and I'm not worried."

Huh. Cute. Awkward. Definitely a little weird, but cute. "This whole parking lot thing," Jack said, attempting conversation. "Fetish of yours?"

Julian's laugh was muffled against Jack's jacket. "One of yours, more like. I just go along with it because I have a fetish for *you.*"

"I appreciate your indulgence," Jack said dryly. He reached down to make sure he was tucked into his boxers before zipping and buttoning his jeans. Then, a little awkwardly, he wrapped his arms around the other man, who, he now noticed, had not put on a coat. It wasn't *that* warm. "Doc, do you have some kinda death wish? You're gonna catch your death. Aren't you supposed to be smarter than that?"

"Sorry. If I'd've known you were going to molest me in the parking lot, I'd've worn a cock warmer."

Laughter bubbled up inside Jack and he shoved Julian playfully. "Smartass."

"Uh-huh. That's not all it is."

The man was incorrigible. Jack thought maybe he liked it that way. "Come home with me," he said impulsively, almost regretting it the instant he said the words out loud. Fuck, it was going to be a lot harder to keep this secret than he'd originally thought—and even harder to keep it casual.

"I can't." The doctor was still speaking into his shoulder. It was kind of adorable.

Jack didn't know whether to be disappointed by the answer, or relieved. He settled on a bit of both. "Okay."

Julian must've been able to sense part of what he was thinking, because he pulled far enough away to look Jack in the eye. "I want to; don't get me wrong. But I've got to work in the morning, and I haven't got anything with me except hockey clothes, and I don't think my patients would appreciate that. Never mind my co-workers."

Snickering as he imagined Dr. Dan's reaction to that, Jack felt some of his misgivings give way. It was definitely going to be a challenge not to get too close to this man, a challenge he could sense he was already failing. Damn it, he was in a good mood and he wasn't going to think about it right now. "All right, Jitterbug, up you get. You're not the only one who has to work in the morning, and if I don't make it home soon, Robot's gonna tie herself in knots trying not to go on the carpet."

He could almost hear Julian's smile in the night. "You named your dog Robot?"

"My next-door neighbor named my dog Robot. She used to walk really stiffly when she was just a puppy, before I put carpet down so she wouldn't slide all over the hardwood."

"Hallie Klein?" Julian asked, adjusting himself as he leaned against the truck, next to Jack.

"Yeah. You met her at the bar the other night."

Julian smiled. "She was the only person there I wanted to dance with besides you."

Damn. Jack felt his face heat, and was glad for the darkness. The last thing he needed was to be accused of being a teenage girl. "Been carrying a torch for me, have you?"

"Something like that." Julian glanced over at him, eyes mischievous. "Bet you'd like to know *where* I was carrying it."

Groaning, Jack tried to discourage his cock from taking an interest. It was a losing battle. "If you're not coming home with me, you're not allowed to talk like that." He leaned over and planted a firm kiss on Julian's mouth, allowing himself to be pulled in further. Then he gave Julian another little push away from his truck, and swatted him on the ass. "Get going, before I refuse to take no for an answer."

Julian blew a ridiculous kiss in the darkness. "See you later, hot stuff. Call me."

Chuckling to himself, Jack fished his keys out of his pocket. Maybe the next few days wouldn't be easy, but he was willing to bet they'd be fun as hell.

Chapter 10

BRUSHING the snow from his hair, Julian stomped into the kitchen, toed off his boots, and put the groceries on the kitchen table. He was not ready for winter, but winter didn't seem to care; it was more than ready for him. This morning he'd been obligated to put the tire chains on the trucks, just in case he slid through an intersection on his way to the damn grocery store. The only person in town happy about the onset of the snowy season was Mr. Bender, and that was because it meant people would stop driving to other towns to get more variety in their groceries.

Luckily, Julian had managed to snag the last box of strawberries Roz had begged him to pick up, pointing out that he and Jack had devoured the last ones without saving her a single berry. Bender's Grocery hadn't had any more in since then, and that had been over two weeks ago. Julian suspected these would be the last of the season, and he was tempted to keep them for himself, but knew what Roz would likely do to him if he tried.

"Roz?" he called. "You wanna help with dinner?"

Roz breezed into the kitchen, dressed in her Saturday night best, putting in an earring. "Dinner? Nah. Got a hot date." She winked at him, and then spotted the groceries. "Oh, my god, the strawberries." Forgetting about her earring, she grabbed the little plastic carton and had it running under the kitchen sink before Julian could even comment. "I can't believe you and Jack ate all the ones I bought last time. I was so jealous." She picked the biggest one of the bunch and took a huge bite of it, sighing. "God, they're perfect."

Julian shook his head. A container of strawberries was a small price to pay for all the wonderful things Roz had done for him over the past few weeks, and he was more than happy to pay it. Jack still wasn't exactly comfortable eating with him in public, and they didn't go to the convenience store together to pick out videos to watch or anything overtly coupley like that. Neither of them had even stayed overnight yet, which had troubled Julian at first, before he had come to realize Jack wasn't going anywhere. They had planned to once; Julian had had his bags packed and even brushed his teeth before bed, but he'd received a page on his cell phone notifying him that Star and Melanie Hamilton's oldest had a fever of a hundred and four, so that had put a stop to that night.

However, if Roz was going out tonight, maybe she could drop him off at Brenda's. He'd meet up with Jack and they could take things from there. "Where are you off to? Seeing anyone I know?"

Roz shook her head, swallowing the rest of the gargantuan fruit. "Couple girls from work and I are going out in Copperfield for a late-night movie, then maybe a club. One of them has a cottage there, so we're staying the night."

Good for her, Julian thought. Roz had never been one to befriend other females easily. Other women were often jealous of Roz's good looks and easygoing nature, and the fact that she got on a little too well with men made some of them resent her even further or slander her behind her back. Julian had missed the worst of those years, Roz's last two years in high school, because he'd been out of the province, but she'd called him in tears a time or two after being confronted by a friend regarding a faux pas she hadn't realized she'd made, such as talking to so-and-so's boyfriend at lunchtime. Because she found it difficult to identify with women her own age, Roz had a lot of male friends—and a lot of boyfriends, which had given her a further reputation. It would probably be good for her to go out and have fun with someone with a uterus. "Have fun," he told her, "You deserve it. You've been working too hard; I can tell you've been exhausting yourself."

"I need to hire a second swimming and aquafitness instructor," she admitted, biting into another berry.

Outside, a car horn honked. "That's my ride," Roz told him cheerfully, pecking him on the cheek. "See you tomorrow, little bro. Don't do anything I wouldn't do."

Julian didn't bother asking about things she wasn't physically capable of doing. She was out the door before he realized she'd taken the entire box of strawberries. "Safe sex!" he shouted after her.

Roz flipped him the bird as she climbed into the passenger seat of an old Jimmy.

He had the phone in hand before he could overthink it, and was dialing Jack's number from memory almost before he'd even made up his mind to do so.

"It's me," he said when Jack picked up the phone. He looked at the bags of groceries on the table, then at the empty kitchen. He didn't much feel like cooking a meal for one....or even two. "You want to pick me up on your way over?"

"WHERE'S your sister? Doesn't she usually come to these things with you?"

Julian looked up from his Guinness-and-mushrooms steak to see the fiddle player standing opposite him. He kicked out the chair across from him so the other man could sit down. "She's out with the girls," he explained. "She doesn't get along with a lot of them, so she tends to take advantage when she can. I think they went to Copperfield for the night."

"Ah." Roy grabbed the chair and sat, flexing the fingers on his left hand. "I guess you were cramping her style."

Snorting, Julian shook his head. It was more likely the other way around, if privacy and time apart were what Roz had wanted out of her impromptu vacation, but he wasn't going to explain that to Roy. Besides, he was pretty sure that hadn't been her motivation at all. "Probably," he agreed anyway, but he put down his fork and knife in an unspoken challenge to pursue the subject further.

Thankfully, Roy had the sense to quit while he was ahead. "How are you adjusting, anyway? It's got to be a big change from Toronto."

Jack chose that moment to join them at the table, and Julian caught his eye for a second before answering. "Yeah, it is, but it's definitely got its perks." He looked around. "Where's Hallie, anyway? Don't you usually bring her along?" He hadn't seen the girl all night, and Roy had stayed for both sets, when he normally headed home after the first. Julian had been picking at the remains of his dinner for almost an hour.

"She's at a sleepover," Roy explained. "Her first. She's trying to cut the apron strings already."

No wonder he was still at the bar, Julian thought. He couldn't bear to go home to an empty house. Julian could relate to that.

"Poor Roy," Jack said sympathetically. "Want me to give you a ride home so you can sit in the dark and mope?"

Roy opened his mouth to retaliate just as Julian shot Jack a warning glare. Thankfully, Roy was distracted by Brad waving him over to the bar before he could accept the offer. Brad's eyes were fixed on the television screen, where the Oilers and the Flames were locked in a two-all game with three minutes left in the third period. Roy gave Jack a brief, unconvincing glare and made his way up to the barstool. "Five bucks on Edmonton."

Jack snickered, kicking Julian under the table. "Delusional. Come on, help me get the stuff in the truck and I'll take you home."

Pulse pounding, Julian stood to help him take down the equipment. The two microphones and mic stands, effects pedals, and patch cords all fit neatly into a gig bag whose primary function was to cart them back and forth to *Brenda's*. By the time Julian had finished packing up the smaller bits and pieces, including harmonicas in two different keys and a tambourine (watching Roy play the tambourine still made him laugh, though he couldn't have said exactly why), Jack had loaded up everything else except for the older acoustic-electric guitar.

Julian hoisted the gig bag on one shoulder and waved goodbye to Brenda, who was just coming out of the kitchen with a dish tub to collect the dirty flatware from behind the bar. She gave him a covert wink as they passed, and for once Julian managed to grin in return without blushing.

Once everything was in the truck, the night seemed to grow quiet, as if all sound was muffled by the still-falling snow. Jack was the last one in the cab, and huffed a breath that made the interior windows fog for a minute before he turned to look at Julian. "You're sure you want to do this?"

Julian raised his eyebrows at him. He felt oddly secure in his belief that, for the first time in weeks, Jack wasn't trying to get him to back off. Maybe they were making progress after all. "Hey, I'm the one who's a bear in the morning hours you like to wake up in. I should be asking you that question."

Jack started the truck, and Julian gratefully put his hands on the heater. "I'm sure I'll find a way to get you up before ten," he said innocently.

Laughing, Julian finally relaxed against the back of the seat. "I guess we know what kind of bear I am in the morning."

"What kind?"

Julian grinned at him. "Horny."

He might've imagined it, but he thought Jack increased pressure on the gas pedal, just a little.

"THAT tickles," Julian mumbled into the pillow, not yet awake enough to try to get away. Instead, he made a valiant effort to go back to sleep, keeping his eyes shut and snuggling his face down into the fluffy pillow.

Unfortunately, it seemed that Jack wasn't ready to leave him alone. He brushed his stubble over the back of Julian's neck again, nuzzling his face in the crook of his shoulder. "Mmm," came the sleepy, noncommittal response. Jack's arm tightened around his waist.

Julian groaned. The renewed embrace brought his backside into direct contact with Jack's morning erection. There'd be no going back to sleep now that his own prick had noticed the fun and decided to join in.

"This is nice," Jack purred in his ear, sliding a hand slowly down Julian's naked chest. Julian's nipples hardened against a not-quite-accidental touch. Jack ground his hips against Julian's ass again.

"You would say that," Julian griped, the grumpy tone he'd meant to use somewhat lost in the fog of lust that seemed to be permeating the morning. Oh well. He couldn't really complain, since he didn't remember the last time he'd woken up to someone groping him. "You're a morning person."

"I am now," Jack confirmed, grasping Julian's cock loosely, running his thumb through the moisture gathering at the tip.

Sighing happily, Julian arched his back into the touch, resting his head on Jack's shoulder and feeling Jack's definitely awake cock nestling between his cheeks. "Um. Not to ruin the moment, but where's Robot?"

The excitable dog had taken an instant liking to Julian, and the feeling was mutual, but he didn't like her *that* much.

"I let her out to run in the backyard. I can't believe it didn't wake you up."

Shamelessly, Julian rubbed his whole body into Jack's touch. "I didn't hear a thing."

Jack bit down lightly on his shoulder and Julian shuddered, gasping. "You were sleeping on my leg," Jack accused, voice fond but raspy from lack of use. He dragged his teeth up Julian's neck and Julian was sure his spine had just melted. "Like that?"

"Uhn," Julian agreed frantically. He thrust his hips forward lazily, following Jack's hand. "Yeah."

Jack's knee came up between Julian's legs, holding him open. The movement stretched muscles that were still a bit sore from last night's activities, but it was a good kind of sore. "Relax, Jitterbug," Jack grumbled against the back of his neck, setting the hairs there standing straight on end. Something blazed a cool trail down his back, from just between his shoulderblades all the way to the crack of his ass.

Jack's other hand, fingers clearly already slicked with lube. God, he'd been planning to wake Julian up this way. Not that Julian was complaining.

Jack's finger grazed over the little pucker of muscle, and Julian felt his body opening to the invasion. Except for his cock, still leaking steadily under Jack's ministrations, every muscle in his body felt loose and languid. "I could not possibly be more relaxed," he mumbled happily as Jack's finger slid inside of him, stroking his prostate with unerring precision.

"Hmm, we'll see about that," Jack laughed, adding a second finger. "I bet I can think of something that'd…relax you a little more."

"It's too early in the day to fuck me into unconsciousness," Julian groused, not really meaning it. His hips were starting to pump forward into Jack's fist and backward onto his fingers without his input.

Snorting, Jack closed his teeth around a piece of skin at the juncture of Julian's neck and shoulder, sending sparks all along his central nervous system. "It's never too early." He added another finger and tightened his grip around the base of Julian's cock.

"Umm, that's good. You may have a point."

Jack curled his fingers mercilessly and the languid ease that had taken Julian's body disappeared in a flash of urgency. "Again."

"What's the magic word?" The fingers twisted.

Julian's whole body hovered on the edge of abyss. "God, please. Jack…."

"Yes?"

"Fuck me."

Jack's tongue licked a hot line from Julian's shoulder to his cheekbone. "Thought you'd never ask." His fingers retracted for a moment, but before Julian could even complain about it, there was a crinkle of foil and a snap of latex and he was being filled, surrounded, overcome.

"Yes," he whispered, and the languid, half-there feeling returned, and he was floating outside his body, feeling nothing but Jack's hands on him, Jack's prick in his ass, Jack's stubble, Jack's lips, Jack's teeth on his neck.

Julian couldn't have said how long it was before the pleasure became too much; it could have been thirty seconds or thirty minutes. He took one last, deep breath before the inevitable all-over tremble took him, and then Jack bit down on his neck hard while flicking his thumb over the head of Julian's shaft and that was it. He came with his eyes open, staring at the wall and seeing nothing, a wordless moan slipping from his lips as his body clamped down hard around Jack's.

A second later, Julian felt Jack stiffen and pulse inside of him, one arm wrapped around Julian's waist. "Fuck."

"Again?" Julian said incredulously. "Already?" To his own ears, his voice sounded far away.

"Smartass," Jack grumbled. He fisted one hand in Julian's hair—ow, that pulled a bit—and turned his head for a distinctly unfresh kiss. Julian couldn't have cared less. "Now that's what I call a good morning."

"Hmm," Julian hummed in agreement. He glanced at the clock. Ugh. Eight-thirty. It did nothing to dampen his good mood. "You know, I could get used to this."

A bark from the back door interrupted the almost-cuddle. Jack made an apologetic noise and sat up, looking for his jeans. "Sorry. Guess it's breakfast time for Robot."

Ah, well. Of course it had been too good to last. Julian wriggled out from under the sheet—he must have kicked off the rest of the blankets during the night, as Jack gave off an unbelievable amount of body heat—and winced. Off Jack's amused glance, he untucked the corners of the bottom sheet from the bed and bundled it up along with the top one. "Laundry room?"

"Downstairs, left of the kitchen," Jack said with a smile. "Hungry yet?"

"Always," he answered with a wink, leaving no room for interpretation as to what he really meant. He set the sheets down just long enough to pull on jeans and a T-shirt. "Got any breakfast sausage?" Julian asked hopefully as he followed Jack down the stairs.

Laughing, Jack reached the bottom and crossed over to the sliding rear door, opening it for Robot. "Sorry. Eggs and bacon?"

Robot came charging in, skittering a bit when she'd got past the mat at the rear door, and mauled Jack's hand with her tongue before half-bounding, half-sliding over to Julian. "It's a good thing you're a dog,

Robot," Julian said seriously, tossing the dirty bed linens into a laundry basket on the floor, then shutting the door behind him. "You have no idea where his hands have been."

He noticed with a grin that Jack made a point to wash them before they got any closer to breakfast.

An hour passed and breakfast turned into a long, hot shower. Jack didn't have a dishwasher, so once they were clean and, more importantly, satisfied (again; Julian noted to never let it be said that Jack lacked stamina), they spent a few minutes doing the dishes. It was such an everyday activity that it felt normal—so normal it was *weird,* in fact. Julian kept the thought to himself as he dried another dish.

He was just putting away the spatula when he heard his cell phone ring.

Jack caught his eye for a second and looked away. Julian groaned inwardly. They had been doing so well, just being together, the two of them ignoring the outside world. But now it was Sunday morning—soon to be Sunday afternoon—and sooner or later he was going to have to go back out into the real world again, back to sleeping alone in his own bed. And waking alone, too.

"You should probably get that," Jack said quietly, sticking his hand into the dishwater to unplug the sink. "It could be important."

Julian sighed, knowing Jack was right, and trudged up the stairs to retrieve the phone. "Hello?"

"Dr. Piet?"

He held the phone away from his ear for a second and frowned at it. No, he hadn't misread the number. It was coming from his house, but he didn't recognize the voice. "Yeah?"

"It's Marianne," the woman on the other end of the line told him. "From the complex. Listen, we just got home from Copperfield. Roz is feeling pretty under the weather. We were all pretty wild last night; maybe she just had too much to drink, or maybe it was something she ate. Anyway, I wanted to let you know…you'll probably want to check on her in an hour or two, just to make sure she's feeling better?"

Julian resisted the implication that he didn't know what to do with a sick woman and focused on his sister's symptoms. "What's wrong with her? Has she got a fever? Is she vomiting?"

"Uh…." Marianne's voice trailed off for a moment, and he thought he could hear Roz's voice, hoarse like it had been when she'd had strep throat as a kid, in the background. "No fever, but she's got no color. I think she threw up before we left the house this morning."

"Could be food poisoning," Julian reasoned, searching through the mess of the bedroom to find his socks. He finally located them under the dislodged comforter. "She ate a whole box of strawberries herself yesterday. Maybe she didn't wash them well enough."

"Julian?"

He blinked. That was Roz, now, certainly. Marianne must've given her the phone. "Yeah, it's me. Hold on tight, okay? I'll be there in a few minutes."

"Julian, I feel like shit," she continued. She sounded it, too. He hated to think what she was going to look like when he got home.

Julian sat on the top step to pull on his shoes, holding the phone with his shoulder. "Eat some crackers if you think you can keep them down, and take a painkiller. I'll be home soon."

There was a deep, shuddering breath. "Oh, no," she said, and her tone was firm even if the delivery was weak. "You stay where you are. I will be fine in a few hours."

Fat chance of that happening. He tied the laces quickly, looking up at Jack, who'd appeared at the bottom of the stairs. His hands were shoved defensively in his pockets, and his gaze was anywhere but meeting Julian's. "You're a terrible liar. See you in five." Shutting his phone, he stood and gave Jack an apologetic look. "Sorry," he said, managing not to shut down completely as he walked down the stairs. They'd never get anywhere if they both kept closing off like this every time the outside world intruded on theirs. He even managed a quick kiss before delivering the bad news. "Could you give me a lift home? I have to go play nursemaid. Roz has the flu. Or food poisoning. Or something. It's a little easier to diagnose in person."

Jack relaxed a little under his touch. "Yeah," he said, meeting Julian's eyes again. "Sorry, I—" He took a deep breath, and Julian watched, rapt, as Jack made a seemingly concerted effort to unknot himself. "I'll get my coat."

Chapter 11

THE ride back home was tense, with Julian basically sitting on his hands so that he didn't fidget too much. After thirty seconds he couldn't take it anymore and flicked on the radio, trying to relax to the strains of an old Canadian folky tune playing on CBC Radio 1.

That took the edge off, but not by much. Julian didn't have a lot of family, and what he did have, he couldn't afford to lose.

Jack pulled into his driveway four minutes later and put the truck in park. "Do you want me to stay?" he asked awkwardly.

Surprised, Julian looked up from unbuckling his seat belt and planted a kiss square on Jack's mouth. He supposed he was probably lucky that Marianne had gone. "You'd better not. She might be contagious, and I don't know what I'll do for a week if you both have the flu." He managed half a smile. "Thanks for the offer. I'll tell Roz you said hi."

Shutting the truck door behind him, Julian made a beeline for the back porch. Just inside the door, he picked up his travel bag and took the stairs two at a time up to Roz's bedroom.

He paused at the door, knocking gently. "Roz?"

She was huddled under her blankets, face ashen, hair plastered to her scalp. "Hey, little brother. I'm not having a good day. Sorry to interrupt your fun."

Julian dropped the bag at the door, pulled out his digital thermometer, and went in to sit on the edge of the bed. "Don't worry about it. This is more important." He put the dial in her ear and clicked the button to get a reading. Normal. Okay, so it probably wasn't the flu.

"I feel like shit."

"You look it." He reached down and touched her cheek. "Open your mouth."

Roz turned a dull gaze up at him. "You don't want me to do that."

"I guarantee you I've smelled worse. Come on, open up."

Sighing, Roz tilted her head back and opened her mouth. Julian felt her glands with one hand and flicked a penlight on in the other. No swelling. *Well, there goes that theory.* He shone the light into her eyes and checked her pupil dilation. Normal. He took her pulse. A little rushed, but not anything to worry about.

"What's the verdict?"

Julian gave her a wry look. "I've been looking at you for thirty seconds!" he protested. "I don't exactly have a lot of diagnostic tools at my disposal, here. Any other symptoms you haven't mentioned yet?"

"My stomach hurts. And I never want to see another strawberry again."

"Been seeing them from the wrong side of digestion, huh?" He pulled back the covers and poked the right side of her abdomen. No reaction. Good. At least it wasn't appendicitis.

"Both wrong sides," Roz said miserably.

Julian winced. "Okay. I'm going to get you something to settle your stomach. Other than that, there's not much I can do for you until tomorrow. I think it's a fair bet you're going to have to cancel aquafitness. I can call for you, if you like."

"You're going to make me go to the clinic, aren't you?"

"Oh, yeah. If you're not feeling better we're doing a full blood workup." He smiled. "It was probably the strawberries, or something else you ate. I'll get your medication. In the meantime, get some sleep. I'll be in to check on you in a few hours."

Roz groaned, half-pulled the pillow over her head, and peeked up at him. "Thanks, Julian. I appreciate you looking after me."

Julian planted a kiss on her forehead. "Anytime. Goodnight, Roz."

JULIAN was already waiting in exam room one when Roz came in, weaving slightly as if she was dizzy. He watched her sit down, then wheeled over to his computer. "Morning, sunshine."

Roz rolled her eyes at him and sat in the chair opposite. "Let's make it quick. I want to go back to bed."

"All in good time." He reached into a drawer and pulled out a small plastic cup with a screw top. "First, I need a sample."

"You're kidding me," Roz said flatly. "Julian, I'm your sister. Please, don't make me pee in that. Take the blood instead."

"Oh, we're doing that too. But we need a urine sample. All the ladies, every appointment. It's policy. Usually we have the nurses take care of it, but since you're my first appointment of the day, I got the honors. You can leave it on the back of the toilet when you're done."

Snatching the cup from his fingers, Roz stormed off to the bathroom, the door swinging shut behind her. Julian took the time to call up her medical file, reviewing the hard copy as he went.

"You're due for a pap smear," he told her when she came back in. "Nice try evading them by listing me as your gyno, though."

"Damn, I meant to change that before you were back in-province." Roz flopped into the chair again with a sigh. "All right; hit me with it."

Julian clicked in the proper field on the computer screen and dated the entry. "Okay. Let's start at the beginning. Have you noticed any changes in your appetite?"

"Yeah. I'm not hungry," Roz said flatly.

"Except for your strawberry thing," he pointed out. "Maybe you've got some kind of vitamin deficiency. We'll look for that on your blood tests. Any tenderness, soreness, unexplained bruising, yada yada?"

Roz leaned back in the chair, twirling a bit. "My boobs and stomach hurt, but I'm probably due for my period and I spent yesterday throwing up."

Probably due, he noted. Julian assumed that Roz's menstrual cycle was still as irregular as it had ever been. He'd tried to convince her that she should start taking the birth control pill, but she wasn't interested. "Are you taking any medication I need to know about?"

"Just my vitamins. And the anti-inflammatories I sometimes take when my knee acts up, but I haven't needed one for almost two months."

"When was your last period?"

"About three and a half weeks ago, I guess."

"Okay." Julian saved his work, grabbed his test kit and clipboard and a pair of gloves, and stood. "I'm gonna go test your pee. Make yourself comfortable on the table. I'll take your blood pressure and all of that good stuff when I get back."

He left her in the exam room and pulled a paper strip from a container in his pocket, gloved up, and dropped the test strip in the cup. He started the timer on his watch and waited, the seconds ticking away, then did his analysis.

The color was normal, and the urine was clear, indicating that her diet was fine and there were no bacteria present. No nitrites, so she didn't have a UTI. Julian ran down his mental checklist as he walked back to the exam room.

When he entered the room again, Roz was leaning back against the wall, her knees dangling over the edge of the table. Scratching the back of his neck, Julian slumped into the chair she'd vacated. He set the clipboard down on the desk and faced her as directly as he could. "So, when's the last time *you* got laid?"

Roz sat forward, hands on her knees. "What?!"

"You heard me. Trust me, this is relevant."

"A little over six weeks ago, I guess. Why?"

There was not going to be an easy way to say this. Julian pinched the bridge of his nose with one hand. "Because you're pregnant."

He heard Roz's sharp intake of breath and looked up to see her face had lost all expression. "What?" she said shakily. "Julian, I just had my…."

"But you've always been irregular," he prompted. "And this one was different. Wasn't it? Less steady?"

"Shit," Roz said. "Oh, my God."

"It happens sometimes during early pregnancy. Everything is probably fine, but of course I'll do a sonogram to check." Julian took a deep breath. "What're you going to do?" he asked, abandoning all pretense at clinical detachment. "I mean, uh, what are you going to do? I'm guessing this wasn't exactly planned."

Roz slumped. "I don't know! This is the sort of thing that only happens to other people!"

Julian meant to disagree; this was precisely the kind of thing that happened to Roz all the time, just not usually this seriously. But he couldn't quite bring himself to tell her so at a time like this. "I, uh, do you know if there's a counselor in town? I seem to have completely forgotten." He just barely resisted the urge to pace.

"Um, Beanstalk—"

Julian looked up again, meeting her gaze. "Yes?" he hedged.

Roz was grinning slightly. "I'm gonna be a mommy."

Oh, thank God. He breathed a sigh of relief and stood to sit beside her on the exam table. He put an arm around her shoulders and Roz leaned into him, wrapping her own arm around his waist. "Yeah, you are."

"I guess that means I have to grow up, huh?"

"I think you can probably fake it 'til you make it."

Against his shoulder, Julian felt Roz shaking slightly. At first, he thought she was crying—but then he heard her laughing. "God. Okay, okay, I can do this, but you have to tell Mom."

"No deal," he said. "You tell her. The only thing I did was the pregnancy test. And I still have to draw blood."

Roz groaned, pressing her face against his shoulder. "I thought I'd got out of that."

"No chance. I have to make sure mamma and baby are both healthy. I'm going to schedule a sonogram for next week, make sure everything's okay. That all right with you?"

"Not now, Julian. I'm kinda overwhelmed."

Fair enough. Julian was pretty floored himself. "Sorry. Just going on autopilot, you know. It's the doctor part of me taking over. I can't help it."

"Well, help it." Roz punched him in the shoulder. "*Uncle* Julian."

Huh. He kind of liked the sound of that.

"HOW'S your sister?"

Julian turned around, surprised to find Jack standing behind him in his kitchen. He put down the knife he'd been using to chop carrots. Being somewhat at a loss for cures for the side effects of the early stages of pregnancy, he was doing the only thing he could think of: making soup.

"She's fine," he smiled, standing on tiptoe for a moment to welcome Jack with a leisurely kiss. "Mmm. Hi. Yeah, she's, well, there's not anything actually wrong with her."

The corner of Jack's mouth quirked up in a half-grin. "You rushed home because she had a hangover?"

"Ah, no. Actually, she didn't even finish her first drink." Julian yelped as Jack squeezed his ass.

"No?" Jack released him, wandered over to the stove, and stuck his face over the soup pot. "Smells good. So what's the problem?"

He scratched the back of his neck. "There isn't one."

Turning, Jack leaned against the countertop. "No problem, huh? She's still sleeping, isn't she? She hasn't been back to work in a couple of days. I do go to the rec complex every day, you know. Hallie's been asking after her."

Fuck it. It wasn't like Jack was going to tell anybody, and Julian could *not* keep any more secrets from him. The one he already had to bear was hard enough. He sighed, hooked his fingers through Jack's belt loops, and pulled them close together, nestling between Jack's wide-planted legs. "The thing is, Roz is pregnant."

"No shit?" Jack returned the embrace, settling his hands on Julian's hips. The gesture seemed so natural, and yet it made Julian's heart skip a beat. "She happy about it? She's pretty good with kids."

"Actually, she's ecstatic. Not that it was expected, or anything. We're both still sort of in shock."

Jack pulled him close, slanting his mouth down over Julian's. Julian opened under the onslaught, welcoming Jack's tongue into his mouth. He hummed happily as Jack worked his hands into his back pockets, and Julian wrapped his arms around Jack's neck.

"Hi," Jack mumbled around his tongue.

Julian grinned into the kiss, finally breaking away. Jack was so affectionate lately, it was getting harder and harder to remind himself that they weren't even officially a couple. He thought Jack might be forgetting, too. "Hi, yourself."

"Oh, spare me. I'm already nauseous."

Jack turned his face toward the doorway over Julian's head. "Hi, Roz. Feeling better?"

"I was," Roz grumbled. Julian squirmed around, trying not to dislodge Jack's hands, which were still settled comfortably on his hips. In the doorway, Roz was wearing mismatched pajamas, her blonde hair mostly falling out of its rough ponytail. "You guys are so sweet it turns my stomach. Not that it takes much right now," she added pointedly with a glance at her brother. "I'm assuming you did tell him?"

Julian didn't know whether to shrug, nod, or blush, so he settled for a mixture of the three. Jack added, "Congratulations."

Roz acknowledged him with a wry smile. "Thanks. So. Did I smell food?"

Chuckling, Julian reluctantly disentangled himself from Jack's arms. "You must be feeling better. The soup should be ready in about twenty minutes."

"Good." Padding barefoot over to the kettle, Roz flipped it on and grabbed a mug and tea bag from the cupboard. "This peppermint shit is absolutely disgusting, but it works."

Julian leaned in to Jack conspiratorially. "One day, she will trust my physicianly knowledge without doubting me."

"I'm just worried that she's now got an excuse to be all mood-swingy," Jack stage-whispered back.

"I can hear you," Roz pointed out. Julian watched in amusement as she spooned a truly gluttonous amount of honey into her mug. "It's just lucky for you that right now my mood is swinging toward hungry. And *physicianly* is not a word."

Julian nudged Jack's shoulder with his own. "You staying for a bowl of soup?"

He saw the panic flash briefly in Jack's eyes. Family dinners were awfully domestic for him, Julian knew. But the expression was gone as soon as it had come. "I could eat," he agreed after a second. "Count me in."

Chapter 12

"Do you think this is too much?" Julian asked, picking out yet another stuffed animal and adding it to the cart. "I mean, am I taking doting uncle too far?"

Jack's bemused expression said it all. Julian could barely see him over the mountain of stuff he'd piled into the cart. "I think you might be, yeah. I mean, how many stuffed polar bears can one kid need? Save something for your parents to get her."

Sighing, Julian started putting the stuffed animals back. "It's too early, anyway," he sighed. It was December, and Roz was pushing three months pregnant, but as her doctor, he was hyperaware that she was far from out of danger of losing the baby. It was hard to focus on, though, because he was so excited for her. He'd had a hard time not buying out the entire Toys "R" Us.

It had been Jack's idea that they take a weekend to go Christmas shopping in Calgary, and Julian had been happy enough at the thought of spending the better part of two days alone with Jack, not bothering to pretend that they weren't together at least in some sense, that he'd agreed without thinking. He was still trying to figure out if he could squeeze in a trip to see Jack's mom without either betraying her confidence or making Jack suspicious. Maybe it was better if he left it alone; he didn't want to seem like he was pushing too hard for something more than what they had.

What they did have was becoming more and more difficult to define every day. Their relationship wasn't official, or even officially exclusive, though Julian was fairly certain neither of them had any interest in seeing anyone else. Most people in town seemed to assume that Jack was seeing

Roz. Apparently word had gotten out about the flowers he'd brought her, though to Julian's amusement, the story about what had happened to the flowers had yet to surface. Maybe that should have bothered him, but somehow he couldn't bring himself to care much. He hadn't been this happy in a long time, and he wasn't going to wreck it the way he'd ruined his first—well, okay, *second*—relationship.

Shaking his head as if to clear it, Julian put the last stuffed animal— a polar bear puppet cute enough to melt even the coldest heart—back on the shelf and turned around to find Jack's eyes on him. "What?" he said. "You're looking at me funny. Do I have something on my face?"

"Not yet," Jack said wickedly, advancing to back Julian up against the shelf of toys. It was nearly closing time, so the store was almost empty, at least for holiday shopping season. Julian's startled yelp probably drew a few curious glances, but he wasn't going to worry about it. Jack's lips brushed his ear. "What do you say we forget the shopping and call it a night?"

Julian swallowed hard, shivering. "That sounds like a great idea to me. Let's get out of here."

AS it turned out, Julian needn't have worried about meeting Jack's mom again. When they woke up in the morning, the weather forecast was calling for snow, and they had to hurry up and pack their purchases into the truck in order to be home before the worst of the storm hit. They had just pulled into the driveway when the flurries thinned out into the harsher, stinging snow of a blizzard. The wind picked up and the sky turned dark above them, though it was not quite two in the afternoon.

Grabbing the last of the packages out of the backseat, Julian looked up and whistled. "That got ugly fast."

"Yeah," Jack agreed, managing somehow to close the door with his butt. "I'm almost glad we skipped the morning sex."

Julian snorted. More than likely he was regretting having skipped it; they could have been snowed in and stayed another night. That was okay, though. "Liar."

Roz opened the door for them as they approached, her eyes

widening at the sheer number of bags there were. "Good grief. Did you forget the kitchen sink?"

"They were sold out," Julian said smartly. "Close your eyes; I know what you're like around presents."

Roz obediently covered her eyes, though he could see her fingers spreading so that she could look through them. With her arms up like that, he thought he could see her abdomen starting to swell with the baby. Maybe she was just getting fat.

"I think your secret's out," Jack said a fraction of a second later, setting down the armload of bags in the pantry. He motioned to her stomach. "You're normally so in shape that people are going to notice that right away."

Roz dropped her hands from her sides and patted her belly affectionately. She probably could have gotten away with wearing loose clothing for a while, except for the fact that she was still teaching three aquafitness classes a week. "That's okay. I'm sort of looking forward to being able to tell people. Although it is always so awkward when people ask who the father is."

"Aw, come on. Even *I* knew better than to ask you that."

Roz smacked Jack halfheartedly, casting a put-upon expression Julian's way. "Are you going to let him get away with that?"

Julian shrugged out of his coat and hung it up, accepting Jack's scarf and hat without comment. "Considering that half of the town is probably going to think he's the father, and the other half really is too smart to ask, I think he can get away with whatever he likes!"

"I bet that's the truth."

Jack just gave them both a smug look. "So! Who's going to feed me?"

"Julian, if you don't want food poisoning. The fetus made me eat all the leftovers." Roz motioned at the clean, empty container sitting on the counter. "I was just putting away the dishes when Mom and Dad called."

"I missed them?" Julian said, disappointed. Oh, well; he could call them back later, find out what they were up to. Right now, he apparently had hungry mouths to feed. Well, three hungry mouths and one umbilical cord. "Did they say when they're flying up?"

"Sometime in the new year," she told him as he rifled through the cupboards, checking out the dinner options. It was early, but he and Jack had skipped lunch, and his stomach was starting to let him know exactly how displeased it was that he had made such an egregious oversight. "Some friends of theirs invited them to spend Christmas with them. They were going to come here for Christmas, but Mom tried to book the tickets online in October, and you know how that usually goes."

Julian did know. Their mother was not what you might call techno-literate. "You tell them yet?" he asked conversationally, pulling a bag of linguine noodles from a cupboard. *Hmm, maybe a nice Alfredo sauce and some vegetables?*

Roz hopped up onto the counter, swinging her legs against the lower cupboards; Jack, Julian noted in his peripheral vision, was already getting out the plates and cutlery. "Nah. I figure I'll tell them when they're down. It's not like I'll be able to keep it from them."

"Mom'll be so excited she'll probably shit a Frisbee." Julian rolled his eyes, filled the pasta pot with water, and set it on the stove.

"That would be something."

The three of them busied themselves with preparing dinner, and it turned out that it was a good thing they'd started early. Almost the moment they were done cooking, the power flickered and went out, leaving them in a bluish darkness, listening to the howl of the wind. They ate their dinner in the living room by the light of the fireplace.

"Looks like I'm not going home tonight," Jack commented, peering out the window. From what Julian could see, which wasn't much, the blinding snow was coming down as hard as ever, and by now, the roads would be treacherous. It was only a five-minute drive to Jack's place, but it certainly wasn't worth the risk.

"Yeah, because that's a major newsflash," Roz teased. "I don't know who the two of you think you're fooling."

Julian caught Jack's eye for a brief instant before the other man looked away, and felt himself flush. He didn't think anyone would notice in the near-darkness, anyway.

"I'm going to take a nap," Roz announced, stretching. "Possibly until tomorrow morning. Have a good night, guys."

After she'd gone to bed and the dinner dishes had been collected and deposited in the kitchen sink for consideration when there was hot running water, the two of them settled back into the living room. Tired, Julian leaned his head on Jack's shoulder and tried to hold back a yawn. They watched the fire for a few minutes in silence, the hypnotic effects of the flames lulling Julian into a sort of trance.

Jack snapped him out of it by speaking softly. "You know, I've been thinking…."

Julian lifted his head, feeling the beginnings of a smile tugging at the corners of his mouth. "Uh-oh."

"Cute. As I was saying…." Julian turned to look him straight on, smile fading. He sounded a little nervous about this, unsure. "Since your parents aren't coming up for Christmas anymore, I thought maybe you would like to spend it with me and my mom in Calgary."

Julian stared at him for a full minute.

"I mean, I understand if you don't want to go, I just thought it might be nice if—"

Realizing Jack had mistaken his silence for a refusal, Julian darted forward and cut off his babbling with a fierce kiss. "Don't be stupid. Of course I'd love to come." He had to bite his tongue to keep from saying too much. It seemed that Jack was finally starting to treat what they had as a real relationship, and Julian wasn't going to push it. "It's just, I can't leave Roz here by herself at Christmas. That wouldn't be right."

"So bring her along," Jack suggested. "There's plenty of room. And I've got to tell you, Mom is a fantastic cook."

"Okay, yeah. I'll ask Roz about it. But it sounds like a good idea to me." Julian bit his lip. Well, he'd known it would come to this sooner or later. He was hoping Flo wouldn't blow his cover and let on that they'd met before, or the fragile trust that existed between the two of them would be broken. Then again, keeping their acquaintance on the down-low had been her idea in the first place. "Um, does your mom know you're seeing someone?"

Jack groaned as if this had just occurred to him, and Julian's heart sank. "God, if she's been talking to Bella at all, she'll probably think I'm the one who knocked up Roz." He put his hand around Julian's knee and squeezed, making him jump. "I guess I'll just have to tell her the truth. She's going to have a bird when she realizes I've been seeing someone without telling her."

Julian realized he was staring again, but he couldn't help it. It couldn't possibly be that easy. Could it?

"Her brother's gay," Jack added unnecessarily. "Freaking out should be minimal."

Shaking his head, all Julian could say was, "You are amazing."

"Yeah? You're not half-bad yourself." Jack slid his hand into Julian's hair, fingernails scraping delicately over his scalp. The teasing touch made Julian's nipples pull taut under his shirt.

"Umm," Julian said around Jack's tongue in his mouth. "Hold that thought." He broke away from the kiss and half-galloped up the stairs, yanking open the drawer to his bedside table and fishing in it for the half-empty bottle of lube. Julian considered the rest of the drawer's contents for another few seconds before slamming the drawer shut and racing back downstairs again.

Tossing the lube onto the couch beside Jack, Julian launched himself into the other man's lap.

"Oof," Jack grumbled as Julian settled his legs on either side of Jack's thighs. "What's got into you?"

"Nothing yet," Julian wriggled, feeling Jack's body respond to his provocative movements. "I think we can fix that, though. What do you think?"

Jack grabbed him by the hair, sending little sparks of interest from Julian's brain to his already hardening prick, and crushed their mouths together. Surprised, Julian opened automatically under the onslaught, relishing the hot slide of Jack's tongue over his lips and teeth. Moaning contentedly, Julian chased after the wet muscle with his own tongue, breath hitching when Jack sank his teeth into Julian's bottom lip. He felt Jack's cock starting to strain against the confines of his jeans, and he realized his own cock had gone from zero to a hundred in about three seconds without ever once being touched.

"Umm," Jack agreed, fingers fumbling with the hem of Julian's pullover. "Take your shirt off already."

Julian did, taking the T-shirt he'd worn under it with it accidentally. The cool air caused goose bumps to raise on his skin, chased by Jack's fingertips tracing the muscles of his back from his shoulders down to his waist. "Your turn." Julian made short work of the buttons on Jack's shirt and helped him peel it off of his arms before rising up on his knees to grasp the back of Jack's undershirt and tug it upward. He let it drop to the floor.

Jack's hands were back on his skin in record time, massaging small circles into the skin of his back as they kissed languidly. Time seemed to slow down as they explored each other with their hands. Julian shuddered as one of Jack's thumbs migrated upward from his back and ghosted over his nipple, causing the sensitive bud to harden.

Shuddering, Julian dug his blunt fingernails into Jack's shoulders, pulling him closer and sliding his mouth along Jack's cheek to his neck. Jack's rough stubble branded his tongue as Julian followed his jugular from his jaw to his collarbone, his own skin thrumming with anticipation the whole way. His cock pressed insistently against the fabric of his jeans, but Julian wasn't going to take a single step away from Jack until it was absolutely necessary.

"Cold?" Jack murmured, his lips hot against Julian's neck.

Breathing heavily, Julian managed to shake his head no, his body arching into Jack's gentle touch. Jack must not quite have believed him, because a half-second later he was standing, sliding Julian off of his lap, and retrieving the lube and a pillow from the couch. "Over here," he said, stretching out in front of the fireplace.

Jack was good-looking in the worst of lighting, but in firelight he was otherworldly. His skin glowed in the light cast by the flickering flame, highlighting the plateaus and crevasses of his cut abs, the thin sheen of sweat only adding to his allure. His lust-dark eyes and hair were painted with red and orange, and his jeans had to be getting uncomfortable; the stark relief outlined his hardening cock just right. Julian almost fell to his knees beside him, then straddled him again for a kiss that took his breath away. Jack's hands inched up his thighs until they met at his groin, framing the bulge in his jeans. Subconsciously, Julian pressed forward into the touch, fists clenching convulsively where they were planted on either side of Jack's head.

Jack's fingers made quick work of the button fly, tugging the two opposing flaps of fabric down roughly to free Julian's trapped erection.

"A guy could get used to this," Jack drawled, thrusting his hips upward a bit as he stroked Julian's cock.

"You mean you're not...already?" Julian managed with some difficulty. After all, they had been sleeping together for three months. His jeans started to slip the rest of the way over his ass.

With a sudden surge of determination, Julian managed to slide backward far enough to attack the fly of Jack's pants. "You keep me on my toes," Jack groaned, lifting his hips so that Julian could tug his jeans and boxers down to his knees.

"Funny," Julian said, slipping to the side and laying down so that their bodies were flush from chest to toe. He rubbed his dripping cock into Jack's hip, belly clenching at the sensation. "You seem more interested in keeping me on my back."

"You complaining?" Jack took that as a cue and kicked off the rest of his clothing, then sat up straight just long enough to take care of Julian's. "It sounded like you were complaining." Jack insinuated one of his legs between Julian's thighs, and Julian threw his head back. Jack's erection was wet and hard against his hip, and his thigh was providing delicious friction.

"No chance," he managed weakly, his hands fastening to Jack's hips without his input. "No complaints. Definitely not. Oh, God, do that again."

Julian could barely make out Jack's wicked grin in the partial darkness. Then he felt his right leg being raised. Sharp stubble against his calf made him gasp out loud; then Jack settled Julian's ankle on his shoulder and scooted forward, knees under Julian's ass. "What? This?" A dry finger brushed across Julian's opening and he bucked, balls tightening.

"Yes," he hissed, feeling his own prick leaking pre-come on his belly as Jack returned to his hole again, fingers now slick with lube. Jack prepared him slowly, sliding in the first finger a knuckle at a time until Julian was cursing and pressing against it. His mind went white the first time Jack brushed against his prostate, and he groaned again as Jack continued to rasp his stubble against the skin of his legs as he worked.

"Are you sure this is okay?" Jack teased darkly, adding another finger to the first, slow and methodical. "You don't seem comfortable. Maybe you'd like to try something different?"

Incapable of answering, Julian just moaned as a third finger filled his ass, stretching him almost perfectly. The only thing better would be to have Jack's dick inside of him, fucking him into the floor. In this position, Julian couldn't even reach it. "I...uh...."

"Not interested?" Jack said blithely. The twist of his fingers in Julian's ass brought his hips clean up off the floor, despite his lack of leverage. "That's too bad. I thought you might like to ride my cock for a change."

Fuck, would he ever! Julian's hard-on jerked against his stomach. "Shit, let me get up."

Jack released his leg—none too quickly—and pumped his fingers in and out of Julian's hole a few more times before backing off, once more laying flat on his back in front of the fireplace. "Tell me you brought a condom down here. I can't wait another second to be inside your sweet ass."

Swallowing hard, Julian just shook his head, heart beating double time in his throat.

Jack's eyebrows raised slightly in the darkness, and Julian thought that maybe his green eyes had darkened all the way to black, the way he was looking at him. "No, you forgot, or no, you want to fuck without one?"

Yeah, right. Odds of Julian actually forgetting a condom were pretty slim. "The second one," he said a little nervously, distracting himself by taking Jack's cock in hand and slicking it up with lubricant. "I know I'm clean and I'm sure you would have said something by now if you weren't. Besides, I sort of have access to your medical records, remember?"

"How could I forget?" Jack moaned, thrusting upward into the touch. "I had Bella do a full panel two weeks ago anyway, just in case. You've got nothing to worry about. Except the possibility of me going completely crazy if you don't get up here in the next three seconds."

Stomach clenching in anticipation, Julian crawled up the older man's body until his ass was right above Jack's thick staff. He bit his lip and watched as Jack gripped himself in one hand, the other guiding Julian downward.

The second Jack's bare cock touched the ring of muscle, Julian knew he was in trouble. He bit his lip hard as first the wide head, then the long shaft, of Jack's dick forced its way into his body. The smooth sensation of a bare Jack sliding into him was indescribable, and he leaned back, resting his weight on his hands, breathing hard as Jack was seated fully within him.

"Jesus," Jack groaned, sliding his hands up Julian's thighs again. "This, I don't think I can get used to."

"Oh, I don't know," Julian panted, raising up experimentally. "I think it's worth a try."

Jack's laugh was cut off by a grunt as Julian lowered himself back down again, all the way so that he could feel Jack's lightly furred balls against his ass. "I think I can get on board with that idea." His hands dug into the flesh of Julian's hips and Julian felt himself being lifted until just the head of Jack's prick was inside of him. Then Jack pulled him back down again, hard, striking right at Julian's prostate.

"Fuck," he half-shouted, trying to keep his voice down. They'd never fucked with someone else in the house before, and it was difficult to start trying to restrain himself now. Julian felt his hands curling around Jack's legs behind him and his thighs burned from the exertion. Faster and faster they moved, Jack's upward thrusts timed to match Julian's. He could feel bruises forming on his hips, but he didn't care.

Nothing mattered, nothing but Jack's rock-hard cock in his ass and his own erection jutting proudly between them, leaking fluid copiously now as Jack's cock struck his prostate repeatedly.

"God, you feel good." Jack reached a hand between them to stroke Julian's swollen member, callused hand sliding easily through the natural lubricant. "So fucking hot and tight. I can't wait to feel you come apart around me."

Mouth open, it was all Julian could do to keep from coming at the words. He loved it when Jack talked dirty. "Shit. Shut up; you're going to make me come."

Jack played his thumb across the head of Julian's cock, and Julian felt his balls draw up close to his body. God, any second now he was going to lose it. Without meaning to, he looked down and met Jack's eyes. "Maybe that's what I want," Jack said. "Yeah, it is. I want to feel your whole body shake, Julian, with nothing between your hot ass and my cock. I want to feel your hot little hole tighten around me. I want to feel your hot come all over my hand, on my stomach, on my chest. And then I'm going to shoot my load inside of you, fill you up with it, watch it run down your legs—"

Julian's head rolled back and with a wordless howl he came, body convulsing around Jack's dick. His own prick jerked and spurted hot, sticky semen between them, covering Jack's hand and stomach. Inside him, multiple bursts of wet heat told him that Jack had fulfilled his promise, filling him up with his seed. The knowledge made his dick pulse again, spewing what had to be the last drops of come his body could produce.

Breathing hard, Julian let his head fall forward. His body curved with it, and he rested his forehead on Jack's chest, Jack's own harsh breath tickling his scalp. "Just when I think you couldn't possibly come up with something dirtier to say, you prove me wrong."

"You like it," Jack accused mildly, shifting his body until his softening cock slipped from Julian's ass.

"I fucking love it," Julian corrected, trying to sit up without pressing his own chest or stomach into the semen covering Jack's. He finally decided on rolling onto the floor as a safer option. "I don't know how you do it."

"What can I say, Jitterbug? You are an inspiration."

Rolling his eyes, Julian sat up and stretched, reaching for the Kleenex box on the coffee table. "Only to you," he said, wiping the last of the seed from his dick before attending to Jack's stomach. Wincing, he felt some of Jack's come start seeping out of him. That was less than romantic. "Okay, I don't know about you, but I think a shower's in order. Kleenex just isn't going to cut it this time."

"Couldn't agree more," Jack said, holding out a hand for Julian to help him up. Julian did, making a face when he heard Jack's knees crack. "No old man jokes or I won't fuck you for a week."

Julian snorted. He'd like to see Jack *try* to resist him for that long. Well, no, actually, he wouldn't. "Empty threats. Come on, cowboy. Let's go before I drip on the floor."

"GOT everything?" Julian asked, taking Roz's backpack from her and squeezing it into the back of the truck. It'd be a bit uncomfortable for her back there, but luckily Jack had a cover for the back of his pickup, so most of their luggage and all of the gifts were safe and dry back there. Roz, however, needed access to food, water and anti-nausea medication, just in case, so she was stuck in the backseat with all of her goodies.

"I'll be fine," she told him, hopping in. "Unlike some people, I am capable of packing for myself without forgetting the essentials."

Julian wanted to make a quip about having forgotten condoms at one point roughly three months ago, but decided not to risk a pregnant lady mood swing, especially since they'd be in the car together for the next few hours. "I forgot my toothbrush *one time*," he protested instead. "I was twelve!"

"Uh-huh. Summer camp when you were ten?"

Narrowing his eyes, Julian crossed his arms over his chest. "Don't think I don't know you're the one who unpacked my underwear, you little shit."

Roz grinned. "I can neither confirm nor deny your accusation. Now close the door; it's freezing."

Julian did, turning and digging his hands into his pockets afterward. The sky was clear for once, promising good weather for at least the time it would take them to reach Calgary.

"Nervous?"

Whirling around, Julian was about to make excuses for his skittish behavior, then realized that the blood rushing to his face had already given him away. He *was* nervous; not just that Jack would find out his mother was sick and that Julian had known about it. Now he had to contend with fears that Jack's mother wouldn't like him now that they were, well, whatever it was that they were. Or that she wouldn't like Roz. Or that she wouldn't like her Christmas gift.

"You might say that," he answered ruefully. *Terrified* might have been a better choice of word. He scratched the back of his neck with one gloved hand. "I've sort of never…done this before."

"You've never had Christmas with someone else's family? Not even when you were in Toronto?"

No, that wasn't it. Julian steeled himself. "No, I, uh…" Was there a way he could put this that wouldn't send Jack running for the hills? Too late to worry about that now. "I've never, um, met anyone's parents before. In this context."

The context of *Hi, your son and I are screwing each other's brains out*. Because he didn't think there was another way to put it.

"Really?" Jack looked genuinely surprised, like he couldn't believe everyone wasn't trying to drag Julian home to meet the parents. That would have been touching, except that it had taken Jack three months to get to this point and he was probably only doing it because it was Christmas. "Well, I wouldn't worry. Mom'll love you. Just don't let her get you alone or she'll ask you all kinds of embarrassing questions you won't want to answer. Oh, and for my sake, if she goes for the photo album, fake a bathroom emergency."

Laughing in spite of himself, Julian relaxed. It was unfair of him to pass judgment on Jack's actions, especially since he hadn't told his own parents about their…arrangement. "What, you don't want me to see pictures of you as a kid? Were you fat?"

"Enormous," Jack said, playing along. "And I had acne. Ooh, and poor fashion sense. Lots of plaid."

"And braces?" Julian suggested, going with the theme.

"Headgear," Jack confirmed solemnly. "And glasses! With coke-bottle lenses."

"You're full of shit," Julian told him with a grin. "You just don't want me to realize how old you actually are when I see a picture of you in line for *Return of the Jedi*."

Jack raised his hands in surrender. "All right, all right, you win. Go ahead and get your fill of the dorky pictures of me as a child. But don't say I didn't warn you. I'm an only child. There are a *lot* of photos." He paused. "And I never stood in line for *Return of the Jedi*."

"That's because there probably wasn't a theater on Cape Breton at the time. Now would you get in the truck before Roz has to pee again? We're never going to make it on time."

Chapter 13

TWO and a half hours and three bathroom stops later, Jack pulled into the driveway of a modest brick two-storey house in a suburb. Aside from the sidewalk, roof, and driveway, everything was covered in a deep layer of white; Jack knew the rooftop itself was only free because of the snow-melting wires he'd installed himself to prevent damage from heavy snowfall. There was a large green wreath above the door, and a string of lights wound up and down the bushes on either side of the front walk. "This is it," Jack said, doing his best to sound nonchalant. Julian could probably still hear the apprehension in his voice.

"Are you sure you want to do this?"

Well, that pretty much proved him right. Jack gave what he hoped was a winning smile. "Sorry. You're not the only one who's a little nervous, I guess. I haven't introduced anybody to my mom since high school, and she had the annoying habit of running most of them off."

"I like her already," Roz quipped from the backseat, "but can we go inside now? I've got to pee again."

Chuckling, Jack steadfastly ignored the butterflies in his stomach and reached for the door handle. He busied himself unloading the essentials from the back, handing half of them to Julian to carry. By the time they made it up the front walk to the house, Roz was shifting her weight from foot to foot. Jack made a valiant effort not to roll his eyes at her and rang the doorbell.

He caught the sound of hastening footsteps on hardwood, and then his mother was at the door, throwing it open and more or less suffocating him in a giant hug. "Jack!" she said exuberantly, sounding breathless.

"Merry Christmas!"

"Hi, Mom," he managed to squeak out. His mother didn't get like this often—just at Christmas. It was like she reverted to a kid during the holiday season, which was totally okay with him, since he tended to share her enthusiasm. "Merry Christmas to you, too. Um, this is Roz. She needs to use your bathroom."

"Oh, go right ahead, dear. We can make our formal introductions later. It's just inside and to the left." Flo pulled back from Jack's chest and shot an appraising look at the man standing beside him. Jack could almost hear the blood rushing to Julian's face. *Damn, the man is adorable.*

"You must be Julian," Flo said, a sparkle in her eyes. "I could just kiss you. In fact, I think I will."

Jack couldn't decide whether to be amused or mortified, but he was fairly certain his mother didn't care either way. She reached out and grabbed Julian's face in both hands and planted a kiss on each cheek. "Um, hi," Julian said, doing an uncanny impression of a stewed tomato. Jack grinned. At least he was capable of speech. Jack's first girlfriend had squeaked in terror and hidden behind Jack all day. "It's nice to meet you."

Flo beckoned them inside, and as he and Julian bent to pick up the duffel bags, Julian hissed, "When did you tell her?"

Jack shrugged, taking Roz's stuff in one arm and a laundry basket full of presents in the other. "The day after I asked you."

He didn't need to turn around to know that Julian's mouth was hanging open like a stupid fish. "You came out to your mom *on the phone?*" he said in his best I-cannot-even-believe-the-nerve-of-you voice, only at about a quarter volume. "You are such a chicken shit!"

Jack *had* told her on the phone. She had said, "Is that all?" and he'd sat there gaping like a frog until he remembered to tell her he was bringing guests for the holidays. "You're just grumpy because I didn't warn you I'd already told her. Suck it up and let's get inside before it starts snowing in there."

Julian gave him a dark look, but followed him into the house anyway. Everything about the look said Jack would be hearing about this later, but everything about Julian said that Jack would like it, so he wasn't worried.

"I think I'll put Roz in the upstairs bedroom," his mother was saying from the kitchen. She still sounded overexcited, like she couldn't quite get enough air. Jack felt guilty; he really should make more of an effort to visit more often. "I thought she'd appreciate having her own bathroom. I remember what it was like to be pregnant."

"That's very thoughtful of you," Julian said, shooting a questioning glance at Jack, who shrugged. He hadn't told his mother Roz was pregnant, but apparently his mother was even more perceptive than he'd thought.

Flo came in from the kitchen with a tray of cookies that smelled delicious and four glasses of eggnog. "It's the way she's walking," she explained, correctly interpreting their silence. "Oh, honestly, I did prenatal scans for twenty years. I know a pregnant woman when I see one." Julian was starting to look a little spooked. Inwardly, Jack sighed. It was no wonder his mother had scared off so many of his high school sweethearts. Not that he wouldn't have done it himself, eventually.

Roz chose that moment to reappear from the bathroom, looking, Jack noted, distinctly relieved. "I'm sorry," she said without a trace of her brother's flush, holding out a hand. "I see you've already guessed the emergency. I'm Roz; this is my gender-undetermined fetus. It's nice to meet you." God, she was an awful lot like Julian. It was odd to think that they weren't actually all that closely related. Nurture over nature, Jack guessed.

"You can call me Flo, honey. Would you care for some gingerbread?"

Jack tuned out their conversation and finished hanging his jacket, absently grabbing Roz's and Julian's as well, stuffing Julian's outrageous spotted scarf into his sleeve. No one would ever conclude Julian was gay based on his wardrobe, he thought drily, but God forbid anyone ever conclude he was straight, either. He toed off his boots and left them drying on the rack, then joined the others around the coffee table.

Domestic, he thought: two men, two women, cookies, beverages, polite conversation—but not conventional. He could do this. Letting out a breath he hadn't realized he'd been holding, Jack slid an arm around Julian's shoulders and settled down onto the couch beside him. Piece of cake.

JACK awoke in the middle of the night, disoriented. At first he didn't know where he was, and Julian's presence didn't clear much up. Then his eyes adjusted to the darkness and he remembered he was in the second guest bedroom in his mother's house in Calgary, sleeping away the last few hours before Christmas morning with his.... *Boyfriend* was somehow too high school. *Lover* and *partner* were too serious, too committed, too *much. Fuck buddy* failed to adequately cover the bases. With his Julian, then. Whatever.

He glanced at the clock and laid his head back down on the pillow again, blinking and trying to remember the strange dream he'd been having. It had been so odd. He vaguely remembered....

Roz pushes an empty stroller down a deserted street in summertime, a blank expression on her face. In the harsh sunlight she looks like a bleached china doll, eyelashes too long, eyes too wide and unseeing.

Jack shivered at the memory. Oh yeah. He was never going into a toy store with Julian again. If he never saw another one of those dolls, it'd be way too soon. He frowned. That hadn't been the end of the dream. Something else had happened, something even stranger....

Roz's stroller squeaks slowly past a tableau of faceless people standing on a street corner. Further down the road, Julian stands in the middle of a shaded yard, his back to Jack, arms splayed at his sides. Robot is chained outside the gate, barking her head off but not making a sound. As Jack approaches, he can see that there is liquid dripping from Julian's hands, running in thick rivulets and coalescing in puddles before soaking into the dry earth.

Jack's breath caught in his chest and he dug his knuckles into his eye sockets, hoping to distract himself, but it was too late. He remembered the rest of the dream.

He comes around to Julian's other side and stops dead, realizing where he is. The street has disappeared now, faded into the background. As far as the eye can see there are nothing but tombstones with dates but no names and graves that have been dug but not filled in. The holes go down all the way to the center of the universe, the fires of hell burning at the bottom.

Julian says nothing. When Jack looks at him, he stumbles back a step in shock. Julian's mouth is a black slash across his face, his eyes are hollow over sunken cheeks, unseeing. His hands are covered in blood. That's what has been pooling on the ground; that is what has soaked the earth. Jack doesn't know if it's Julian's or someone else's. He tries to move forward to touch him, to help, but the ground lurches beneath his feet and he falls backward, into an open pit, he falls and he falls and he falls....

Jack shivered and made an effort to steal some of the blankets back from Julian, who was about the worst blanket thief Jack had ever shared a bed with on a semi-regular basis. Then again, Jack hadn't shared a bed with anyone on any kind of regular basis since his undergrad, so that wasn't saying much.

What a fucked-up dream. Jack wrestled away a few square feet of comforter and snuggled up to Julian's back to get warm. There; that was better. He was already starting to relax; he could feel the tension drain out of him. Julian was fine. He was fine. Everyone was fine. The living proof was right there in front of him. Jack wormed a hand over Julian's body and crawled it up his bare chest, letting it settle against the steady heartbeat. Nothing to worry about, he thought drowsily.

Just a stupid dream.

By the time he woke again, he'd forgotten all about it.

JACK came to with a heavy weight on his chest and a raging hard-on, neither of which was particularly comfortable. When he opened his eyes blearily the room was still mostly dark, but he could just make out the whites of Julian's eyes, narrowed sleepily. That explained the weight, anyway.

"Merry Christmas," Julian said perfectly wickedly, and continued to rub his body against Jack's in the way that was at the very least responsible for his erection, if not the actual cause of his awakening.

"So it would appear," Jack groaned, not bothering to resist the temptation to thrust his hips into Julian's. "I thought you weren't a morning person?"

"I make special exceptions for Christmas and birthdays." Julian turned his sinful mouth to Jack's chest and started making very good friends with Jack's nipple, laving it with the flat of his tongue before biting the little nub almost hard enough to cause pain. "I figure it's early enough that we won't get interrupted."

Oh, so *that's* why he was up so early. "What?" he teased, "You're afraid my mother won't approve?"

"Hey, being walked in on by parental units is distinctly unsexy. I'm just looking out for you." Julian pinched the inside of his thigh. "Now, can I get on with what I was doing, or would you like to criticize some more?"

Well, when you put it that way.... "Nope. Sorry. Don't mind me. You just do your thing."

"It's your thing I'm interested in." A hand crept up his leg to cradle his balls just as Julian's teeth scraped over his hip bone. "That's not going to be a problem for you, is it?"

Oh, Jack had no complaints. Nope. Definitely not. Julian could be as interested as he liked. In the meantime.... Jack reached down to tangle his fingers in Julian's already perpetually messy curls and tugged him upward, capturing his mouth in a sloppy kiss. Julian rubbed against him provocatively, hands wandering shamelessly. Jack bit his lower lip, skimmed his fingertips down Julian's body, raking his fingernails down his back. "Hmm," he murmured as Julian started worming his way south again. "Hold that thought." He half-sat, grabbed for Julian's thighs and swung his body neatly around.

"What are you—*oh.*" Julian's hands gripped Jack's knees as Jack dug his fingers into Julian's hips and guided his prick into his mouth. "*Oh.* Hello to you, too," Julian said, his cheeriness underwritten with a tone of definite manic lust. He rubbed his stubbled cheek against Jack's thigh and reciprocated in kind, engulfing Jack's shaft in one long swallow.

Damn, the good doctor was good at that. Jack hummed in satisfaction around a solid mouthful of Julian's dick and let his fingers wander backward over the perfect curve of his ass to nestle provocatively between his cheeks. He heard Julian's rapid intake of breath and almost smirked in satisfaction before being rendered almost completely incoherent by the rasp of teeth across the crown. Oh, yeah. Julian was a biter, and Jack didn't mind it at all. He would have sworn, but his mouth was busy doing other, more important things, like licking away the moisture leaking from the tip of Julian's shaft. He thrust lazily into Julian's mouth, tilting his head back as Julian began to do the same.

Jack slid one hand around to cup Julian's sac, rubbing his perineum with his fingertips. The cock in his mouth jerked against his tongue, and Jack felt his own swell sympathetically. Julian made an impossible noise, throat muscles contracting wildly, and he spasmed in Jack's mouth, sharp taste flooding over Jack's tongue. Unable to restrain himself, Jack thrust roughly a few more times before arching his back and spilling his seed into Julian's throat.

Julian released him slowly, and Jack watched in a lazy and bemused fashion as he stretched his body tight, then relaxed every muscle at once and nuzzled his face into Jack's thigh. "Hmmm," he said happily. He sounded completely blissed-out.

Jack didn't blame him. He wasn't feeling any pain, himself. And, okay, it was completely adorable when Julian did that snuggly thing to his leg. "Merry Christmas to you, too," he chuckled, sinking his teeth into Julian's calf playfully.

"You might make a morning person out of me yet," Julian conceded. He wiggled around until he was lying more or less parallel to Jack instead of on top of him. "Time is it?"

Jack didn't need to look at the clock to know that, at least by Julian's standards, it was still ungodly early. "Go back to sleep," he recommended. Jack himself wouldn't be able to—he just wasn't programmed that way—but he wasn't going to let that spoil the morning for Julian, even if he did get the impression that under normal Christmas circumstances he was a six o'clock riser. The doctor had clearly worn himself out just enough to justify going right back to sleep. He didn't even bother turning around, just closed his eyes where he was and dropped off, bare-assed and dead to the world.

Shaking his head, Jack sat up straight and wrangled some blankets around to preserve his modesty. Yeah, he could admit it, at least to himself when they were alone like this: The kid was adorable, and Jack doted on him shamelessly, and even if it made them both a little uncomfortable at times—on those rare occasions when the doting occurred in a safe but public forum, or the increasingly more frequent ones when it seemed too intimate at home—he wasn't going to stop. He didn't think he *could* stop. Julian was quirky, energetic, funny, gentle, kind, and, importantly, insatiable. He was crazy, or maybe he just drove Jack crazy, or maybe it was just that Jack was crazy *about* him. It didn't really matter. The point was that Jack was starting to recognize how incredibly easy it would be to fall in love with him, and how little will he had to stop himself from doing so. It was terrifying, and exhilarating, and exasperating, but there it was. Jack was completely fucked, and he didn't even care.

Well, not much. There was the whole issue of the world thinking he was straight. The world continuing to think he was straight would be something of an issue. The Roz cover was only going to work for so long, and they all knew it.

Belatedly, Jack realized he'd been staring at the sleeping Julian for a good three minutes without moving himself. With a sigh, he picked out a set of clothes from his duffel bag without really considering it and headed for the shower.

"WELL, I'm stuffed," Roz said cheerfully from across the table, leaning her head back against the wall behind her. "Where's the pie?"

Julian snorted beside him, and Jack felt his leg, which had been brushed up against Jack's comfortably for most of dinner, sweep out as if to nudge Roz under the table. "That eating-for-two excuse is getting old."

"You did see your pie, right?" Jack asked. The latest in the long line of unutterably adorable things Julian had done so far this trip was bringing along the ingredients for an apple crumble pie, which he had promptly thrown together for tonight's dessert. The smell could induce drooling at fifty paces.

Apparently his mother agreed with him, because she emerged from the kitchen four seconds later carrying three pieces loaded with vanilla ice cream and plopped them down in front of the unsuspecting eaters. Jack's stomach rebelled. He ignored it in favor of his taste buds and picked up his fork.

An agonizing fifteen minutes of dessert consumption followed. Jack eventually pushed his plate away empty, stomach protesting at the extra sugar. He leaned back in his chair happily, stretching his legs out beneath the table.

Julian made a happy noise beside him, nudging his foot under the table. Roz belched loudly, had the presence of mind to blush and excuse herself, then, when Jack's mother just laughed at her indulgently—so long and loud that it ended in a coughing fit that had Julian patting her back awkwardly—pushed back from the table and unbuttoned the top button on her fly.

Julian snickered. "Get used to it."

Roz shot him a betrayed look and aimed her foot at him under the table, but it connected with Jack's shin instead. "Ow."

"Sorry."

At the head of the table, Flo made a contented sound, wiping away moisture from her eyes. Jack guessed it was more due to the energetic laughing than the wistful expression she wore. "You know, I always wanted a house full of kids. Your father and I just met at the wrong time for them. And now here I am, thirty years later, and I've got a bunch of eight-year-olds masquerading as adults at my table."

Jack felt the tips of his ears turning red, and Julian reached out beside him and laced their fingers together. When Jack chanced a look at him, he thought he saw a drop or two of extra moisture hiding in the corner of Julian's eye, too, but he wasn't going to call him on it. Instead, he just squeezed Julian's hand and looked across at Roz. "So. Presents?"

This normally required a bit of a soft touch, since Jack's mom usually insisted that the dishes be washed before any presents could be unwrapped. Tonight, however, it looked like she was softened up enough already. "Oh, have it your way. I've made you children suffer long enough." Flo shooed them over to the tree and pulled the ragged old Santa hat from the mantel as she went, turning to Roz and Julian. "Which one of you is the youngest?"

Jack's lip twitched as Roz and Julian exchanged glances. Instead of answering straightforwardly, they each wordlessly held out a fist and counted to three. Julian won the rock-paper-scissors match and Roz sighed. "I'm the youngest," she said. "Technically."

Grinning, Jack snatched the hat from his mother and tugged it down over Roz's ponytail. "Congratulations. You've just been nominated for Santa of the Year. Presents, please."

Roz just rolled her eyes at him, adjusted her hat jauntily to one side, and got busy under the tree, sorting presents into piles and handing them out accordingly. Jack noticed bemusedly that an extreme number of presents seemed to have her name on them, but then, that wasn't surprising, since he and Julian had both spoiled her terribly. Roz was the sort of person it was just too easy to spoil—not that Julian's own stack was anything to sniff at.

Jack waited contentedly as Roz delivered the first round of presents, starting with Flo, since she was the oldest. It was a big box, but mostly empty, he knew, since he'd wrapped it himself. He'd weighted it inside with newspapers and odds and ends—toothbrushes, socks, an umbrella—and wrapped about fifteen different boxes inside each other, just to keep her busy.

By the time Flo got down to the envelope he'd taped inside a Kleenex box, she was cursing him viciously, but not without a smile on her face. Finally, she opened it, and Jack held his breath. "Jack? What's this?" She seemed genuinely touched, and if he didn't know any better, he would have sworn there were tears in her eyes.

"It's a trip," he said. "Two tickets out to the Cape. I know you haven't been back in years, and I thought you might like to go— together." He squirmed a little. He hadn't anticipated having to justify his gift, especially not with an audience. "We can visit Uncle Pete and David. I know you haven't seen him in years, and you must miss him.

I...I want to visit Dad's grave again, you know? I thought maybe at Easter time...."

That was as far as he got, because he had an armful of hugging mom. "Thank you," she said fiercely, doing what had to be her utmost to squeeze the breath out of him. She pulled back, green eyes bright, and coughed a little as if to cover some strong emotion. "It's wonderful. I can't wait."

"I'm glad you like it," Jack smiled, touched and relieved. "My turn!"

Roz tossed a present at him. "This one's from me," she said. He caught it, wondering at its lightness, and shook the package. It rattled. Jack raised his eyebrows. At least if it was making that sort of noise it was probably something he could open in front of his mother. Warily, he slid his thumb under the tape at the corner and tore the paper open.

Jack blinked. What on Earth? There were about ten little envelopes, all taped together at the ends like a paper chain. Colors of various intensities offended his eyes. Daisies. Lupins. Roses? Who the hell started roses from seed, anyway? He looked up at Roz, confused.

She smiled at him sweetly, one hand folded over her belly. "Payback's a bitch."

Jack looked down at the packets in his hands and recalled vividly exactly what Roz had done with the flowers he'd bought her. God, he'd been such an *ass*. He hoped the worst of *that* was over. Laughing, he balled up the wrapping paper and sent it flying at her head. "Thanks, Roz. I guess I deserved that."

Julian and Flo were shooting them both inquisitive looks, but Jack and Roz just smiled secretively across the room at each other. This would be their little secret, he understood. That was nice, that he could trust her not to tell Julian—or his mother—what a fuck-up he was.

"Yeah, you did, but you got over it." Roz smiled at her brother. "Your turn, Beanstalk. Let's have it."

Julian looked at the label. Jack looked at the shape of the package. The label clearly read "Love, Mom," in Flo's spindly handwriting. Jack watched as Julian traced over the letters on the card, a faint, far-away smile on his face. He felt a sudden rush of affection that he wasn't prepared for, and really appreciated for the first time how Julian was able to accept that people could care for him as their own. He was instantly likable, and people were drawn to him, wanted to protect him. Funny, because Julian was probably stronger than all of them. He flashed Flo a brief grin in thanks, then tore the paper from the package.

Jack leaned forward unconsciously, wondering what his mother could possibly have found in the space of the less than a week's notice he'd given her that he was bringing a significant other, and one she hadn't met at that. His stomach did a funny flip when he recognized the angular construction of a small photo collection, and he groaned. "Uh-oh."

Flo's smile was positively beatific, which did nothing to alleviate Jack's sudden sense of foreboding.

Finally, Julian cracked the cover on the album, one corner of his mouth turning up in an absolutely (Jack hated himself a little for admitting this) adorable smile. God, Jack wanted to lick that dimple there on his cheek. What sort of a degenerate was he turning into, anyway? "Mom, what exactly did you give him?"

Neither Flo nor Julian deigned to answer, and when Jack looked beseechingly at Roz, she just scooted up onto her knees to look over Julian's shoulder and started snickering.

Uh-oh. "Oh, Mom, you didn't."

"Didn't what?" she said innocently.

Roz let out a peal of laughter as Julian turned the page and Jack's curiosity got the better of him. He reached over and plucked the album from Julian's too-slow hands, scowling. She *had*. The album was filled cover-to-cover with photographs of Jack in very compromising positions at various ages, ranging from the stereotypical naked-on-the-bear-skin-rug shot (he was four months old in that one) to the one she'd taken at his high school graduation. The gowns had been open at the back and as a grad prank, he and his closest friends had worn nothing beneath them.

Jack shot a betrayed look at his mother, who just smiled at Roz indulgently. "Give him the other one," she instructed.

Roz did. Julian tore into this package gleefully, then promptly flushed the color of an overripe tomato as he unwrapped a small digital camera. Laughing helplessly, he held it up for Roz to see.

"An entire album full of blackmail," Jack complained, though he was pretty sure everyone could tell he was just as amused as anyone.

"And the potential for so much more," Julian grinned, holding up the camera. "Thanks, Flo. It's perfect."

Jack was aware of a few seconds of misty silence before his mother made a flip you're-welcome comment, and then Roz was busting in. "My turn!" she said gleefully, and reached for the biggest present in the pile.

Flo looked at Jack pointedly. Jack shrugged and looked at Julian. Julian's lips twitched in that knowing way he had and he spread his hands in a what-can-I-do gesture. Jack got it. Roz might be having a kid, but right now, it wasn't going to stop her from being one.

The cycle of gift-opening more or less decayed after that, with Roz tossing out presents seemingly at random as soon as she noticed someone with their hands empty. Jack couldn't help but notice she'd set two gifts aside. One of them, he knew, was his gift to Julian. He assumed the other was Julian's gift to him. He didn't know if Roz was keeping them separate because she thought they were naughty, because she wanted to make a spectacle of it, or because she wanted to give them some privacy, and he didn't get the chance to ask her. By the time the rest of the presents were open and the wrapping paper had been more or less consolidated into a recycling bin, Roz was yawning and claiming it was bedtime, and Flo was backing her wholeheartedly. "We ladies need our beauty rest," she said with a completely manipulative smile. She kissed Jack's forehead—he felt about three years old—then did the same to Julian, ruffling his hair almost the way Jack liked to. They both reveled in his flushed cheeks. "Goodnight."

That left the two of them sitting together, across from each other on the thickly carpeted floor by the tree, the two gifts left sitting between them. Some serious butterflies were dancing an energetic tango in Jack's stomach, but he did his best to ignore them. This was important to him, an actual honest-to-God relationship. The mere fact that he wasn't running screaming right now was testament to the crazy things Julian did to his mind without even exerting any obvious effort. Biting the bullet, Jack reached out and picked up the squarish package, pressing it into Julian's hands. "You first."

There wasn't a card. Jack hadn't found one with the right sentiment. Apparently there wasn't much demand for a greeting card that said *I'm crazy about you; don't push me.* Julian definitely noticed—Jack noticed him noticing—but he didn't comment.

Julian unwrapped the iPod with a strange expression on his face, not necessarily ungrateful or surprised, just perplexed. He'd been wanting one and Jack knew it; they'd planned to go MP3 player shopping together. But he was still…. Well, Jack had to admit it wasn't the most romantic of gifts.

Not on the outside.

"Open it and turn it on," he said before Julian could comment, curling his fingers toward his palms to keep from fidgeting. "That's the important part."

It had taken a lot of doing on Roz's part. Jack hadn't had a clue how to use the software he needed, and most of it wouldn't run on his computer anyway. Roz had generously lent him the use of her Mac and, after a quick tutorial, he'd been off to the races.

Speaking of racing, his heart was pounding like he had just run a marathon. There were things Jack couldn't just come out and say, couldn't even *think,* not even to himself. The depth of emotion he felt for Julian was frankly terrifying, and he avoided classifying it like the plague because it made him feel utterly helpless. But there were things he wouldn't say and couldn't think that could come out of him in other ways, so he'd spent a good week in front of a borrowed laptop with some rented sound equipment and a guitar, all of which had led to the most agonizing two minutes of his life.

Julian found the tiny earbuds and inserted them, thankfully foregoing the lecture about how bad this type of headphone was for your hearing. He switched the iPod on and checked out the playlist Jack had loaded.

He'd loaded up the thing with as many of Julian's Saturday-night-at-Brenda's favorites, everything from "A Really Stupid Kind of Love" to Gordon Lightfoot and back again. Julian would claim he was too young to appreciate Gordon Lightfoot, but he was full of shit and they both knew it. There were also a couple of songs he'd never quite dared to perform, at least not for the past several months, afraid that baring his soul in public like that would make this whatever-it-was between them not only patently obvious but explicit and more real than he was prepared to own to just yet.

He was owning to it now, even if it was in private. One step at a time.

Julian's eyes stayed fixed to the song list for a long time before he scrolled down and selected one, as far from randomly as was humanly possible. Then he looked up at Jack, pulling the iPod in close to his body. "Jack." His voice was so quiet, Jack thought for a moment he was hearing things. "It's perfect," Julian said, deadly serious. "I love it."

Jack heard what he wasn't saying and smiled. "Good." Okay. That was enough heavy-handed emotional stuff for one night. "Now, gimme my present."

Shyly, Julian handed it over, their fingers brushing. Jack traced the seams of the wrapping paper for a moment before slipping his thumb under the tape and tearing it off.

The small, black box was heavy, about eight inches long and three deep. Jack lifted the lid carefully and turned back the soft blue cloth inside.

"I was talking to Roy," Julian said carefully as Jack lifted the delicate silver harmonica, "last Saturday when you were playing. I noticed you played that one song in a key that was awkward for you, and I asked him why." Jack raised the instrument to his lips and blew a few notes. "He said you used to have a harmonica in this key but you lost it and wouldn't buy another one. He didn't know why."

Roy. Of course. "The one I lost belonged to my dad before he died," Jack said softly, playing for a few minutes more before he could speak again. "It was a family heirloom, I guess you could say. He used to sit and play that thing for hours. Once it was gone, I couldn't bring myself to get another one." Reluctantly, Jack set the harmonica down and looked up at Julian. "This is the same brand, the same model even. It's identical. How did you find it?"

He was sure Julian was blushing, but it was impossible to verify in the darkness. "I, um, I e-mailed your mom and she sent me a picture." He fidgeted with the wrapping paper at his feet. "I spent a few hours on eBay," he admitted. "And then I spent a few more scouring pawn shops and music stores."

Touched, Jack ran his fingers over the surface of the harmonica one more time before sliding the lid back on and setting the box aside. "C'mere," he commanded, uncrossing his legs and beckoning with both arms.

Julian scooted forward and planted his knees between Jack's. Impatient, Jack grabbed a handful of his sweater and pulled him off-balance, leaving him with a happy lapful of squirmy Julian. Instead of leaning forward to meet his eager lips, Jack allowed himself to fall the rest of the way back, Julian landing squarely on his chest.

"Hi," he said with a slight smile.

Julian bit his lower lip. "Hi yourself," he said back, and then the time for words was definitely over. Jack wiggled a little to get comfortable and opened his mouth, welcoming Julian's tongue as it slipped inside, brushing over his teeth for a second before tangling enthusiastically with Jack's.

Sighing happily, Jack planted his hands firmly on Julian's fantastic ass, then slipped them up and under the hem of his shirt, stroking slowly over the smooth skin. Julian practically purred, rubbing his hardening cock firmly over Jack's own growing bulge, the pressure and friction spiking the desire low in his belly. "I fucking love your ass," Jack murmured happily as Julian sank his teeth into the flesh at his collarbone, following up with a particularly vicious thrust. "The rest of you ain't bad either."

Snorting, Julian managed to work a hand in between their bodies to hike Jack's shirt up. "Yeah, I know. Why aren't we naked yet?"

"Because we're in my mom's living room?" Jack suggested, working his fingers around to undo the clasp of Julian's jeans anyway. "I feel like a naughty teenager."

"I have that effect on people," Julian said smugly, wiggling as Jack worked his pants down.

"If you're being naughty with anyone else I think it's only fair I get to watch," Jack grumbled around a mouthful of tongue. "And beat him up after," he added after a moment of consideration.

"Yes to the first, no to the second," Julian chirped. He managed somehow to support himself on one arm and work the button fly on Jack's jeans open, freeing his aching cock. "Although I seriously doubt you'd be willing to just stand by and watch."

Yeah, that would be a bit of a sticking point. In fact, just the thought of Julian with another man made him twitch—which didn't mean he couldn't watch Julian by himself. A little shiver went through him at the idea. "Speaking of watching." Jack pushed up and rolled a little, sending Julian sprawling onto the floor, hooking his fingers into the younger man's belt loops and jerking down sharply. "You feel up to a show?"

Julian's eyes went liquid dark, hands resting on his belly. "Depends. You going to reciprocate?"

Hell, yeah, he was! Jack rolled up onto his knees and shoved his pants down past his thighs, taking his cock into his hand. "That answer your question?"

Julian groaned, hiking up his shirt and sliding his open palm down his belly, fingers curling loosely around his erection, stroking up and down slowly, his eyes never leaving Jack's.

"You're so hot," Jack complained, mirroring Julian's actions. "I want you all the time."

"I'm not seeing a problem here," Julian smirked, spreading his knees.

Jack's view improved immeasurably. He rubbed his thumb through the bead of moisture at the tip of his cock, drawing it down the length.

Julian swallowed audibly, and Jack reached out with his left hand to tweak a nipple. "Not a problem in sight," Jack agreed. Watching Julian stroke his dick was unbelievably arousing.

"Can you—God, come closer."

Jack did so, collapsing next to him in a heap. He slid his lips over Julian's, moaning a little as their hands and cocks connected. "Like this?" he murmured, writhing furiously against Julian's body.

"Shit," Julian groaned. Jack could smell the pre-come scenting the air, taste the thin sheen of sweat on Julian's upper lip. "Jack. I want you."

Jack could get on board with that. He wrapped Julian's dick in his fingers, keeping up the rhythm Julian had so relentlessly set for himself. "Here?" he asked, licking at Julian's mouth distractedly. Not that the idea of screwing Julian into the New Year right here on the floor of his mother's living room didn't appeal. He just wanted to make sure it was okay with all parties involved.

Julian wriggled enthusiastically beside him, eventually pulling a couple of single-serving lube packets from the pocket of his discarded jeans. "Here," he confirmed a little breathlessly as Jack circled his thumb over the head of Julian's prick. "It's not polite to keep a guy waiting."

"Not all that polite to fuck you on the floor, either," Jack pointed out, reaching as far as he could to snag a throw pillow from the couch.

"That's never stopped you before!"

It wasn't going to stop him now, either. "Lift," Jack instructed firmly. He was pretty sure the last time they'd done this on the floor he'd almost done permanent damage. Julian obliged and he slid the pillow under his hips.

"You're too far away," Julian protested. Agreeing, Jack leaned forward for another bruising kiss, leaning on his left hand while he worked the little plastic twist off of a garishly green packet.

"Sorry," he said, not particularly apologetically, as Julian nipped at his lower lip. He was pretty sure this working one-handed thing was going to make a mess but they were both too impatient to care at the moment.

Julian's hands smoothed over his back and shoulders as he managed to slick his fingers. Jack felt his breath hitch when he circled Julian's hole lazily. He might be impatient, but he wasn't careless. He pressed his index finger forward, gut clenching at the silky heat.

The muscles under the skin of Julian's stomach flexed as he exhaled slowly, lifting his pelvis encouragingly. Jack curled upward, rubbing in slow circles until Julian was panting and squirming. A second later Jack sank his teeth into Julian's hip bone and slid a second digit in alongside the first, scissoring his fingers gently.

Julian's body jerked, his cock leaving a sticky trail of clear fluid on his stomach. Patiently, Jack worked his fingers in and out, his own prick throbbing sympathetically as Julian writhed and moaned.

"Jack," he murmured, head flat against the floor, heels planted. "Quit teasing me. I need you."

Jack ignored him for as long as he could, adding a third finger and massaging his prostate almost brutally, until Julian's vocalizations threatened to wake the rest of the house. Balancing on his knees, he reached up and covered his mouth with his left hand. to stifle the noise. "When I'm ready," he said into the top of his thigh, still working his fingers in and out inexorably.

Julian licked his palm.

Jack figured that was enough of a sign for him. He twisted his fingers one more time, watching as Julian's cock leaked pearlescent fluid into his navel, then withdrew them to yank the top off of another lube packet. He squirted a liberal amount into his palm and slathered it over his dick, releasing his hold on Julian's mouth.

He eased forward, sliding into the tight sheath. Julian hissed softly, his legs wrapping around Jack's waist, ankles hooking together. Jack groaned as Julian drew him forward until his balls were resting against Julian's ass. Then Julian's fingers twined in his hair and yanked him down, taking his tongue as well as his cock. Jack grunted at the change of angle, ground his hips forward firmly and growled as Julian bit his lower lip hard enough to draw blood.

The sharp jolt went straight down his spine and into his groin, and Jack broke away from the kiss as he pulled his pelvis sharply back, slowly pushing forward again as Julian dug sharp fingernails into Jack's ass.

"Jack." Julian buried his face in Jack's neck, his dark curls tickling Jack's chest and chin. He licked a trail up to Jack's ear, as Jack fucked him long and slow, knees burning on the carpet, nails digging into his palms as he balanced on the floor. "God, that's good."

He was so hot, and so tight, so alive and so close that he was almost under Jack's skin, eyes open in the dark. Jack scraped his teeth along Julian's jaw, breathing in the scent of his sweat, tasting the salt on his skin. "Tell me," Jack murmured, moving his hips unhurriedly, watching the expressions flicker over his face.

Julian groaned wantonly, reaching down between his legs to fist his cock. "Deeper," he begged, gaze fixed on Jack's.

Jack obliged, shifting his knees around until he could comfortably rub against Julian's prostate on every stroke. Julian shuddered beneath him, his fingers moving quicker over his swollen cock.

"Harder."

Shit. Maybe telling Julian to tell him what to do was a bad idea. Jack shuddered, running his tongue over the cut on his lip and swallowing as he pistoned forward again.

Julian practically mewled, and Jack lowered his head to catch the noise from his lips, rubbing their noses together. "God…. Julian…."

"Yes," he whispered, and Jack couldn't help it. He looked deep into those huge dark eyes and saw Julian for the first time.

Shit, shit, shit. He knew what this was, now, knew it without a doubt. He knew. He was terrified, and nothing had ever felt this good. Not in thirty-six years.

Hand shaking, Jack uncurled a fist and cupped Julian's face in one hand, laying his palm flat against his cheek. Julian took a shuddering breath and released it with a whimper, then his whole body arched and spasmed, clenching furiously around Jack's prick. Jack came almost soundlessly, his head falling forward as he pulsed inside Julian's ass, hot seed spilling over, collapsing down onto his elbows as the adrenaline rush faded into post-coital tremors.

"Jesus," Julian whispered softly after a long moment.

Jack concurred, shaken to the core. He pressed his uncertain smile into Julian's temple and followed it up with a kiss. "Come on," he said, rolling over and tugging Julian's hand. "Let's go to bed."

Chapter 14

"DON'T be stupid," Julian said from the laundry room as Jack put away the last of the dishes. Jack looked up in time to see Robot plant her paws on his belly. "My parents will love you. Everyone loves you."

Jack wasn't so sure, although his mom had certainly liked Julian well enough. She'd even invited the two of them back for New Year's, though they'd chosen to stay behind in town with Roz. It was a good thing, because everyone at Brenda's had figured out exactly why Roz wasn't drinking and the lineup of well-wishers had been enormous. Julian had had to field hugs and smiles for her for a good half an hour. Eventually they'd had to facilitate her escape and take her home, which was just as well, since she'd been exhausted and Julian had been horny. There had been more than a few speculative glances thrown Jack's way, but luckily, nobody had asked.

"Whatever you say," Jack agreed noncommittally, closing the cupboard door. He turned just in time to find Julian's body pressing against him.

"Promise?" Julian asked huskily, biting his chin.

Jack's knees went to jelly. Right then—not just right then, but any time in the recent past or foreseeable future—Julian could've asked him for anything and Jack would have moved mountains to do it for him. He spread his legs to make room for Julian between them, leaning back against the kitchen cupboards.

Julian's cell phone rang.

"Fuck," Julian said, mouth full of Jack's lips. "Never fails." He moved back far enough that Jack wouldn't overhear if it was confidential and flipped open the phone. "Dr. Piet."

Jack watched as his body stilled in confusion and resigned himself to a night alone. It looked like it might be serious.

Julian frowned and turned aside, pressing a hand to his free ear despite the fact that Jack wasn't making any noise.

Then all the color went out of his face. "Roz?"

Oh, fuck. Jack froze, staring as Julian slouched against the counter. His knuckles were white against the phone. "Roz, slow down, I can't understand you. I…." Julian stopped, held the phone away from his ear, and looked blankly at Jack. "She's not there," he said. His voice was soft and quiet. "I…I think she passed out."

Jack said, "I'll get my keys."

Julian ran for his shoes as Jack slammed the key drawer, tearing after him at a run, shoving his feet into his shoes. There was a foot and a half of snow on the ground that soaked into his socks as he ran out the front door without locking it, but the roads had been plowed, thank God.

They didn't look at each other during the five-minute drive back to Julian's, Jack's foot hard on the gas the whole way. He hadn't even parked yet before Julian was out the door, skidding across the slush in front of the back door and ripping into the house. Jack followed hot on his trail, his heart hammering in his chest. "Roz!" he heard Julian shout as he followed right on his heels.

"Jack, get up here!"

Fuck. Jack didn't bother wiping the snow from his shoes. He just thundered up the stairs as fast as he could, heading for Roz's bedroom.

Julian wasn't there. Neither was Roz. "In the bathroom!" Julian shouted.

Jack whirled, ran down the hallway, and stopped dead in the bathroom doorway.

Roz was curled unconscious in a ball on the bathroom floor, a small pool of blood spreading steadily from between her legs. The phone lay beside her on the floor, the status light flashing. Jack could hear the busy signal over the roar of blood in his ears.

Julian was kneeling beside his sister, looking very small, two fingers on the pulse point in her neck. "It's thready," he said, intensely focused. "We're going to have to carry her down the stairs. Hold her head and shoulders, okay?"

Jack did as he was told, lifting when Julian did, and they managed to bring her to the top of the stairs. There was no way they could bring her down like this, though. Not without serious injury to Roz or to themselves. "I've got her," Jack said, shifting so that he could grab her legs. "Go get in the back of the truck and call the hospital. Let them know we're on our way."

For a minute, he thought Julian was going to protest, but then he was gone, cell phone pressed to his ear. By the time Jack got Roz down the stairs, out the door and into the truck, Julian had it started and was sitting in the backseat of the pickup with the throw blanket from the back of the couch. Jack laid her down next to him, with her head resting on Julian's chest, and was surprised to find Julian almost completely calm. He took Roz's wrist in one hand, presumably to keep track of the pulse he'd called *thready,* and the other on her lower abdomen. "Drive," Julian instructed.

Jack drove. Fast. They made it to the hospital in forty minutes, riding in terse silence the whole time, save for Roz's occasional groans. She woke up once along the way, her voice soft and pained and confused, and Jack heard Julian's tone falter in the backseat as he answered.

By the time he pulled up in front of the emergency room, Roz was unconscious again, and a team of hospital staff was waiting with a stretcher. Jack practically fell out of the truck.

The team had the back door open and Roz on the stretcher before he could say anything. Julian was rattling off medical terms at a pace Jack couldn't keep up with, shooting Jack the briefest of glances before running to keep up with the staff. Jack looked helplessly at the security guard and the nurse that had been left behind, tossed his keys at them and took off after the siblings, but they had disappeared into an elevator.

The nurse at the emergency station wouldn't tell him where they'd gone.

Lost, Jack just looked at her. "Listen, my friend is three months pregnant. We found her passed out on the floor of her bathroom in a pool of blood less than an hour ago. I need to know where she is!" Just as importantly, he needed to know where Julian was, so that he could be there for him.

The nurse—Michelle Renaud by her name tag—gave him a sympathetic look. "I'm sorry, but I can only release that information to family members. She's probably in surgery right now. Why don't you give me her name, have a coffee, and take a seat? I'll let you know when she's in a recovery room." She paused. "If you can see her. She might not want company."

That was as much as he was going to get, and Jack knew it. Trying not to think about what that last comment might—probably did—mean, he ran a hand through his hair. Coffee, waiting. Phone? "Her name is Roslin Piet. That's P-I-E-T. Roslin with an s." Jack waited until Michelle had scribbled down the information, then gave her his own name and cell phone number so that she could call him when Roz had a room.

When he didn't move after that, Michelle attempted a small smile. "Decaf?" she suggested, motioning to the coffee pots on a small table near the outside door.

Jack flashed her a grateful look, or what he could manage of one, anyway, and drifted over to pour himself a steaming cup. It was so hot, it was almost flavorless. Perfect.

He sat there feeling worse than useless with no idea what he could or should be doing for almost half an hour. Then he took a deep breath and did what he always did in tough situations.

He called his mother.

JACK'S cell phone buzzed. He jerked awake with a start, looking around guiltily until he caught the eye of the nurse at the station. Not Michelle, a different one this time. He wondered how long he'd been asleep.

Swallowing hard, Jack stood and walked over, trying to keep his emotions in check. He couldn't even imagine what Roz and Julian were going through right now. They would need him to be strong, no matter what had happened. He would be there for them. He would not let them down. "Yes?"

The nurse—a man probably close to Julian's age, with blond hair and dark shadows beneath his eyes—said, "Dr. Piet's been asking for you. Room D-518. That's up five floors, take a left when you get out of the elevator, past the nurse's station, then turn right. You got that?"

Jack nodded mechanically. "Thanks." He looked at the bank of elevators, wondering. What would he say when he got to the top? Should he have brought flowers? That might, at least, have got a smile. But it seemed so inappropriate.

Deciding he needed a few minutes to pull himself together, Jack headed for the stairwell, climbing the flights mechanically until he reached a landing labeled D5.

He found D-518 without any trouble. Julian was sitting outside it on the floor, legs splayed in front of him, wearing someone's borrowed scrubs and a lab coat a size too large for him, head leaned back against the wall. Jack slumped down beside him and put his arm around him before he could think better of it. Fuck it. Some things were more important than public perception of his masculinity, or lack thereof. "Lean, Julian," he commanded when the doctor resisted.

Julian did, exhaling slowly as he let his head rest against Jack's chest.

"Now talk."

It was as gentle a way as Jack knew to put it, but Julian still flinched a little and picked at the hole in Jack's jeans while he spoke. "Roz is, I mean she, I don't think...." After several more abortive attempts at a sentence, Julian sighed and went limp. "She's sleeping now. Well, sedated. I.... That's for the best."

Jack's heart ached for the two of them. He pressed a chaste kiss to the top of Julian's head and then leaned his own back against the wall, utterly wiped. This emotional shit was draining. "I'm sorry," he said softly, at length. "I can't even...."

Against his chest, he could feel Julian shudder. "Me neither. God. Being orphaned is one thing...."

Without his permission, Jack's arm tightened around Julian's shoulders. He wanted, irrationally, to promise Julian he'd never have to be alone again, but it was stupid. Julian hadn't been alone then, and he wasn't now, and Jack had no right going around making grand gestures like that when he couldn't control how long he'd be around for and hadn't even been comfortable enough to hold hands in public. Until now, apparently.

"She's devastated," Julian finally heaved. Jack's fingers curled into his upper arm supportively. "And there is absolutely nothing I can do about it and, damn it, Jack, I don't know how to *fix* things like this. Roz always knows what to say or do to make me feel better and I am utterly, utterly *hopeless* when it's time to return the favor."

"Julian." Jack managed somehow to pull him closer, so that Julian was sitting between his legs, using him for a chair. The hallway here was mostly deserted except for a few scattered hospital staff, and they seemed to be ignoring the scene playing out here. They'd seen their share of breakdowns in this ward, he decided. "There is *nothing* you can do or say right now to make this better. That's not your fault, okay? You did everything you could. I was there, remember?"

In front of him, Julian's head bobbed in a nod, and then he was very still for a few long minutes. Jack held him without moving until his ass went numb, wondering if he'd fallen asleep, and then wiggled only just enough to work some blood back into his butt. It was late now, some ridiculous hour of the morning, late enough that it was actually early, and people were starting to arrive for shifts. Jack was about to ask one of the passing staff if there was a gurney his exhausted doctor could nap on for a few hours—or days—when Julian stirred against him, jerking fully awake in seconds.

"Is your ass numb?" was the first thing he asked once he seemed to have figured out where he was and just whose arms were holding him upright.

Jack couldn't resist squeezing a little, but he let go quickly, wanting very much to stand up, stretch, and pee, not necessarily in that order. Julian jumped to his feet without a hint of hesitation, and Jack glared up at him resentfully. His own hip and knee made embarrassing old-man noises as he dragged himself up off of the floor. "I guess that answers your question."

Amusingly, Julian seemed to be very engaged in massaging feeling back into his regrettably still-clothed backside. "Need a hand?" Jack offered.

Julian gave him a darkly amused look. "Now you decide to molest me in public? No offense, Jack, but your timing sucks." He stretched, the skin showing between the halves of his scrubs making the roof of Jack's mouth go dry. Tease. "I'm going to check on Roz," he said, and the severity of the situation flooded back so quickly that Jack just nodded.

"I'll be in the waiting room at the end of the hall," he said, intending to round up some coffee. If there was a vending machine around here maybe he'd scrounge Julian some orange juice. "Call me if you need me?"

Julian nodded, not quite smiling, and opened the door to Roz's room. It was dark inside, but Jack could see Roz's silhouette against the brightening window, looking curled up and small.

Wandering off down the hallway, Jack opted to locate a cafeteria rather than drink the sludge that was trying to ooze its way out of the spigot on the D5 coffee machine. He took the scenic route, hitting the bathroom first. Afterward, he wandered through the just-opening gift shop, then played a game of pinball in the small arcade. He detoured into another quiet lounge area to make a quick phone call to work, let Hamilton know he might not be coming in Monday, then sidled into the cafeteria to stock up on pocketable goodies to sneak to Julian throughout the day. Hell, maybe Roz would feel up to something loaded with sugar and delicious trans fats. He picked up a few extras, just in case. Pockets full of pastries, Jack meandered back up to the lounge on D5, sipping his coffee slowly. Still scaldingly hot, and oh so good. He had a bottle of OJ for Julian, too, but he'd wait until Julian came out to get it himself.

Jack had just sat down to polish off the last of his coffee and bagel when the last person he'd expected to see walked down the hallway. He put down his drink and stood, suddenly uneasy for reasons he couldn't explain. "Roy?" Jack fidgeted, made even more uneasy, if that were possible, by the large bouquet Roy was carrying. "Is that you?"

It definitely was. Roy froze at the sound of his voice and turned slowly in his direction. If his posture was anything to go by, he was every bit as on edge as Jack. "Oh, hi, Jack. I came as soon as I heard."

Heard? "Heard what?"

"Come on, Jack," Roy said impatiently. "It doesn't take a genius. I got a phone call this morning saying Hallie's swimming lesson was cancelled tomorrow because the instructor had a family emergency. Roz is her swimming instructor. I put two and two together."

Okay. That was…believable. But it didn't explain what Roy was doing here. Was he just dense? Did he not realize Roz was not going to be in a particularly social mood? "Right," he hedged. "I don't know what to tell you. She's not exactly up to having visitors right now, you know? I'll drop off the flowers for you, though, if you like, and tell her you stopped by."

Roy's eyes narrowed just slightly. Jack felt the hair on the back of his neck stand up. This was totally unlike the Roy he knew. He seemed almost spiteful. Then the expression was gone, replaced by something milder and almost sympathetic. "Look, I don't know what Roz told you, Jack, but you aren't that baby's father."

Jack blinked. *Roy? Roy was Roz's baby-daddy?* Wow, that one had gone right by him. He tried to be sensitive. "There is no baby, Roy," he said gently. "And Roz isn't up to visitors. Trust me, no matter how much you think you share her pain, she doesn't want to see you."

Roy put the flowers down on the lounge table and stepped back. "I guess you would know, huh?"

Ah, shit. This was really not going to go well. At least Roy sounded more resigned than angry. So far. "I don't know what you're talking about," Jack lied. He knew perfectly well what Roy was implying; it just happened to be way off the mark.

"Right." Roy snorted bitterly. "It's all right, Jack. I get it. You don't have to worry. After today, I won't get in your way. You won't ever have to see me again." He swiped the vase off the table and stormed toward the hospital rooms.

What the hell? Jack was *not* losing a friend over this. This was ridiculous. There was also no way he was letting Roy in to see Roz. He was, quite possibly, the last person she needed to see. He headed Roy off before he could get to the door. "Roy. There is nothing to be in the way of! But I am *not* going to let you go in there. It'll be bad news for both of you."

"Quit denying it!" Roy finally said furiously. "Do you think I don't see the way she looks at you? I'm not *blind,* Jack! You're always there, and if you're not, her truck is parked in your driveway! I'm not angry with you for it. You didn't know there was any history there. But the least you could do is own up to it!"

"For the last time," Jack told him, exasperated, "there is *nothing going on.* I don't know why you won't believe me, but it's not my problem."

"THEN WHY WON'T YOU LET ME SEE HER? WHAT ARE YOU DOING HERE?"

Oh, for fuck's sake. "Because I'm in love with her *brother,* you idiot!"

Jack was vaguely aware that Roy had very nearly lost his grip on the enormous vase he was holding. His blood was pounding furiously in his ears, adrenaline coursing through him, and all he could think was—it felt good to have it out in the open. It felt…great, in fact. Fuck Roy if he didn't get it.

"What?"

Okay, Lucy. You've got some 'splainin' to do. Jack steeled himself. "I'm gay, Roy. That's what you've been seeing. Roz looks at me like that because I make Julian happy, because we get along, and because I'm her friend. It's Julian's truck that's been parked in my driveway, and it's Julian I've been visiting at the Piets'. I'm sorry you got the wrong idea, but I *won't* be sorry for that. And you still aren't going in there to see Roz."

Roy opened his mouth to reply, but Jack heard the door open behind him before Roy could get a word out. "You guys are awfully loud," Julian admonished, cheeks pink and eyes dancing. "Think you could keep it down a little?"

Jack felt an answering blush creeping up the back of his neck and grinned. He'd been going around thinking Julian was a midlife crisis. More like a rest-of-life crisis, he figured. He wondered how he'd missed it. "Sorry, boss."

"Uh-huh," Julian said, mock-severely. "Just don't let it happen again." His head disappeared back into the room, then reappeared a half-second later. "Oh, and Jack?"

"Yeah?"

Julian's answering smile lit Jack's whole body from the inside. "Me, too."

"I think that's my cue," Jack told Roy flatly. "Do you want me to take the flowers or not?"

Roy handed them over, still looking completely steamrollered.

"Thanks, Roy. You're a pal. See you later."

Maybe Jack was being rude, but, well, Roy had started it. Roy would either forgive him for making an ass out of him or not. Jack wasn't about to lose any sleep over it now, although he'd certainly miss seeing little Hallie if Roy decided to hold a grudge. There was nothing he could do to influence that situation now, so he turned his mind to the task at hand.

"Hi, Roz." Jack plonked the flowers down on her table. "I won't ask you how you're feeling."

"Don't you know better than to bring me flowers?" she grumbled, not quite smiling. She looked—okay, she looked devastated, like she'd been crying her eyes out for as long as she'd been awake, but all things considered Jack thought she was a rock for acting as normally as possible.

Jack appreciated the effort. "You know me. I couldn't help myself." He glanced sideways and caught Julian's eye again. "I, um…."

Roz peeled one arm off of her mattress long enough to fling an ice chip at him. "Get a room, guys. This one's mine."

Taking that to mean he was forgiven for being totally at a loss, not to mention excused from the room, Jack let Julian drag him out the door and into the nearest supply closet.

The nurse taking inventory raised her eyebrows in a decidedly amused expression. Julian said, "So sorry; need to borrow the supply closet for a minute. Medical emergency," and shooed her out.

Jack didn't bother suppressing the snort of laughter at that, and didn't have to. Half a second later he found himself pressed up against the door, two armfuls of warm, happy doctor. Being manhandled by Julian was something new for him, although if preliminary tests were anything to go by, he kind of liked it.

"I should have told you weeks ago," he mumbled, tongue tracing the roof of Julian's mouth.

"You do pick your moments," Julian acknowledged, nipping Jack's lower lip. "I can live with that." His hands wandered down Jack's sides to hook fingers into his belt loops. "Tell me."

Jack's head went fuzzy, his senses filled with Julian's scent, his taste, the feel of not-quite-clean-shaven skin against his own. "I love you," he said, letting the words take him away.

The hands at his waist tugged him closer. "Again."

A lazy grin curled on his lips. "I love you," Jack practically sing-songed. Who knew three little words could be so liberating?

Julian kissed him again, a long, slow, burning kiss that had every nerve ending in Jack's body standing up and taking notice. "I like the sound of that."

The grin turned wry. "You're kidding."

Julian reached around and grabbed his ass. "No joke." He leaned his forehead against Jack's, so close that all Jack could see was the deep, mesmerizing brown of his eyes. "For the record, I love you too. And I am going to show you just how much." He tilted his hips forward into Jack's, just for a second, then said mischievously, "Later. Maybe I'll even get out that Christmas present from your mom."

"Tease," Jack pouted, willing his erection to go away. It throbbed insistently, demanding someone give it some more attention. The idea of incorporating a camera into their, uh, bedtime routine, was definitely worth exploring. "Five more minutes?"

"Optimist." Julian pinched his butt, then pulled him away from the door by the belt loops. Jack would have been offended, but, well, he had a point. Actually, right now, they were *both* a little pointy in certain areas. "Come on, get. Ooh, is that a pastry?" It was a little squished, for obvious reasons, but Julian tore into it as they not-so-discreetly evacuated the supply room.

Jack rolled his eyes a little, feeling flushed and exposed, but oddly not afraid, not ashamed, and unfortunately not any less aroused. He was beginning to think he had a...thing...about public sex. "I got you an orange juice, too. I think I left it in the lounge."

"I knew I kept you around for a reason." Julian stifled Jack's token protest with another brief kiss, then gave him a little shove in the direction of the lounge. "You go get it. I'm going to go make sure Roz hasn't tried to escape."

Yeah, that would be something she'd try. Maybe not yet, but soon enough. Jack sauntered off to the lounge—not on purpose, but because with his dick this hard there was really no other way to achieve locomotion. The bag with the rest of the pastries and the bottle of orange juice were still on the table. Snatching them up, Jack was just getting ready to head back when he heard familiar footfalls in the hallway. He looked up to see his mother coming at him at a full run, face full of worry.

"Jack! I got here as soon as I could. They kept telling me visiting hours weren't until eleven on Sundays!" She swept him into a hug that felt more fragile than it looked. "How is she?"

"About as well as can be expected," Jack said automatically, hugging back gingerly. "Which is to say, she's a wreck but she's also a rock. She'll be okay, but not for a long time."

Flo nodded, releasing him to stand at arm's length. "You look different," she said after a second of scrutiny. "Is everything okay with you and Julian?"

Jeez, Jack might as well just tattoo it on his forehead: "Property of Dr. Julian Piet." It'd save him from people and their nosy, occasionally well-meaning questions. Then again, maybe his ass was a more appropriate location. "Peachy," he said wryly. "Thanks for prying."

Flo tsked at him, then segued into a cough. Remembering she'd seemed a little under the weather at Christmas, Jack frowned. "Have you still got that cold?"

"I'm fine," she protested, waving him off and covering her mouth with her hand. Her whole body seemed to shake with it, and for a second he thought she wouldn't be able to catch her breath. Then she straightened up. "There, you see? Just a little tickle."

Jack blinked. There was a smear of blood on the corner of her mouth. He reached out to touch it. "Mom?"

She wavered in front of him, then started to fall. Jack only barely managed to catch her, panic rising deep within him. "Mom?! Mom!" She was limp in his arms, and her breathing was shallow. "Julian! I need a doctor!"

I need you, he thought at his mother, but her eyes were closed, and even if he'd said it aloud, she wouldn't have heard him.

"MR. STRANGE?"

Jack looked up, squeezed Julian's hand briefly, and stood. "That's me."

Julian flashed him an indecipherable look, then stood himself and left the counseling room. "I'll catch up with you later." Jack watched him go a little forlornly. They'd agreed that his mother would appreciate Jack hearing this by himself, but that didn't make it easier to bear alone.

"How is she?"

The doctor put down the clipboard and motioned for him to sit again. That did not bode well. "It'd be best if you were sitting down for this."

Jack's stomach flipped. "I...can't. I feel helpless sitting down."

"I understand." The doctor leaned against the counter. "I'm Dr. Wilson. Before we start, you should know that I'm not your mother's usual physician. She's been seeing Dr. van Hissink in Calgary."

That sounded ominous. "Dr. van Hissink?"

"The oncologist?"

Off Jack's blank stare, Dr. Wilson released a long sigh. "Your mother is a very difficult patient. I can see that just from Dr. van Hissink's notes. She didn't tell you?"

Jack shook his head, his whole body shaking slightly. Maybe it wasn't such a great idea to stay standing after all. He sank down into the chair, numb. "Tell me?"

Dr. Wilson took the chair beside him. "Well, at least you're not alone. Mr. Strange, your mother has stage-four small cell lung cancer. She was diagnosed last summer. Treatments were ineffective in reducing the cancer or stopping its progress, so she opted to decline treatment a few months ago."

Jack's mouth dropped open slightly. "Cancer?" His mother had *cancer* and she hadn't told him? Hadn't even mentioned being sick? And now she was declining treatment? "What…how long…?"

"The cancer is causing her lung tissue to collapse. We've put her on a ventilator, but it's only a temporary measure. I'm afraid she probably only has a few weeks, but it's impossible to say with any degree of accuracy. I'm sorry."

God. All those times he should have called, should have visited, should have made more of an effort to be the son he could have been. He'd never have the chance to do any of those things. He would never take her back to Cape Breton to see Pete and Dave. "I…. Oh." His mouth went dry and his head felt empty. He thought he maybe should have cried a little, but nothing was sinking in. "Thank you. I…. Could you send Dr. Piet back in here please?"

Dr. Wilson gave him a tight smile. "Sure."

The door swung open a couple of times and Julian slunk back in, slid back into the chair beside him, and slipped an arm around his shoulders. Jack accepted the touch, let Julian comfort him with his presence for a minute, then straightened up a little. When he turned to look at Julian, he felt the moisture in his eyes. "My mom's dying."

WHAT seemed like hours later, Dr. Wilson returned to say Jack could go in and see his mother.

"Is she awake?"

The doctor shook his head. "Not yet. She's had a bit of a shock. She probably won't wake up until tomorrow at the earliest. Right now, it's best that she stays sleeping."

Jack nodded, and Julian squeezed his hand. "Do you want me to…?"

Feeling selfish, Jack shook his head. He wasn't the only one who had lost something. No, he shouldn't think of it that way; not yet. Roz needed Julian's support at least as much as he did. "It's okay," he told him. "Go be with your sister. There's probably only room for one, anyway."

He was right.

Jack let the door close behind him. The room was tiny, and crammed with all sorts of medical equipment that he was glad he couldn't identify. The calm blue walls were bathed in an unearthly glow of greens and reds, and the steady hiss of the respirator was the only sound in the otherwise desolate space.

Jack took the seat beside his mother's bed and flopped forward with his head in his hands. Someone had picked up the contents of his mother's purse, which had spilled over the ground when she had fallen, and put everything in a clear plastic bag. Not yet ready to face his mother on the bed, he grasped the bag in both hands and turned it over.

The detritus of his mother's life had no answers for him. A half-used package of Kleenex, patterned with pink cats, was squished in the bottom corner; half a dozen pill bottles in varying degrees of consumption, a small wallet, and a cell phone that was losing its charge were all that remained. Absently, Jack opened the bag, spreading its contents on the bed in front of him. He ran his fingers over the objects absently, turning them in his hands.

The labels on the pill bottles attracted his attention for a few moments, but none of them made any sense to him. Six- or seven-syllable words with instructions like *twice daily with food,* refill instructions, and prescribing physician, Dr. van Hissink. Pink pills, blue ones, big ones, small ones. Jack picked up the last bottle in his right hand, leaning his forehead on his left. He traced the letters with his thumb, not really paying attention.

D.

R.

J.

P.

I.

E.

Jack blinked once and rubbed his left hand over his eyes, his vision blurring. Was he that tired?

No. There it was, in plain sight: Dr. J. Piet. Julian. And his mother's name, Flora Strange. And a date. Which could mean only one thing.

Julian had known. The whole time they had been together, Julian had known his mother was dying.

And Julian hadn't said anything.

Jack closed his fist around the bottle and closed his eyes. *Fuck.*

⟍⟋⟍ Chapter 15

JULIAN closed the door quietly behind him and took a moment to scrub a hand over his eyes. Roz would be released tomorrow, with no lasting damage that wasn't psychological or emotional, and for which he was mostly grateful. For now, she was sleeping, something she'd probably be doing a lot of for the next few weeks. Roz tended to deal with this kind of intense and negative emotion by being unconscious for as much of it as she could manage.

He sighed, making his way toward the lounge. With any luck, there was coffee left in the pot with his name on it. God, he was slipping back into old habits, but he couldn't help it. What the hell else could he do? He wasn't exactly sure what time it was. Sometime after four; that he knew because the shifts had changed. That made it, what, close to thirty-six hours since he'd had any sleep?

Pouring the last of the coffee, Julian slumped into a chair. Now Jack's mom was…well, here. It made everything a lot more complicated. He had been grieving for Roz, and now he was grieving for Jack, too, but on top of that he had to deal with the guilt of having known this was coming. Everything was compounded by the fact that he'd been where Jack was now, though granted at a much younger age. Not to mention that not eight hours ago Jack—*Jack,* who had been purposely distant from day one—had practically shouted to the world that he loved Julian.

Julian took a sip of the hot liquid, wincing as it burned down his throat. He felt like his skin was too thin, like anyone could just look at him and see through everything he was feeling, all of the conflicting emotions tearing him in every direction at once. He thought he'd split under the sheer variety of things he had to think, feel, or do.

"What the hell is this?"

Julian managed not to spill the coffee on himself, but only because he dropped the whole cup, instead of reacting with just a jerk. His nerves must have been completely shot. A brown vial flew across the lounge and hit him in the chest, then rolled off of his lap and bounced onto the floor with an empty, plasticky tick-tick-tick. "I think it's a pill bottle," he said reflexively, watching as it rolled into the puddled coffee.

"It's my *mother's* pill bottle," Jack snarled, stalking across the lounge. Julian noted detachedly that his eyes were red and wondered if he'd had a little too much caffeine.

"Okay," he said non-argumentatively. Carefully, he placed his hands on either side of the chair, letting them rest in plain sight. He'd never really seen Jack angry, but it could just be a natural part of the grief cycle. Tiredly, he let his head fall back. If Jack needed to vent, he'd let him vent.

"It's got your fucking name on it as the prescribing physician!" Jack hissed. "Dated months ago, Julian! What the fuck?"

Fuck. Fucking perfect timing, that was what this was. Julian didn't have the energy to defend himself. "She accidentally dumped her prescription down the sink when she was visiting you," he said dully. He tried not to flinch when Jack blocked out the light from the overhead halogen bulbs. "I wrote her a refill."

"That was before we were even together!" Jack was not doing a very good job of keeping his voice down. Some of the nurses and other staff were starting to take notice. "You've known this whole time and you never said anything?"

"What exactly could I have said?" Julian countered, eyes falling closed. Could they have this conversation in the morning, maybe? He never had gotten that coffee. This was such a huge mess that it had to be a dream, anyway. Nobody's real life was this dramatic. "Oh, Jack, hi, remember me, the doctor who stitched up your leg and gave you a boner in the exam room? Guess what? Your mom's dying of terminal lung cancer. By the way, I think you're hot. Want to go out sometime?"

The silence was deafening, so much so that Julian forced his eyes open again past the fog of sheer exhaustion. He must be getting soft;

thirty-six hours had never been a problem before. He looked up. Jack was staring at him, fists clenched, eyes open, mouth hard. "You know what?" he said. "Maybe I was wrong about you. About us."

That stung, even through the haze of conflicting emotions, but Julian couldn't exactly come up with a counterargument. "Maybe you were." He couldn't quite bring himself to meet Jack's eyes when he said it. One more emotion to add to the ever-growing pile.

"I don't think I want to see you for a while," Jack said at length.

Julian could only stare at his shoes in the spreading puddle of cooling coffee until he walked away. Then something inside of him splintered, and he pulled his feet up into the uncomfortable chair to press his face into his knees. If he were lucky this would all be some terrible dream.

"JULIAN, baby, you look worse than Roz."

"Thanks, Mom," he sighed, sagging into her hug anyway. Roz had gone to bed early—no surprise there—but she did seem to be improving, bit by bit, as the days went by. Having their parents here certainly helped, since it had been agreed that she shouldn't be alone for extended periods and Julian did have to go back to work. Besides, Roz needed a woman to talk to, and she was shy on lady friends.

His mother squeezed him tightly for another thirty seconds and then let go, holding him at arm's length. "You're sure there's nothing you want to talk about? I know this can't be easy on you."

You have no idea, he thought. The last week had been nothing if not trying. Public exposure of his sexuality had been inevitable—several of the hospital's nurses lived in town—but the fallout had been mostly in the form of strange looks. One of his patients had refused to see him, but on the other hand, he had a new pair—high school students—who had wanted to know all about the ins and outs of sex with another man. When they'd left, Julian had laughed himself silly for a solid three minutes.

He wasn't quite sure if it was the only time he'd smiled genuinely all week. "It's not Roz, Mom. I'm just…tired. You know?"

"Does this have something to do with that man you were seeing?"

We could keep it secret for months, but the whole town knows the second it's over. With an inward wince, Julian turned and started going through the motions of making tea. "Jack. And yes. Or no. It's complicated."

His mother insinuated herself at his side, wrapping an arm around his waist. Julian let himself lean into her wiry frame, now shrinking with age, but still strong. She smelled the same as she always had, and her gray eyes were as kind as ever. "It's okay," she told him, patting his hip fondly. "I know *complicated* means you're not ready to talk about it. I won't push."

Julian wasn't even ready to *think* about it, but that didn't stop him from rehashing everything every waking moment and several of the sleeping ones. "Roz so takes after Dad."

That got him a smile. "That she does. I'm surprised he hasn't tried to blunt-force-trauma the truth out of you yet."

"I don't think he wants to know that badly."

"Honey, not even I want to know that badly, and no one needs to know more than I do. But at least you and Roz have each other." Sara Piet took the last clean dish out of his hands and stacked it in the cupboard. "Are you sure you'll be okay with just the two of you? Your father and I could stay another week."

Julian shook his head. "You'll get snowed in. We're expecting a big storm. Besides, Dad's arthritis is already driving him nuts. Don't think I didn't see him limping up the stairs last night. I see his physician upped his dosage again."

Not that he wanted to get rid of them. Far from it, in fact, especially now that he'd had a sharp, unnecessary reminder of how mortal parents were. He was never likely to forget the pain of losing his birth parents, but right now what he really wanted and needed was to be left alone for a few days.

"Your father will suffer in silence if he knows what's good for him. And I don't know why we sent you to med school. Honestly, all you do is criticize us for unclean living." She pinched his cheek and he rolled his eyes.

"I'm not exactly in a place to lecture anyone about *that*," he sighed, kicking out a chair from the kitchen table and slumping into it. "Sorry. That was supposed to sound ironic, not bitter."

"Julian, honey…. Are you sure you made the right decision? Staying away from him, I mean? You're obviously unhappy, and I can't help but think…."

He offered her a tight smile. "Jack made his feelings pretty clear, Mom."

She ruffled his hair affectionately. Julian tried not to remember all of the times Jack had done that, with the same lack of calculation. Julian was there, so Jack touched him. If only things could have stayed that simple. "If you say so," she conceded finally. "He obviously doesn't know what he's missing. Now, how about helping your dear mom pack? It'll be fun."

WHEN Roz had moped for nearly two weeks, working only the classes she couldn't pass off and heading to bed at no later than nine-thirty, Julian decided they both needed an intervention. He himself had spent a disproportionate amount of time these past days sitting in a corner booth alone at Brenda's (never on a Saturday night), drinking Jack Daniels very slowly or, if it was before serving hours, eating pie. Brenda hadn't asked him any questions, though she had known what was going on far longer than most if he was any judge. She did comment that last week, Jack's performance had included new lyrics to that song of his everyone seemed to know.

"A Really Stupid Kind of Love," Julian had supplied dully, and that had been that.

Now it was Friday night, at not quite eight o'clock, and Roz was looking like she wanted to flee back up the stairs and cocoon herself in her bedroom for another ten or twelve hours. This was pathetic, and unlike both of them, and Julian was going to put a stop to it the best way he knew how.

Okay. The first thing he was going to need was a strategy. "Do you want to go out?" was not going to work. It hadn't worked for the past week and he saw no reason for it to start now, and variations in the form of movie invitations and physical exercise had bombed. Similarly, "Get dressed," its close cousin, had been striking out. There was one fail-safe he hadn't tried yet, though, and he was banking on its success. "So," he said bravely, crossing his fingers behind his back, "me and this club in Calgary have a hot date. Wanna dress me?"

Roz's eyes didn't exactly light up in the way he had hoped for, but her smile at least seemed genuine. "Sure thing, Beanstalk. Getting back on the horse?"

"Not tonight," Julian rolled his eyes at her suggestive tone. "I just need to do something or I'll lose my head. You know? Not that I don't enjoy your company, but I'm not exactly used to sitting at home by myself anymore. Think of it as filling the void with dancing."

"That thing you do is more like dry humping with strobe lights," she said drily, "but I see your point. Now get upstairs and open your closet."

Breathing an inward sigh of relief, Julian complied. After two weeks of waiting with baited breath, finally there was a sign that Roz might someday be her old self again. His world had shaken but not crumbled around him. Glory hallelujah. Julian threw open his closet doors and presented arms.

"Reporting for duty, *sir*," he said sharply, saluting crisply as Roz entered the room after him.

"Smartass." She peered into his closet and immediately started pawing through his shirts, tossing some on the bed as she went. "Lieutenant Piet. Your mission, should you choose to accept it, is to—" Roz paused, a pair of pants in each hand. "What exactly is your mission? Are you picking up, or are you just teasing?"

Hey! What kind of guy did she think he was? "Roz!"

"Teasing," Roz answered for him, and tossed the leftmost pair back onto their hanger. "These," she said, holding them out. She glanced briefly through the pile of shirts on his bed, then retreated into his closet for a minute. "I know you have a red T-shirt in here somewhere," she grumbled, sifting through the folded shirts on the top shelf until she found the one she was looking for.

"Roz...." Julian looked down into the pile of clothes he was holding. Roz had bought the shirt for him almost a year ago. It was a size too small, which she said was how he should wear all of his shirts. As for the pants.... "I haven't worn these since my undergrad!"

"More's the pity," Roz sighed. "You still have Patrick's old biker boots in there somewhere, right?"

"Yeah, I think they're in the Rubbermaid container with the summer shoes." Julian watched in equal parts awe and horror as Roz fished out his old motorcycle jacket to complete the ensemble. Good grief, he was going to look like a tart. A really hot tart, but a tart nonetheless. If he'd ever gone out in public wearing that Jack would have—

Well. Never mind.

She brushed off her hands and looked down at her handiwork laid out on the bed, looking less preoccupied and more self-satisfied than he'd seen her in way too long. "Well. I think my work here is done."

In for a penny, in for a pound, Julian supposed. He could hardly say he was surprised. Steeling himself, he opened his mouth to insist she be his bodyguard if she insisted on dressing him like such a slut.

"Give me ten minutes," Roz said before he could bother. "There is no way I'm going to miss this. You're going to cause a *riot*."

She was down the hall before he even had a chance to be relieved, and back again before he'd managed to get his fly undone. *"Thank you,"* she said fiercely, her arms wrapped tight around him and her face in his neck. "Julian. *Thank you.*" He thought she might be crying.

Then she was gone again, and fifteen minutes later they were on their way to Calgary.

Chapter 16

JACK shifted the flowers to his left hand, unaccountably nervous. This was stupid. It was so, so stupid. He could do this. He shouldn't be nervous. His heart should not be pounding, his throat shouldn't be dry. He was strong, and he'd been through this all once before.

He knocked twice with his right hand, then pushed open the hospital door.

His mother was sitting up in bed, resting back on her pillows but otherwise looking as well as could be expected. The oxygen tubes running into her nose were reflecting the light at a funny angle, making it almost look like she had a sunny blonde mustache.

She was also in the middle of a conversation.

"Hi, Mom," Jack said, wishing he didn't sound like such a loser.

In the chair next to the bed, Julian flushed right up to his eyebrows and stood, stammering excuses. "I'm sorry, Flora. I'll have to talk to you later. I didn't mean…. I'll go."

Jack couldn't think of a single thing to say to him as he brushed by. The contact still sent a jolt of electric energy through his system, but seeing Julian again here—hell, at *all*—left a sour taste in his mouth and a lead butterfly in his stomach. It didn't help at all that Julian was walking stiffly, like he had sometimes after he and Jack had—well, anyway, Jack couldn't have said how he felt about that, other than sick. He closed the door once the doctor had left. "You never told me he'd been coming to see you."

"You never asked," his mother rasped at him. "Those flowers for me or for Julian?"

Jack flinched and set them on the table. "No. They're for you." He sat, awkwardly, in the chair Julian had just vacated. "I didn't mean for that to sound so snobby. I just didn't realize he was still your doctor."

"He's not," Flora said flatly. "He's visiting. He's good company."

"Oh." He folded his hands in his lap, unsure what to say.

"Jackson Strange," his mother finally snapped, her voice so like its old self he almost forgot where they were. "If you aren't the stubbornest man I have ever met I'll eat that shit they serve as gravy. That boy didn't do a blessed thing wrong except love you with everything he had and look how you thanked him! He is *suffering,* Jack!"

He hadn't looked like he was suffering to Jack's eyes. In fact he'd looked like he was getting along just fine, but he couldn't exactly say that Julian looked like he'd been well-laid very recently to his mother. "He kept secrets from me, Mom. He made me believe he'd never met you before. He lied! He lied to me about you. How am I supposed to trust him?"

"Oh, you know damn well he couldn't have told you a damned thing if he'd wanted to," Flora bit out. Her slow words and frequent pauses let on that Julian wasn't the only one who was suffering. It twisted Jack's guts to see it. "There's this little issue called doctor-patient confidentiality. It's kind of a legally binding agreement."

That was the crux of the matter, yes. Jack knew that, legally, Julian had effectively had his hands tied. That didn't excuse it, and it didn't stop Jack from hurting, and Julian hadn't even *tried* to defend himself. What was Jack supposed to think? The whole thing had obviously been a sham from the beginning. If only he hadn't gotten so involved in the first place, he could have saved himself a lot of hurt. "Why didn't *you* tell me?" he finally asked, changing the subject.

It was something he hadn't brought up until now, mostly because he was afraid of what the answer might be. His own mother hadn't told him she was dying. Was it because she was afraid he wouldn't come? Or because she was afraid he would?

"Jack, when your father died, you pulled away from us. From me, from your Uncle Pete, from your friends. I didn't want you to do it again. I could see you had friends, you had that Star Hamilton, and your Roy and his little girl." Her dry hand curled around his own. "I thought that if I just gave you enough time…you would find someone who wouldn't let you pull away."

Shit. It had been a setup from the beginning, and not the way he thought. "Mom…." he started, his throat suddenly close. There was moisture behind his eyes. "You would have been alone. At the end, you…you would have been alone."

"But you wouldn't have," she said gently.

Oh, God, he was such an ass. He had taken his mother's sacrifice and thrown it in her face when he'd gone off on Julian, and now it was far, far too late to take it back. "You asked him not to tell me."

"I had to beg him not to tell you," she countered. "Your Julian is a very persuasive young man. He said you had a right to know, a right to say goodbye, but I said you had a right to happiness, too."

Jack had never thought about how hard keeping that secret must have been for Julian. "He lost his parents unexpectedly," he said quietly. "When he was eight."

"Oh, Jack." When he could look at her, there were tears in Flora's eyes, too. "I should never have asked him that. He hardly even knew you then, but he knew you wouldn't take it well. I told him…what had happened with your dad, and he let it alone, but…it must have eaten at him."

Yeah, Jack reckoned it must have. How had he managed to walk around with a secret like that? He had never slipped up, never let on. He'd certainly seemed as happy with Jack as Jack had thought it was possible for anyone to be. It was frankly astounding. "Mom, what else did you tell him?"

She gave him an approximation of a sly smile. "I might have mentioned what else you started getting into at that age. When I see fertile soil, I plant a seed." For a second there he was afraid she was going to make a really terrible pun, but thankfully she refrained.

"Mom! You knew I was gay?!"

"Honey, I'm your mother." She raised her palm to cup his cheek, her breathing obviously labored. "I probably knew long before you did." She let the hand fall to the bedside.

He stared at her for a moment. "You never said anything."

"It wasn't for me to say," she reminded him gently. "Julian…. He liked you, even then. I could tell. He just needed a little…push."

"Divine intervention, huh?" He sighed. Flora ex machina. *"And I would have gotten away with it, too, if it weren't for those pesky kids."*

His mother laughed slightly, and even though he could hear the pain behind the sound, it was okay. "I love you, Mom."

"Oh, honey. I love you, too."

JACK'S eyes snapped open to the phone ringing and he blinked furiously a few times, only to realize it was dark. He'd taken to sleeping with the phone in his hand ever since his mom had been hospitalized. Groping for it one-handed, Jack struggled to sit up, heart pounding. The time on the alarm said 1:57. "Hello?"

"Something's wrong with Hallie."

Jack shook himself, looked at the phone, and kicked at the covers to free his feet. "Roy? Is that you?" He hadn't really spoken with Roy in close to a month, though he'd continued to pick Hallie up from her various after-school programs. Since their confrontation at the hospital, their friendship had been more than a little strained.

Or perhaps nonexistent would have been a more accurate word. Still, this wasn't the time for grudges.

"She's got a fever of a hundred and four," Roy said, sounding panicked. "She's been up since six this morning throwing up; she can't even keep water down. I don't know what to do."

"Calling an ambulance to take her to the hospital would be a good idea," Jack said, finally managing to stumble out of bed.

"Look out the window."

Jack yanked back the curtain and squinted into the night. Shit. It had been snowing steadily since before dinner, and there were at least eighteen inches of fresh-fallen snow accumulated on the ground. There was no chance the snow plows had cleared the road from here to the hospital already. "Can she walk?"

"She can't even sit up. Jack, I don't know what to do."

And Roy couldn't carry her, since he'd injured his back years ago. "Okay. I'm coming over. Get her things together and wrap her in a blanket. I'll be there as soon as I can."

Jack hung up the phone and threw it back on the bed, snagged a pair of sweatpants from the bottom drawer of the dresser and threw on a T-shirt. Yanking his cell phone from the charger, he dialed one-handed without looking while running down the stairs. He shrugged into his coat, shoved his bare feet into his boots and grabbed the keys to his truck, running outside into the driving snow.

"Hello?" came a sleepy voice on the other end of the line.

"Roz," Jack said, digging bare-handed through the back of his truck for his tire chains. Fuck, they had to be in here somewhere. "Don't hang up. It's Jack. I need you to wake up Julian."

"Are you insane?" she grumbled, voice hoarse with sleep. "I'm not waking him up so you can give him some lame-ass self-flagellating apology. He's barely slept for a month. Go to hell."

"It's a medical emergency," Jack said tightly, doing his best to ignore the sting of her words. "It's Hallie."

"I'll wake him," Roz said immediately, sounding much more alert. "Are you at your place or Roy's?"

"I'll be at Roy's when he gets here," Jack answered, finally clasping fingers around cold metal. He yanked until the tire chains came free. "Roz, tell him to hurry." He knelt in the snow, beginning the buckling process, and added belatedly, "But not too much."

The line went dead. Jack shoved the cell phone in his pocket and concentrated on the task at hand. Three minutes later, he was pulling into Roy's driveway. Jack threw the truck in park, but left it running, slogging through the snow to the kitchen door.

"Roy!"

"In here!"

Jack followed the sound of his voice into the living room and stopped in his tracks. Hallie was lying on the couch, skin gleaming with sweat, cheeks flushed. Roy was kneeling beside her on the floor, face pale. "Shit," Jack said, dropping down beside him. He touched her forehead for confirmation of the high fever. "Okay, talk to me."

"She's been like this since this morning. It's like every time she moves, she loses whatever she's been able to keep down. The fever didn't get bad until about twenty minutes ago. I don't know what to do."

"Get me some ice," Jack told him, going for the blanket. He peeled it off, noting that the little girl's pajamas were soaked with sweat. The top was riding up a little, and he thought there was some slight discoloration on the right side. "Shit." He touched his fingers to the area lightly and Hallie moaned and squirmed without opening her eyes. The skin felt too hot.

Jack flipped open his phone and dialed Julian's cell. He waited for the call to click through, but not long enough for Julian to offer a greeting. "I think it's appendicitis," he said. "You'd better hurry."

BY the time Julian got there, Jack had applied Roy to the task of the ice compress and taken to pacing the kitchen, waiting for Julian to show up. He finally ran inside, snowflakes clinging to his hair and eyelashes, dressed in a ratty T-shirt, pajama pants, and a lab coat and carrying his bag. Jack directed him to the living room and tried to stop freaking out unproductively.

The diagnosis only took Julian thirty seconds. Leaving Roy to look after his daughter, he met Jack in the kitchen. "I need to operate. If her appendix hasn't burst already, it won't be long. If I wait much longer, the septic shock might kill her." He looked Jack in the eye for the first time in a month. "Jack, even if I operate right now, she still might die."

Jack's blood went cold. "Okay," he said, hands shaking. He shoved them into his pockets. "What do you need me to do?"

"Call Dan," Julian said immediately. "Find out the nearest place I can do an appendectomy and get him to meet us there. I'm going to get Hallie in your truck."

Jack could do that. It was only when he didn't know what to do that he was paralyzed. Directions, that he could do. "Dr. Matheson? It's Jack Strange. I'm sorry to wake you, but it's an emergency." He paused. "It's Hallie Klein. Julian says her appendix is bursting and he needs to operate as soon as possible. He wants to know where…." Jack listened. "Where?!"

Julian popped his head back into the kitchen and gave him a look. "Okay," Jack said. "We'll meet you there."

He grabbed the ice scraper and brushed the newly accumulated snow from the windshield and jumped back in the cab. Roy was fidgeting compulsively in the passenger seat, and Julian was in the back with Hallie. Jack handed the phone to Julian and put the truck in reverse.

"Hi, Dan," he heard from the backseat as he started the window wipers on high. The snow was still falling thickly, and the roads were treacherous, even with tires. "Listen, I need you to pick up some things at the clinic for me before you meet us. I need four sets of adult scrubs and one child-size if you can find them, or a hospital gown, whatever. All of the sterilization equipment, iodine, gauze, a saline drip, the consent forms for emergency procedures, child-safe painkillers and sedatives, the soap. Are there gloves already there? Yeah, all right. We're also going to need…."

Jack found that it was easier to concentrate on driving if he tuned out the flow of medical jargon, so he did, turning on the fog lights to help him see where he was going. The high beams were useless, just reflecting too much of the falling snow to be of help.

"…And call the EMTs," Julian was finishing up as Jack pulled into the parking lot. "Tell them they need to be ready to go in an hour, and call that guy who does the plowing, redirect him on a priority route. Yeah. Bye."

Jack had barely parked the car before Julian was up and out of it. He seemed to have no trouble lifting the sick little girl in his arms, draping her so that her body was almost flat, with her legs hanging down and her head resting against his shoulder. "Get the door, Jack. Roy, get my stuff."

As it turned out, Jack didn't need to get the door. When they approached, the door to the police station swung open, and Jack ushered in his accomplices to the complete bewilderment of the officers on duty. "Hi, Ted," he greeted the senior officer. "Sorry to bother you, but we need to borrow the lab. It's sort of an emergency."

"The lab?" Ted repeated blankly. He was staring at the four of them as if he didn't know what to say. That was probably partially true, since none of the three men had been spotted together anywhere in the past month, and more or less everyone knew why. "The *coroner's* lab?"

"Nowhere else to do an emergency appendectomy," Julian told him. Apparently he already knew the way, because he was off heading toward the back somewhere without so much as a by-your-leave. "I need a sterile environment, and the clinic doesn't have what I need. Open this door, please."

Ted complied, eyes wide, looking about like Jack felt. "Will she be okay?"

If she's not, Jack thought, *neither will we.* "Let Dan know we're ready for him," he said instead, and hustled after the other two, hoping to God he'd be able to make himself useful.

When Dan arrived two minutes later, everything broke out into chaos. Jack was dispatched with Dan's keycard—Dan was currently acting coroner for the county—on a number of fetch-and-carry assignments while the two doctors disinfected, reorganized, and swabbed. He was just coming down the hallway with the last of the supplies when he saw Julian step sharply away from Roy as the older man slumped into Ted's waiting arms.

"What happened?"

Julian held up a syringe. "Sedated. Trust me; it was necessary."

Jack stuck out his arm. God, anything if it would end this nightmare. "While you're at it."

"Sorry. We're going to need you." Dan tossed him a bar of yellow soap and a plastic-wrapped set of scrubs. "Scrubs first, then wash to your elbows. Thoroughly. We'll meet you inside."

When Jack entered the room again—he was trying really hard to think of it as an operating room and not an autopsy lab—Hallie was on the table in a hospital gown that was pushed up to her rib cage. A sterile sheet covered her lower half, and there was an IV in her left hand. Julian and Dr. Matheson were almost unrecognizable in all of their gear, between skull caps, face masks, gloves, and scrubs.

Julian handed him a mask, a pair of latex gloves, and a cap to go over his hair. "Here's the rules. I tell you to do something. You do it when I tell you to. If you are going to throw up, you need to leave the room and wash again before you come back in. Clear?"

Jack nodded, hooking the straps to his mask over his ears.

"Stand at her head," Julian directed, taking his gloved hand and pointing his first two fingers. He put them on the pulse point in Hallie's neck, then set a tiny clock beside her ear. "We don't have any equipment here for live patients, so I need you to count the beats per minute and call them out to me. Make sure she keeps breathing. If she looks like she's waking up, you'll need to hold her down until Dan can administer some more sedative, because if she wakes up while I've got my fingers in there there's no telling what kind of damage we'll do."

No pressure or anything. Jack took a deep breath and held it for a few seconds, then nodded. The second hand on the little clock ticked past the twelve, and he started counting, watching Hallie's steady breathing and tuning out the other sights and sounds of the room. Ten, eleven, twelve. Tick, tick, tick. Twenty-six, twenty-seven.

"Jack."

He looked up, still counting, and met Dan's eyes. Julian was standing next to him, a scalpel in hand, white as a sheet, his gaze focused somewhere on the other side of the ad hoc operating table.

Dr. Matheson shrugged helplessly. "I've been trying to talk to him for thirty seconds. He hasn't responded. You have any idea what's going on?"

Shaking his head, Jack continued counting. "No clue. Want to take over for a minute? We're at eighty."

Dan pressed his fingers to Hallie's pulse, and Jack touched Julian on the arm, drawing him away from the table a few paces. "What's going on?" he said lowly, doing his best to ignore the slight current running between their bodies. This was so not the time. "Julian?"

His arm was shaking under Jack's fingertips. "I can't," he whispered, not looking at Jack.

"Bullshit." Jack's grip tightened. *What the hell is going on?* "You're a fucking surgeon. You've probably done this operation a hundred times. You talk the talk, now walk the walk."

Julian didn't respond.

"Damn it, Julian, a little girl is going to die if you can't pull yourself together and I *know* you don't want to live with that, so suck it up and save her fucking life!"

He blinked, the color returned to his cheeks, and he ducked his head further, but the shaking stopped. "Okay."

Julian returned to the table. Jack resumed his task keeping track of Hallie's vitals, and did his level best not to pay any attention to what the other two were doing. He watched her face so closely for signs that she might be waking that his eyes started to water, but he didn't let his gaze waver. Seventy-seven. Seventy-eight.

"Hand me those forceps," Jack heard Julian murmur to Dan. He tightened his free hand into a fist and glanced at the clock. *Keep counting.* Ninety-three. Ninety-four.

"She's waking up."

The words were out of Jack's mouth before he was even aware of what he was saying, but it was true; Hallie's eyelids were fluttering, and her brow was wrinkling in obvious discomfort. Jack swallowed, pressing his free hand to her forehead, smoothing her brow. The fever flush had faded from her cheeks, leaving her complexion ashy gray. Her lips parted, and a slight groan escaped her.

Julian called out a dosage of sedative and another for a painkiller, not even looking up from his task. Now that Jack was watching, he could hardly look away, as Julian's red-stained fingers worked quickly with a series of wicked-looking and unfamiliar tools to repair the girl's body. Jack's stomach gave an emphatic twist, and his mouth tasted like sea salt, but he ruthlessly quelled the urge to vomit and glanced at Dan instead. The older man was already finishing administering the necessary doses to Hallie's IV drip, and her eyelids were already drooping again, her pulse evening out and her breathing returning to normal.

Jack would have sagged in relief, if he'd had any indication that his work was nearing completion. With no medical training, it was impossible for him to tell how far along in the process Julian was, or how long it might take for him to conclude.

"I'm almost finished," Julian said an interminable amount of time later.

Jack blinked, so thrown that he missed his pulse count and had to start over. He must have zoned out watching Hallie's face after that near disaster when he'd accidentally started watching the surgeon in action instead. Ten, eleven, twelve. Julian asked Dan to hand him some instrument or another, then looked up and locked eyes with Jack. "Get on the cell phone," he said. "Get those EMTs in here as soon as you can."

JACK watched the EMTs load Hallie into the back of the ambulance with a fresh cup of coffee in his hand courtesy of one of the cops he hadn't had a chance to meet formally yet. Roy had come out of his sedation a few minutes ago angrier than a bag full of wet cats, but conveniently, no one was talking and from what Jack had picked up of his actions while Jack had been busy making himself useful, Julian and Ted had made the right call.

Julian hopped into the ambulance in Roy's place, the door slamming behind him, and the look on Roy's face broke through the numbness Jack was feeling. "He's her doctor," Jack pointed out quietly. "If something happens on the way to the hospital, he can handle it. You can't."

"If she dies in there...."

Yeah, that was the exception. Jack sighed. "Come on; get in the truck. I'll drive you to the hospital. Julian will call if anything…."

He stopped, realizing what he was saying. God, would this day, night, morning—all right, how about the whole damn *winter*—never end? "Let's go."

It was still snowing out, and the sky was starting to lighten from midnight black to a heavy velvet blue. The roads were slick, but at least this one had been plowed in the past hour; considering how treacherous the asphalt had been a few hours earlier, Jack counted them lucky. The cab of the truck was eerily silent as they followed the ambulance, lights spinning off the snowflakes. Jack figured the weather was messing with the radio reception, and he knew better than to try to talk to Roy. He followed the ambulance into the darkness with his fingers crossed, wondering if what he was feeling was despair or hope.

Chapter 17

JULIAN splashed warm water on his face until the crusts in the corners of his eyes dissolved, then toweled off his face and sank down onto the bench in the locker room.

"You look like you just pulled a triple," one of the doctors commented, and he groaned.

"I *feel* like I just pulled a triple," Julian admitted. "I'm way too old to be doing this shit," he sighed, then quirked the corner of his mouth up involuntarily. The man in the yellow scrubs couldn't have been much younger than he was. "Out of practice."

"Aren't you the guy that did that emergency appendectomy in the coroner's lab?" The doctor shucked his scrubs and reached for a worn-looking set of sweats. "That must have been pretty intense. The kid okay?"

"God, I forgot how gossip gets around in a place like this." It was a good thing there was nothing for him to lean on; if there had been, Julian would have been asleep in no time. "That was me. I never want to do it again. And there weren't any complications, aside from the fact that she should have had surgery at about four o'clock this afternoon, *before* the appendix ruptured. But there's always infection."

The other doctor sat down across from him, slumping like he'd just pulled a thirty-six-hour shift himself. "I know what you mean. I remember when my kid brother's appendix burst when I was in first-year university. He was in the hospital for a month with infections; looked like he'd lived through the Holocaust."

Julian winced. Ouch. Talk about worst-case scenarios. "Heavy."

Like his limbs. How the hell was he going to get home to bed, Julian wondered? He supposed he could commandeer something to sleep in for a few hours and see if one of the nurses in the area was getting off-shift.

"Speaking of gossip…."

Oh, boy. Talk about kicking a man when he's down. Julian blinked slowly, cautiously. "Yeah?"

The other doctor shrugged apologetically. "I know it's not really any of my business, but you are the same guy, right? You had a, um, oh fuck it, you were seeing that engineer with the crazy hair? You had a giant fight up on the fifth floor a few weeks back?"

"Guilty as charged," he admitted tonelessly. At least the guy wasn't being a jerk about it.

"You guys still together?"

The question took Julian by surprise, so much so that he actually sat up straight. There was no way this doctor—Keegan, he thought he'd seen on his lab coat before he'd hung it up—was making a pass at him, now of all times? "After that?" he raised his eyebrows. "Come on; didn't the grapevine get all the details? I knew his mom was dying and couldn't tell him."

"Right," Keegan hedged. "Just—you know—curious, I guess."

Okay, so maybe his motives hadn't been selfish. He seemed to be withholding something. "Why?" Julian drew the word out, too tired to just let it be.

The other man shrugged. "Because he's sitting in the waiting room two levels down with the kid's dad, drinking coffee like he's anticipating a shortage."

The idea warmed Julian from the inside immediately, filling him with a drowsy kind of hope, but he forced it down viciously. "He's probably just waiting to hear about Hallie," he sighed. "They're close."

Keegan looked skeptical. "Whatever you say, man. He looks like he's got a lot on his mind."

"That, I can believe." Slowly, Julian stood, scrubbed a hand through his hair, then belatedly realized he'd been rude. "Sorry. I should've introduced myself as something other than the sum of the last couple of weeks. Julian Piet."

"James Keegan," the other man greeted. "Nice to formally meet you, Julian. However, if you don't mind, I stink and I'm running on caffeine, so I'm going to head home and crash hard."

Julian smiled. "I remember what those days were like. Thanks for the chat. I'll see you around." He watched Keegan go with a faraway look in his eyes, then shook himself and headed for the door. Time to face the music.

"Hi, guys," Julian half-yawned, stepping out from behind the out-of-bounds doors and smiling wanly at Roy and Jack as they attempted to struggle to some sort of attention. "Sit. Hallie came through the surgery okay."

He waited until they had deflated back into their chairs before continuing. "She's going to need to be in the hospital a while. Her appendix had already ruptured by the time she was in surgery, and there will probably be complications; E. coli or strep or maybe both. Anyway, she could be here for a few weeks, so if you've got some vacation time, Roy, now would be a good time."

"We were going to go to Disney World," Roy said ruefully, sounding a little choked up. Then again, Julian's overtired brain could have made that up. "Thanks, man. You didn't have to come running and step up the way you did. I owe you an apology."

Julian waved him off. "That's my job. It's Jack you owe the apology to, and I'm guessing with everything that's happened tonight, he's probably forgiven you by now. Hallie's in room 1158 in the children's ward; the nurse at the department desk will get you a cot so you can stay. I'm sure she'll want to see you when she wakes up, but it might be a while yet."

He barely registered Roy's handshake and heartfelt gratitude before he was swaying on his feet as the older man walked away. Suddenly Jack was by his side, one arm around his shoulders. "Easy, Doc. You've had a long day. Let's get you home, yeah?"

Oh, thank God, Julian thought. Home. "Yeah," he agreed readily. "Lead the way."

He didn't remember getting into the truck, or falling asleep, or the drive home. He barely even remembered waking up. All he knew was that they were somehow—miraculously—now parked in front of the house, and Jack was getting out. The sun was out, which felt wrong, glaring unforgivingly across the fresh, crisp snow. "Come on," Jack said, opening his door. "You look like you need to sleep for about a year."

That didn't sound like such a bad plan, actually. Julian slid out of the cab and allowed himself to be led into the house. Jack made him sit on the couch so that he could bend to undo his boots, and Julian watched him impassively as he did so, willing himself not to fall asleep here. Then Jack herded him up the stairs into the bedroom and stripped him out of the grungy scrubs, turned back the covers and helped him slide in. Julian heard him closing the heavy curtains and sighed, inhaling a noseful of Jack-scented pillow.

The next second he was fast asleep.

JULIAN shifted, rubbing his face against the pillowcase, sighing and straining to hold on to the last vestiges of sleep. His eyelids fluttered, and he grumbled, turning to lie on his back.

He frowned. The mattress was…wrong. Reluctantly, he opened his eyes.

"Rise and shine."

Jack? God, had he gotten *drunk* after surgery? He sat up, slowly. That explained why the bed felt wrong. It had been over a month since he'd slept in it last. "Uh…hi." He ran a hand through his hair, got it stuck, winced, and disentangled it again. "Did I skip a few chapters or something?" He remembered the surgery, and the ambulance ride to the hospital. He knew he must have gone out into the reception area to talk to Roy. But after that….

"You feeling any better?" Jack asked from the doorway. He was wearing a pair of raggedy sweatpants Julian knew well and not much else, and holding a glass of orange juice.

"Uh," Julian stuttered. His body was just itching to get right back into its old habits, but he wasn't going back there without a fight. Or some convincing encouragement. "Aside from the memory loss? Yeah."

Jack passed him the orange juice and sat next to him on the bed. It should have been awkward, but somehow wasn't. "No memory loss. I'm pretty sure you were asleep on your feet."

Julian took a sip, then set the glass on the bedside table. "How did I get here? I mean, obviously—" he waved his hand around a little, aware that it hadn't been exactly the question he'd meant to ask. "*Why* am I here?"

"Meaning of life? That's a little beyond the scope of this conversation." He looked a little uncomfortable. "I…. It was late, and I didn't want to drive you home."

They both deflated; then Jack went on: "And I wanted a chance to apologize."

Julian froze. "For?"

"I blamed Mom's cancer on you. That wasn't fair of me; I know that you couldn't have told me if she asked you not to."

"Thanks." He picked up the orange juice again, wrapping his fingers around it for something to do. All of a sudden he had the fierce desire to go back to bed and sleep until he forgot about the past, oh, several months. "For the record, I hated having to do it."

"She might have mentioned that."

Julian's lip twitched. Knowing Flo, she'd probably mentioned it until Jack was sick of the subject. She certainly had a knack for bringing up the tough conversations again, and again, and again. "I can imagine." Finally he stood up, swaying a little as his blood pressure evened out. "I should probably call Roz."

He reached down for his scrubs, looking for his cell phone, and wondered exactly what had happened to them that they had ended up on the floor. The phone was in the breast pocket of the scrub top.

"Umm…."

Julian looked up.

"I might have called her last night. That is, this morning."

He raised his eyebrows. Jack's ears turned pink.

"What? I thought she should know Hallie's operation went okay."

Julian kept staring. Jack took that as a cue to keep talking. "I sort of, um, indicated that you wouldn't be going home. And I left a message for Dan that you weren't going in to work."

A reluctant smile tugged at the edge of Julian's mouth as he glanced at the clock. It was quarter past four in the afternoon. "Good call. I hope you called in sick yourself."

"Oh, yeah." He grinned, though it looked a little anemic to Julian's practiced eye. The grin faded under his scrutiny, and Jack's good cheer subsided as well. "Julian, what happened to you?"

Julian flinched. *Gee, I don't know; my boyfriend told me he loved me and broke up with me in the same day?* "What do you mean?"

"At the coroner's office, when you were taking out Hallie's appendix. You just…stopped, like you were somewhere else. You were looking right through her."

Oh, you mean the time I had to do an emergency operation on a little girl on an autopsy table? Because that won't screw with your head at all. "I *was* somewhere else," Julian sighed, throwing his scrubs back onto the floor and slumping back onto the bed again. "Some*when* else."

"You sure as hell weren't in the here-and-now." The words were flippant, but the tone was inoffensive.

Julian figured he might as well tell Jack the truth. If nothing else, it was high time he told *someone*. "When I was in my first year of residency, I fell in love with the first-year supervisor. Richard Warren. He was older—*much* older," Julian amended at Jack's obvious bristling. "We had an affair, which we kept quiet for the obvious reasons. But when the year was up, and he wasn't my supervisor anymore, I wanted to stop hiding." He shrugged. "Richard wasn't ready. He said it would affect his job, his family, his friends. He told me that if he was important enough to me, I'd understand. I didn't, or he wasn't, so I broke it off."

Yeah, okay, that explained exactly nothing. Time to relate the second half of the story. "Then, when I was starting my sixth-year residency, I was performing a surgery on a little girl about Hallie's age, just a routine appendectomy. Hers flared up from time to time; it happens. Everything went fine, until I was closing. All of a sudden, her heart flat-lined. We did everything we could to revive her, but she died on the table. We didn't find out until the autopsy that she'd had a congenital heart defect."

Scrubbing his face with both hands, Julian soldiered on. "I was pretty wrecked, as you can imagine. I mean, patients had died before, but always when we'd known there was a risk, and I'd never lost a child. They sent me home to my boyfriend because I wasn't in any state to be dealing with patients." He felt his mouth turn down at the corners, the way it would if he were going to be sick. "I went straight to Derek's and let myself in. Grabbed a beer from the fridge before I even started to look for him. I'm surprised I didn't throw it at him when I found him in bed with Richard."

Jack's eyebrows disappeared into his hairline. "Richard your ex?"

"The very same," Julian confirmed. He paused. Well, might as well have it all out in the open. "It gets worse."

"I doubt it."

Julian rolled his eyes. "Ye of little faith. They announced their *engagement* a week later. Derek was only a second-year resident."

Jack whistled. "Ho-ly shit. That is worse. Derek was under his supervision the year before?"

"You got it." Julian still didn't know how he'd missed the signs. "Last year was not a good Christmas."

There were a few moments of awkward silence, and then Jack's hand settled onto his knee. Eventually, he asked, in a voice that sounded artificially light, "So what did you do?"

"Called Roz," he answered, as though it were the obvious answer. It was, of course; there was no one else he trusted as much, and Roz had been close enough. And perceptive enough; thank God for that. "She was in London finishing up her degree. I must have really freaked her out. I was drunk when I called, and I think she thought I was going to do something stupid." Julian exhaled slowly. "She showed up two and a half hours later with a speeding ticket and a suitcase and stayed with me for almost two weeks, just watching *Baywatch* reruns on the couch." He smiled a little, secure in the knowledge that his "big sister" Roz loved him very much. "She missed two final exams and had to go back for a semester."

Jack's fingers tightened just perceptibly. "You guys are good for each other," he said, staring straight ahead. Then: "Would you have?"

Blinking, Julian turned to him and gently removed the hand from his leg. There were enough emotions being thrown around right now. They didn't need that, too. "Would I have what?"

The rejected hand and its counterpart twisted furiously in Jack's lap. "Done something…stupid."

Something permanent. Damaging. Had Julian considered it? Certainly. Had he been out of his faculties at the time? Oh, yeah. "I don't know," he said honestly. "I was so sauced that I probably wouldn't have even managed it properly. But I try not to think about it."

"Think I'll take a leaf out of your book," Jack said shakily. His face was devoid of all color, and Julian finally noticed the dark circles under his eyes. "While we're on the subject." He stopped, ran a hand over his face and leaned forward on his elbows.

"The subject?" Julian asked, hesitant. He wasn't sure he was going to like where this was going.

"Ex-lovers. Of a sort." Jack sighed. "I've never done this before, Julian. I'm not good at it. The closest thing I've ever had to a relationship is the ongoing affair I had with my college roommate, and that didn't exactly go well. I never understood what went wrong until years later when a mutual friend pointed out that he'd been in love with me. I'm not *good* with feelings."

God, if they were going to go with full disclosure…. Julian closed his eyes. "On my eighteenth birthday I met someone," he hedged, swallowing. This story was never easy to tell. "Long before I ever met Richard or Derek. We fell in love. It was…easy." He took a breath. "For me. I thought it was the same for him, and I know he loved me, but he wasn't ready." Overhearing that particular conversation was one of the worst ordeals Julian had gone through in his life, and as a surgeon, that was saying something. "I knew he wasn't ready, so I left. But since then—with Richard, with Derek—I was just biding my time. I always thought that one day, everything would fall into place, that he'd be ready to try again."

Now for the hard part. Jack was looking at his hands. Julian swallowed, his tongue thick. Letting go of that fantasy had hurt him deeper than he had realized. Apparently he'd been too busy falling in love with Jack to notice. "I haven't even thought about him for months."

Jack looked up sharply, the sudden light of hope in his eyes. Julian's stomach clenched. "Listen, I have to ask you something else."

"What is it?"

"Is there a chance…. I mean, do you still…. Do you think…." After several false starts, Jack flopped backward onto the bed in apparent frustration.

Part amused, part anxious, Julian wiggled over so they could look each other in the eye again. "Take two?" he suggested.

Jack's eyes softened, and Julian breathed in sharply. "Exactly," Jack said. "That's it exactly. Can we, I mean, if there's no one else…can we take it from the top?"

Julian let the relief and joy wash through him, but kept his face as much of a mask as he could manage. After all, it wouldn't do to let Jack off the hook *too* easily. He might be tempted to try the same thing again. Better to make him sweat a little. "Exactly how many gay men do you think there are in this part of Alberta?" he asked, a wry smile tugging at the corner of his lips.

"Was that a yes?"

"There was doubt?" He settled down onto the bed facing Jack. "It was a yes," he affirmed, warmth spreading out from his chest, making his fingers and toes tingle. "Just in case that wasn't clear. A resounding yes. And now, I think you'd better kiss me to seal the deal."

"I think that can be arranged." Jack's arm reached out to grip Julian around the waist, hauling him closer on the bed. Their bodies lined up perfectly just like they always had, and then Jack's stubbly lips rasped over Julian's, warm and moist and inviting. He lost himself in the kiss, reveling in sensations and emotions that he hadn't allowed himself to feel in far too long. Languishing in Jack's touch, he let his lover take the lead, stretching his body from his fingers to his toes, maximizing the amount of surface area Jack could possibly touch. Jack's fingers teased under the hem of his T-shirt, and Julian sat up, arms above his head so Jack could take it off of him.

A warm, flat hand pressed against the center of his chest and pushed him firmly back against the mattress again; then Jack's face appeared in his field of vision. "What's this?" he asked, gaze unfathomable as he traced a pattern on Julian's abdomen.

The corner of Julian's mouth twitched upward. That tickled. "What's it look like?"

Jack bent his head to lick around the tattoo on the right side of Julian's abdomen—located just above his appendix, in fact. "A caduceus," he said around a smirk. "When did you get this?"

"The day before I saw you at the hospital," Julian gasped, toes curling as Jack bit lightly into his hip bone.

"So that's why you were walking funny. I thought you'd found someone to make you forget me."

Julian's answering snort of laughter was cut off prematurely when Jack wrapped a fist around his boxers and tugged them down sharply. "Never," he denied, and was rewarded when Jack covered his mouth with an exuberant kiss. He'd just been trying to keep from rubbing anything—including his own clothing—against the bandage. Next time Roz got him drunk he was going to make sure he was supervised by a responsible adult. He glanced down when Jack broke the kiss to find him staring at the small black tattoo. "Are you developing a fixation or something? Get on with it."

"Smartass."

"You are still wearing *clothes*," Julian pointed out, in a tone of voice that brooked no speculation as to what a nuisance he thought that was. "When you're naked we'll talk."

Jack made a face at him, but pulled back long enough to strip nonetheless. When Julian yanked him down to the mattress by the arm and commenced molesting him, he murmured, "Thought you said we were going to talk?"

"Body language," Julian said succinctly, and suited action to words by twisting both of his hands in Jack's hair and pulling their heads together for another wet kiss.

Jack hummed his agreement, working nimble fingers down Julian's body, circling around his nipples until they hardened at the sensation. Nipping Jack's lower lip in encouragement, Julian let his right leg fall further to the side, inviting one of Jack's to settle between his own.

"What's that mean?" Jack wondered, sliding his lips from Julian's and trailing them across his cheek, up his jawbone to his ear. Sparks jumped along Julian's nervous system, gathering in a pool of lust low in his belly.

"You want a translation?" Julian hissed appreciatively as Jack's teeth worried a patch of skin at his neck and dragged his nails down Jack's back in return. "Human-to-Jack just happens to be my specialty."

"And it means?"

"Loosely translated," he told him as Jack's leg rubbed gently at his swelling erection, "it means 'take advantage of me now, please.'"

"Which part was the please?" Jack asked, faux-curious. He bit down hard on Julian's nipple.

Julian arched his back and rubbed his hard cock firmly against Jack's hip, leaving a sticky trail of pre-come. "That part."

"Oh, well, as long as we're being polite." Jack reached down one-handed and gripped Julian's shaft lightly, teasing. "God. Do you have any idea the things I want to do to that tattoo?"

"I think I can probably imagine—" Julian started, then stopped, swallowed, and looked down. Jack was rubbing the head of his dick along the darkened skin, slick, warm fluid pooling there as it had on Jack's hip. "Or maybe I have no idea," he amended roughly.

"Can you translate that?" Jack asked, voice low.

Julian shook his head wordlessly.

"'You're shit hot,'" Jack growled, reaching left-handed for the drawer in the night stand, "'and I can't wait to be buried inside you.'"

"For someone who can't wait," Julian complained, "you sure are taking your oh, *God*." It looked like Jack was going to make him eat his words, possibly literally. He scissored two fingers in Julian's ass, stretching him open.

"You were saying?"

Julian spread his legs, planted his feet on the bed, and reached for his own prick, joining his hand with Jack's. "You don't need me to translate this, do you?"

"Nah." Jack bit and sucked until there was a purple mark on Julian's chest, throbbing in time with the pulse in his groin. "That one's universal." He shifted just slightly, removed his fingers with a soft, sucking sound, and replaced them with the head of his cock, pressing inexorably forward.

Julian groaned as Jack breached him, lifting one leg to wrap around Jack's hip, needing to feel him as deep as humanly possible. Jack locked his hands around Julian's hips, stilling his body, and rolled his own a few times, cock brushing against Julian's prostate until he thought he'd burst. Panting, Julian reached out an arm and tugged Jack down for a sloppy kiss, licking across his cheek to his ear. "Jack. This is makeup sex. Fuck me now; you can make love to me later."

"Slut," Jack said fondly, snapping his hips.

Oh, yeah. Sparks shot all the way up Julian's central nervous system and his brain started to short-circuit. He moaned, pulling Jack forward with his legs. "Again."

Jack complied readily, thrusting steadily now, nailing Julian's prostate with every stroke. Julian bit his lip hard enough to draw blood, body thrumming with pleasure. He knew it couldn't last when it was like this between them, all grunts and shudders and startled exclamations. Already he could feel himself tipping toward oblivion.

"God, Jack—"

Jack planted a hand flat on his belly, thrusts coming faster and deeper.

"Let go," Jack demanded quietly, leaning his rough, stubbled cheek against Julian's. "I want to feel it." He licked from his neck up to his ear, latching his teeth onto the soft, tender lobe.

"Yessss," Julian hissed. His body tightened impossibly and convulsed, hot, white semen shooting over his stomach, splattering the caduceus tattoo and the back of Jack's hand.

Jack shuddered, then ran his fingers through the spilled seed. Julian held his gaze until he felt the rush of hot seed inside of him, then let his eyes fall closed as Jack kissed him, oddly sweet in contrast to the rough pleasure of a few moments before.

"I love you," Jack murmured softly, sliding their bodies apart.

Smiling into the curve of his neck, Julian pressed a small kiss there. "You're kidding."

"Nope," Jack said cheerily, wrapping Julian in a sticky embrace. "True story. Scout's honor."

"Good." Too tired to protest that they both really needed a shower, Julian laid his head on Jack's shoulder. He felt so happy that he was tempted to get up and turn the lights out just to see if he glowed. "I love you, too. Do me a favor and don't forget this time."

Jack snuffled laughter into the pillow, and conversation stopped as they both lapsed into post-coital semi-consciousness.

Sometime later, Julian was awoken by a muffled sound. "Something's ringing," he murmured into the pillow.

Across his back, Jack's arm barely twitched. "Nah," he said. "You're just experiencing hallucinations due to lack of blood flow to the brain."

"Am I hallucinating the vibrating, too?" he asked lethargically, rolling onto his side. A quick search with the hand he wasn't currently laying on revealed the cordless from the kitchen. "Here."

"Oh. The phone." Jack reached out and took it from him without looking. It was a clumsy affair.

"Who's experiencing lack of blood flow now?" Julian grumbled. He let the haze of pseudo-sleep wash over him again.

"Hello."

Then Jack sat up. The blanket pulled away from Julian's skin, and he shivered.

"I'm Jack."

Julian's brain registered a note of panic creeping into his lover's voice and he swiped a hand over his eyes, wiping away the last traces of fatigue. He sat up, too, goose bumps rising on his arms and chest.

"When?"

Jack's eyes had gone hollow, and his hand was trembling slightly around the phone. The bottom dropped out of Julian's stomach.

"Yes. I'll be there as soon as I can."

Fuck, Julian thought. *Out of the frying pan.*

"Thank you."

Jack hung up. The phone dropped to the mattress.

Julian curled his fingers around Jack's.

"It's Mom," Jack said, but Julian already knew. "She's dead."

Epilogue

JACK was sitting on the chair in the corner when Julian came in with takeout, closing the door quietly behind him. "Hey."

Jack nodded in response, picking at the quilt on his lap. It had grayed with age, but it still bore traces of the vibrant reds and blues his mother had loved when she'd had it on her bed twenty years ago. After his father had died, she couldn't bear the memories, and she had put it away at her brother's house in Inverness.

"You hungry?"

The scent of warm cardboard filled the air. Jack's stomach turned, rather than rumbling. He wanted—needed—to be alone, but didn't know how to ask for it. Julian had taken him all this way, held his hand through the worst week of his life, two memorial services, choosing an urn before her cremation, and the scattering of his mother's ashes in the Atlantic.

"Jack?"

He blinked. "Sorry. I'm not very hungry."

Julian put down the cardboard container he'd been holding and sighed, running his fingers through his hair. A stab of longing hit Jack low in the belly and he winced, barely resisting the urge to draw his knees up under the blanket. Then Julian turned around, reaching back into the bag of Chinese food, addressing the wall. "Jack, you haven't eaten anything all day. You've got to eat something."

"Stop treating me like a patient."

A pair of chopsticks clattered to the hotel table. Julian faced him again, expression empty, bleak. "Stop acting like I'm your doctor!" Julian fired back.

The words stung Jack across the heart, cutting deeply. Jack broke eye contact before the tears could start to burn behind his eyes.

"Sorry." The apology was almost too immediate to be genuine, but Jack didn't dare look at his lover again yet. "Sorry, Jack. I'm just—try to understand; I'm not trying to be your doctor; I'm trying to do what I can for you as someone who cares for you. Of course I want you to eat, to sleep, to be healthy. I'm *not* your physician."

Jack blinked furiously, swallowed hard, and tried to let go of the hurt. "I know." He did know. Most of the time. But sometimes, on his bad days, in his less charitable moments, he wondered whether Julian was only drawn to him because he saw in Jack a chance to fix his own troubled past. Still, he hadn't meant to play the part so well. "I lean on you too much. I'm sorry."

"That's not it at all." Julian slumped down into the chair opposite him with what was obviously a frustrated sigh. "It's just the opposite. Jack, you have to *let* me help you; you have to let me be there for you— but you have to stop looking at me like I have the answers just because I've seen so much death. Yes, I have seen it, Jack. I've held its hand and closed its eyes and called the time, but I can't tell you anything but the hard facts as I know them, and they are no comfort. There aren't any answers. Not about this."

"I miss her." The words sounded hollow and simple and inelegant after Julian's blunt chastisement.

Still, Julian managed a wan smile. "You will. You will miss her every day for the rest of your life. That's how you know she's still with you."

"Sometimes I think you only stuck around because you don't think I can stand on my own," Jack said absently before he could stop himself. As soon as the words were out of his mouth, he wished he could take them back. God, how needy did that sound?

A month ago, two months ago, it wouldn't even have occurred to him. But with what he had thought of at the time as Julian's betrayal, and then his mother's death hard on its heels, his sense of self, of normalcy, of *reality* even, was shaken and skewed. It was a terrible kind of weightlessness; he barely knew which way was up.

Jack didn't know if he could stand on his own, either.

With a deep breath, Jack raised his head. Julian's posture was quiet and still, but his face gave everything away. His mouth was set and his eyes were sad, so sad, but not with guilt or pity. Inhaling sharply, Jack knew what he saw there was pain—real, intense pain, that Jack had put there himself.

Wordlessly, Julian rose from the straight-backed chair. For a terrifying moment Jack was convinced he was going to walk out, for good this time. But he didn't. Instead, he just moved slowly over until he stood by Jack's chair. He reached out and wrapped his hands around Jack's head and pulled it firmly but gently to his chest, so that his ear was pressed flat against the soft cotton of Julian's shirt. "Do you hear that?"

Jack's throat closed. The steady, solid *thum-thump* of Julian's heartbeat echoed through his whole body. Unable to speak, he simply nodded.

Julian pulled his head away, but didn't remove his hands, instead forcing Jack to meet his eyes. "Do you understand? I love you, Jack, and I know you love me, but this relationship won't survive on love alone. You need to trust me."

"It's not you I don't trust," Jack sighed. He rubbed the back of his neck with one hand and tried to resist the urge to bang his head repeatedly off the table. "It's me."

"Jack, we're guys. We are inherently bad at relationships. And with two guys in a relationship, fucking up is a given."

He blinked, then looked over at Julian again. That shouldn't have made him feel better, but it did. "You know, you may have a point there. Not that it makes me feel any better, but a point nonetheless."

"Luckily," Julian put in with a smirk, "we are both very stubborn. Also, I hasten to point out there are advantages to this whole gay love thing."

Jack didn't bother resisting the urge to grin back. Julian had just segued seamlessly from an important and very serious relationship talk straight into sexual innuendo. Jack knew there was a reason he loved him. "Oh, really?" he laughed.

"What?" his partner said innocently. "You need a demonstration?"

Need? No. Want? Definitely. "Maybe I do."

Julian's eyes took on a wicked gleam, and he stepped back, away from Jack, leaving him lots of space. "That trust thing," he said casually, hands in his pockets, the hint of a smile on his lips. "You feel up to proving it?"

Jesus. The idea alone had Jack hard already, cock swelling in his jeans. "What did you have in mind?"

As if he'd refuse anything Julian asked of him right now. Or, well, ever.

"That's where the trust part comes in," Julian answered with a leer.

Jack swallowed hard, then stood up, taking a step toward him, but Julian just gave him a coy look and took another step back, pulling the hem of his shirt over his head. Jack got the message and stopped, waiting for Julian to come to him.

He didn't.

"Take off your clothes."

Shit. How had it never occurred to him how hot it would be to let Julian make all the calls for once? Jack doffed his sweatshirt quickly, wanting to make it to his jeans before his raging erection split them open.

Julian amended, "Slowly."

God, this was pushing hot buttons Jack hadn't known he'd even had. He took a deep, calming breath and slowly tugged off his T-shirt, the combination of the cold air and Julian's appreciative gaze causing his nipples to harden. He bent to pull off his socks, then popped the button on his jeans.

Julian was watching him carefully, velvet eyes dark with desire. His right hand was rubbing in slow circles over the bulge in his own pants.

The sight set Jack's pulse racing, lust zinging through his veins. Without breaking eye contact, Jack drew down the zipper, exposing himself to his lover's hungry gaze.

"No boxers?" Julian asked, not quite managing to hide the rasp in his teasing tone. "And you call me a slut."

"Are you complaining?" Jack stepped out of the jeans, wrapping his right hand around his cock. If Julian wanted a show, a show he would get. He played with the moisture pooling at the head, drawing it down his length, torn between squeezing his eyes shut in pleasure and watching Julian watch him.

"Complaining is the wrong word," Julian agreed. He motioned toward the hotel bed. "Lay on your stomach."

A thrill went down Jack's spine as he complied. He could feel Julian's gaze hot on his skin; the younger man hadn't even blinked. The comforter was rough against his sensitive flesh, providing just the right friction, just a little abrasive. He felt Julian settle astride his knees.

"Don't fall asleep."

Jack snorted, but it turned into a moan as Julian's warm hands dug into the flesh of his back, kneading and soothing. "As if."

Heat spread everywhere, radiating from Julian's jeans-clad thighs up Jack's legs, down from his strong, nimble fingers. The hairs on the back of Jack's neck stood up and took notice; sensation pooled in his balls and he squirmed a little against the bed, seeking relief for his aching prick.

Julian leaned down and bit his shoulder. Jack's cock twitched in reaction where it was pressed up against his belly. Julian's bare chest was flat against his back, and the thin trail of dark hair that led down from his navel tickled. His legs settled parallel to Jack's so that Jack could feel the entire warm weight of him, solid and not to mention *hard,* from his knees to his shoulders.

In the past couple of months, Julian had been pushing the unstated boundaries of their relationship—specifically, that Jack was a top, period. It was never obvious, and it had never bothered Jack; in fact, it was pretty hot that Julian reacted to him that way. Still, Julian had always backed off or been interrupted before they could talk about it.

Jack wasn't about to interrupt him now. Since he was getting into the habit of being honest with himself, he had to admit that he'd come to crave the feel of Julian's thick cock spreading him open, sliding deep inside of him. It looked like tonight he might finally get it.

It had been ages since Jack had been comfortable enough with another man—or himself—to allow anyone to get that close to him, never mind to actively solicit it. He planned to make the most of it. He wiggled his ass in what he hoped was an enticing fashion.

Julian muffled a snort of laughter in his neck. That tickled, too, in the way that sent an electric current straight to Jack's groin. "I guess that answers that question."

"Get on with it," Jack said helpfully. He wiggled again and was rewarded when Julian thrust his cock against him instinctively.

"You're such a romantic," Julian murmured, mouthing Jack's earlobe. The rush of wet heat that suffused Jack's brain left him completely paralyzed with lust even as Julian eased off of him, kneeling up between Jack's thighs as he drew sloppy moist kisses down the skin of his back. His hands traced soothing patterns on Jack's sides, then moved lower to rest on the globes of his ass.

Jack tried and failed to hold back a groan. "What can I say," he panted, as Julian's tongue painted pleasure down his tailbone, "you bring out the best in me."

Julian didn't even attempt a rebuttal. At least, not the verbal kind. He kept up his steady southward track, gently prying apart the cheeks of Jack's ass and fluttering wet licks down the middle.

Then the hot muscle first brushed across Jack's hole, and his whole body bucked so uncontrollably that Julian had to shift his legs in order to hold him down. *Fuck,* it had been a long time since anyone had touched him like this, and it was good—*too* good. Breathing hard, Jack squirmed, and let Julian draw him up onto his hands and knees. The cool air on his prick didn't ground him any; if anything he hardened further, a drop of moisture leaking from the head. Julian curled his right hand tightly around the base of Jack's shaft, hard enough to take the edge off.

Jack curled his fingers into the comforter, bracing his body for the onslaught of pleasure. Just a touch of Julian's tongue made his head spin so fast he needed something to hold on to, the world bucking and shaking with every flicker, swipe, stab, scrape of teeth. Then, abruptly, the touches stopped, leaving Jack panting, aching hard and ready to beg for more.

Before he could formulate the words, Julian spoke, breath hot against the small of his back. "Turn over."

Jack complied, and got a nice eyeful as he did so. Julian had managed to work his jeans and boxers off completely, and was sporting a healthy erection, dick firm and curved slightly toward his own stomach. His first instinct was to reach out and touch, but Julian caught his right hand with his left, pinning it to the mattress, and forestalled any further attempts by leaning down and swallowing Jack's cock.

"Fuck!" Jack's hips thrust upward instinctively, and Julian allowed it, letting Jack pump in and out of his mouth easily, eyes fixed on Jack's. Jack's balls tightened. "God, Julian, *please—*"

Please fuck me, he was going to say, but he couldn't quite get out the words. There was a *snick* as Julian opened the lubricant one-handed, and a second later he jerked as cool, wet fingers circled his entrance. Julian hummed as Jack pushed back against the gentle pressure, and Jack discovered exactly how good it was to date a doctor. Julian slid his finger past the tight ring of muscle with almost no resistance and stroked unerringly across Jack's prostate.

Sound and color faded into white as Jack arched back on the bed, body convulsing as Julian milked his orgasm from him with lips and hands. The pleasure seemed to go on forever, and then the shuddering took over, easing him down from the high.

"Oh my God," Jack said, when Julian didn't wait to slip another finger inside of him. The stretch burned just right, one knuckle, then two.

"Trust me," Julian said, as if Jack had any choice in the matter. He ran his free hand up the inside of Jack's thighs, playing with the hair there, then continued on to toy with his nipples, pinching them until they were hard nubs. By the time he had worked the third finger into Jack's ass, Jack's cock was swelling again, hardening insistently. Julian winked. "I'm a doctor."

"Love doctor, witch doctor," Jack agreed, his body moving with

Julian's hands of its own accord. "Dr. Zhivago…."

"Dr. Zhivago?" Julian echoed lightly, giving a vicious twist that stroked Jack's prostate just right. "What are you, like, sixty?"

Jack groaned. He certainly didn't *feel* sixty. He didn't even feel thirty-six. The way his body was behaving, he was channeling six*teen*. "It's a classic." He finally realized his hands were free—had been for ages, but he hadn't thought to move them after Julian had told him not to—and reached up to take Julian's face in both of his hands. He drew him down for a long, slow, hot kiss, reveling in the scrape of teeth on lips, his taste on Julian's tongue. His right hand wandered from Julian's face and skimmed down his well-defined stomach instead, fingers carding through the sparse hair low on his belly before wrapping firmly around his erection. "Ready when you are, Doc."

"Patience," Julian admonished. He pulled Jack's hand away, bringing his palm to his mouth and pressing a light kiss there.

Strange, that such an innocent action could make Jack blush when Julian had just had three fingers buried to the knuckle in his ass.

He heard the flip cap on the lube being opened again, and leaned up a bit to watch as Julian slicked his hard shaft thoroughly. Jack's eyes flipped up to Julian's and locked there. Time fell away as Julian pressed inside him, stretching him from the inside out, pushing just the head inside, giving Jack's body time to adjust. "Oh, God."

Julian ran a hand up his leg, the touch soothing. "You okay?"

"Are you kidding?" Jack groaned. "I'm fantastic. Gimme the rest of it."

Snickering, Julian wrapped his hand around Jack's prick, fingers sliding through the pre-come at the head. "Not to question your judgment, or anything, Jack, but ah…." He inched forward almost imperceptibly. "How long has it been since you bottomed for anyone?"

Oh, right. Jack thought about it a second. He'd been, what, twenty-seven? "Oh, you know." Julian twisted his hand around the head, and Jack's breath hitched. "Ten years, give or take?"

Julian's cock gave a noticeable twitch. "Jesus Christ. No wonder you're so tight."

"I was saving myself for you, schnookums."

"Oh, God. Never call me that again." Julian punctuated his request with a roll of his hips and Jack bucked, feeling Julian slide all the way in. The hurt was more of a sting than anything—it *had* been a long time, Jack's body reminded him—but he still couldn't quite repress a low hiss. "Told you. Aren't you glad you trusted your doctor?" Julian shifted his hips, just a little, but it was enough. Pure, liquid pleasure washed up Jack's spine and down again to settle in his balls, and the rest of the discomfort faded with it.

"Well, when you put it that way...." Julian twisted inside of him again. Jack promptly forgot what he was saying. "Can we have this conversation later?" he panted, meeting the next thrust square on.

Julian planted one hand beside him on the bed and leaned over, bringing their faces close together, noses just barely touching. Jack fisted one hand in his hair and kissed him thoroughly, all teeth and tongue and gasping breaths as Julian moved steadily inside of him, feathering light touches across his body, eyes, neck, nipples, navel, before dropping to fist his cock in a still-slippery hand.

"Julian. Oh, fuck."

Julian latched his mouth onto Jack's neck, and suddenly the blood was roaring in Jack's ears. It wouldn't be long now. He couldn't possibly last....

"I've got you," Julian said very softly, right into his ear. His thumb circled the head of Jack's shaft almost leisurely.

Jack threw his head back against the bed and let instinct take over. Julian thrust two more times, rubbing deliciously deep inside of him, and then his body seemed to splinter apart, clenching and convulsing as he shot harder than he could remember, coating the both of them in his release. In his ear, Julian's breathing grew labored and then stopped for a moment as he stilled, mouth open just a little, eyes closed. Jack felt the sudden warmth inside of him and shuddered again, fisting both hands in Julian's hair and kissing him furiously, tasting the helpless pleasure in his mouth as he came down from the high.

Looking as dazed as Jack felt, Julian groaned and pulled his body away from Jack's, sliding onto the bed beside him, their limbs still entangled. "Not to pressure you or anything, but I hope you let me do that again."

Jack was too sated to laugh; he just closed his eyes and turned his head to nuzzle into Julian's shoulder. "Let you? 'Beg' might be a better verb."

"Oooh. Promising." Julian slung his arm around Jack's waist and pulled them improbably closer. "So, did I assuage your unfounded fears?"

Jack opened his eyes again and looked up, meeting Julian's gaze squarely. There was nothing hesitant about the grin he could feel spreading across his face. "Oh, I don't know." He laced their fingers together. "Tell me again."

"I love you."

God, Jack was getting mushy in his old age. He figured he could forgive himself for it just this once. It wasn't every day you found someone to give your life direction. Julian, he was true north, a star to sail by. "Yep," he said cheerily. "That'll about do it."

Julian gave him an unmistakably fond look. "You're so easy to please."

"Only for you." Jack stretched a little, feeling his muscles burn. Damn, he was getting old. Maybe next time he'd stretch first. "I love you."

"Yeah, I know," Julian said mock-seriously. He poked Jack in the belly with one long finger. "So, what are you doing tomorrow, say around four o'clock?"

Jack answered without thinking. "I'll be sitting beside you on a plane cruising at thirty-six thousand feet."

"Too bad."

Jack raised his eyebrows. "Too bad?"

"Yeah." Julian's tone was casual. "See, there was this club I was thinking we could join. No membership dues or anything."

Oh, yeah. The idea had definite appeal. "A club, huh?" he asked, walking his fingers up Julian's sternum. "Tell me more."

BETHANY BROWN is a 27 year old with a BA in English, Language and Literature, and a bit too much time on her hands. Hopefully, her new barista job will keep her occupied enough that her mind doesn't wander too far. Unfortunately, that most likely won't be possible. Her mind is too full of stories.

Having been interested in writing since her first trip to the Young Authors Conference in the fourth grade, Bethany finally gave in to the voices in her head and wrote them a story. Since all that accomplished was to make the voices louder, she's looking forward to continuing the *Lost Boys and Love Letters* Series with Ashlyn.

Bethany spends her free time reading, and watching TV and movies while pairing up her favorite male characters. She is always looking for something new to get Ashlyn hooked on. She also spends a great deal of time trying to convince Patrick, who lives in her head, that just because he won't leave doesn't mean he gets to be in all of the stories. Unfortunately, it's not working very well.

Bethany would like to take this opportunity to address the administrators who wouldn't let her into the Creative Writing Program at the University of Windsor. I have a writing career! Choke on that, suckers!

ASHLYN KANE is a 23-year-old supergeek who graduated cum laude from the University of Windsor with an honours degree in English Language and Literature. When she's not writing, she moonlights as an education student, and is somewhat baffled by the idea that someday someone will put her in charge of a group of children. She is addicted to classic rock, science fiction, and TV on DVD.

In the event that her professors go on strike, Ash can usually be found lounging around in Bethany's basement, making inappropriate sexual comments about any given male character on TV, especially if he's in the Air Force and has stupid hair.

She has a fiancé, a little brother and a bitchy cat.

LaVergne, TN USA
03 December 2010
207194LV00004BA/26/P

9 781935 192428